Merrilee waited until her daughter was out of earshot before turning on her heel, her hands fisted on her hips. "How did you do that?"

At least John had the decency to look surprised. "How did I do what?"

"Never mind." Merrilee shook her head. So what if John had made a tiny crack in the solemn shell Claire had encased herself in this past year? Merrilee's bigger problem was how to keep her daughter from getting hurt by this man. "How long before you head back to your unit?"

"I don't. I've been relieved of my duties."

An odd way of putting it, but then John had always put his own unique spin on words. "Thank you for not telling Claire who you are. You can see she's a different child from the one who wrote you that letter."

"Maybe, but let's get one thing straight. Our daughter is going to know I'm her father," John answered, his voice slashing any hopes she may have harbored that he would fade from their lives once more. "Whether you like it or not."

D0448739

Books by Patty Smith Hall

Love Inspired Historical

Hearts in Flight
Hearts in Hiding
Hearts Rekindled

PATTY SMITH HALL

A Georgia girl born and bred, Patty Smith Hall loves to incorporate little-known historical facts into her stories. Her writing goal is to create characters who walk the Christian walk despite their human flaws. When she's not writing, Patty enjoys spending time with her husband of twenty-eight years, their two daughters and a vast extended family.

Patty loves hearing from her readers! Please contact her through her website, www.pattysmithhall.com.

Hearts Rekindled

PATTY SMITH HALL

HARLEQUIN® LOVE INSPIRED® HISTORICAL

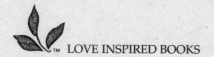 LOVE INSPIRED BOOKS

Recycling programs
for this product may
not exist in your area.

ISBN-13: 978-0-373-28252-4

HEARTS REKINDLED

Copyright © 2014 by Patty Smith Hall

www.Harlequin.com

Printed in U.S.A.

Bear ye one another's burdens,
and so fulfill the law of Christ.
—*Galatians* 6:2

To my parents, Emmett and Margaret Smith,
who are a living example of God's unconditional love
for His children. I love you!

Chapter One

"I've got another assignment for you."

Merrilee Daniels Davenport stiffened at the words, any joy she might have had watching her nephew with his new bride evaporating like the morning mist on Sweetwater Creek. Keeping the Army Air Corps informed on the comings and goings of the folks living in her boardinghouse bothered her to no end, even if it was, as Major Evans had said many times, her patriotic duty to keep the area safe from hidden enemies while the war raged on. The major would not relax his vigilance, not even now that the end of the war was in sight. The United States and her Allies had the Germans on the run in Europe and were making inroads on Japan's hold in the Pacific. Still, the major's surveillance carried on—which meant that hers did, too.

Not that there was anything patriotic about her reasons for aiding Patrick Evans in his new investigation.

The carrot the major dangled in front of her had been enough to enlist her help.

A chance for her daughter to be whole again.

"What do you need me to do this time?" The knots in her shoulder loosened a hair, but not enough to relieve the ache radiating across her back.

"Not one to beat around the bush, are you?" Turning to face her, the major thrust his hat under his arm and leaned back against the supporting post. His expression was relaxed, as if this spy nonsense was as normal as apple pie.

Merrilee shifted to face him, but not before noting the widespread looks of interest on her kinsfolk's faces. Probably thought she could do a lot worse than pairing up with the major, maybe get married again. Well, she'd loved only one man, and while their marriage had brought joy, it had ended in unbearable heartache when her husband—off working with the Civilian Conservation Corps—had filed for divorce without a word of warning. "You're the one who mentioned a new assignment."

Evans's soft chuckle grated on her nerves. "True enough. Guess it just threw me after the fight you put up when I first approached you about following Edie Michaels. But everything worked out in the end." He nodded toward where the bridal couple stood talking to their guests. "I'm betting Beau thinks so, too. He and Edie look very happy together."

"They are," Merrilee agreed. Seemed like everyone who lived beneath her roof radiated the delight of finding true love these days. First, her niece, Maggie, had paired up with Captain Wesley Hicks, then Beau and

Edie. In recent months, whispers that Merrilee's well water was spiked with just the right ingredients to find matrimonial bliss had been making the rounds through the church circle. And just last week, she'd caught Honoria Lee pumping water into her favorite large bucket, babbling some silly nonsense about needing to find husbands for all five of her daughters.

Complete rubbish. If that tall tale were so, Merrilee would still be a married woman herself instead of raising her daughter alone. A vague sense of sadness drifted through her. No sense crying over the past; the present was bad enough as it was. "Why does General Carson think I'm the person for this job?"

The major dropped his gaze to the floor, as if he'd find the words he needed in the seams of the marred boards of her porch. "Because you're friends with the parties involved in this case."

That got her attention. "What's the case? What are the 'parties' involved in?"

"The black market."

Merrilee automatically shook her head. Evans had come up with some doozies over the past few months, but this one had to be the icing on top of the cake! Keeping secrets in a small town like Marietta was nigh impossible—especially a secret that big. Granted, there were many new faces in town since the Bell Bomber Plant had opened more than two years ago, but most were there to earn a fair wage wiring the fuselage or riveting screws on the massive B-29s that the army used in the Pacific. Still, a black market was no good unless people knew it was around. If such a thing existed in Marietta, she'd have heard about it before now.

No, Major Evans was barking up the wrong tree this time, but his allegations had piqued her interest. "Exactly who do you think is involved?"

Reaching into his coat pocket, the major pulled out a folded sheet of paper and handed it to her. "A few days ago, one of the mechanics came to my office with this. He said he found it crumpled on the floor in the men's locker room."

Merrilee glanced down at the flyer in her hand. At first, it looked like any one of a dozen wartime ads printed in the newspaper or posted on the sides of buildings in the Marietta Square. But the more she studied it, the more the message sunk in. "What does this mean, farm fresh eggs without the hassle of ration stamps?"

The major glanced around the yard, then back at her. "We've heard that one of the local farms is supplying restricted goods to the black market dealer who drew up this ad."

"Who's your source?" Merrilee asked.

"Someone I trust."

Her teeth pressed into the tender skin of her inner lip. Probably someone like herself who thought they were doing their patriotic duty. Had Evans made this spy promises like the one he'd made her? What would the major give in exchange for information? Merrilee flicked the edge of the paper with her fingernail. "Then why not go after the dealer? He's the one making a living off the rations."

The relaxed smile he'd flashed for the benefit of their audience flattened into a tight line. "We've tried, but he's a slick one. This isn't the first time he's run this sort of operation. He never stays in one place long enough for us to catch him."

"He moves his market around?"

Evans gave her a stern nod. "That's why we need to catch whoever's supplying him. It may be our only chance to stop him."

No wonder the major was on edge. This modern-day pirate took food out of the mouths of their fighting men on the front.

Merrilee took a deep breath, dread tightening into a hard knot in the pit of her stomach. Despite her disgust at the idea of a black market supplier, she was still uneasy with the role she'd have to play. Which one of her neighbors was she about to betray now? "Who does the army suspect is helping him?"

Major Evans slipped a finger beneath his shirt collar and tugged, as though the words had caught in his throat. "My informant believes it's Aurora Adair."

Merrilee blinked. The man couldn't have shocked her more if he told her Roosevelt himself was dancing a jig down the streets of Berlin. "Your informant has a screw loose."

"I told General Carson you'd say that."

She seriously doubted that. "Anybody who's been in Marietta for any length of time would tell you that Ms. Aurora is the most kindhearted, giving person in the world. She's taken in deserted kids and given them a home for as far back as I can remember."

"Don't you think that's odd?" the major replied. "A woman taking in a bunch of...feeble-minded kids? Why bother with them at all?"

Irritation flashed through her at the major's obvious

disdain for the physically and mentally disabled children Aurora took in. "And where do you think those children should go, Major? Out on the street? Or would you rather they be dropped off at the state institution in Milledgeville?"

He chuckled. "I hadn't really considered it."

Of course, he hadn't. Neither had the doctors who'd evaluated Claire in the last year after she'd contracted polio. That was why this assignment was so important. Claire needed therapy to regain full use of her legs. And the major held the key to making Merrilee's dreams of treatment for Claire into reality.

But could she betray her old friend's trust?

She didn't have a choice, not with Claire's future at stake. "What do you need to know?"

Evans gave her a sardonic smile that made her stomach sour. "Who has she got living out there with her right now?"

"It's been a while since I've been there." Not since the night she'd showed up on Aurora's doorstep, terrified by the possibility of losing Claire to polio. Merrilee shook off the memory. "I only know of a boy and a little girl who have been with Ms. Aurora for years."

"Anyone else?"

"I wasn't really taking a head count the last time I paid her a visit."

Her sarcasm bounced off him like Claire's baseball against the shed door. "So she could have a few older boys who work the fields for her."

The way he said it, as if he'd stated a proved fact, bothered her. "If she did, she'd keep it close to the chest." Aurora had to. If the state learned she harbored those children, she ran the risk of losing them. Worse still, Billy and Ellie would be dragged off and institutionalized.

One dark brow disappeared beneath his major's cap. "That's why the general thinks you're perfect for this assignment. Aurora Adair trusts you, so you can get us information most operatives couldn't."

Merrilee turned toward him, leaning in close. No sense having the whole town knowing Ms. Aurora's business. "You haven't met any of her children, have you?"

"Why would I want to meet them?" The major leaned closer, his gaze stark and unyielding. "Besides, what better way to run an undercover operation than get a bunch of mush heads doing your dirty work?"

The muscles in her throat tightened around the words she wanted to say, but Merrilee decided not to waste her breath. Major Patrick Evans had his own distorted sense of the world, a view that ran completely opposite of her own, and no amount of arguing with him would change that. "Feeding a houseful of kids takes a lot of groceries, and I'm sure Ms. Aurora doesn't get near enough ration stamps to keep food on the table."

"Then how did she get the money to buy the farm next door in cash?"

"Cash?" Church mice had more money than Aurora, not that she ever seemed to mind. Material possessions had never had much of a hold on the older woman. Which made it odd that she would even consider purchasing another farm, much less buying it outright. There had to be a good reason for this, but what?

"Maybe she needed more space for the kids and got a good deal on the land."

Major Evans shook his head. "According to Mr. Todd's son, Ms. Adair offered him the full asking price for the place and had a bank draft the next day."

Merrilee felt sick. To listen to Evans, he'd already tried and convicted Aurora; all that was left to do was for Merrilee to uncover evidence to convince a jury. Her peers would never know how Aurora had smoothed back the matted hair from Merrilee's face just moments before Claire was born or how the older woman had held her when the doctors weren't sure Claire would survive her bout with polio. The woman's common sense and unconditional love had pushed Merrilee to rebuild her life when her marriage collapsed, to be the woman God wanted her to be.

I know the plans I have for you, plans for good and not evil.

Merrilee glanced toward a massive oak, its limbs laden with crisp green leaves that shaded a grassy patch of land where the children played a noisy game of Red Rover. Leaning against the sturdy trunk, her daughter Claire clung to her crutch for dear life, pressing it tightly against her side. Was this God's plan to supply Claire's need for therapy—betray the woman who'd been more of a mother than a friend?

Claire pushed away from the tree, the grass beneath her right foot parting as she tried to catch up with the crutch. Merrilee's lungs stung and she forced herself to breathe. Evans knew what he was doing when he'd made her this offer. "If I do this, when do you think I can take Claire to Warm Springs for therapy?"

"It'll be a while."

The muscles in her jaw began to throb. "Why is that, Major?"

He hesitated. "I'm not at liberty to say."

Which meant that the rumors swirling in the Atlanta newspapers about Roosevelt being in Georgia were probably true. But how long would the president reside in Warm Springs, what with the war going on?

In the meantime the army expected her to spy like some Mata Hari on a woman she cared for, all on the hope General Carson would secure Claire a slot at Warm Springs. But what else could she do? The clinic was Claire's last hope to free herself from her crutch. "I need the general's word that the minute an appointment opens up, I'll be free to take Claire there myself."

"You know he can't do that, Merrilee."

"Then maybe I should wait," she answered. "Claire has been on the waiting list for a few months now, and the last time I called, the nurse thought a slot would be opening up soon. Perhaps I don't need the army's influence to help us after all."

The major gently took her elbow and nudged her toward the swing in the corner of her front porch. After she took a seat, he sat down beside her, giving all the wedding guests the appearance of a gentleman coming to call.

But the words he whispered were far from romantic. "Are you sure you want to take that risk, Merrilee? I know you're close to losing this place with all the medical bills you owe. And the army has a way of burying plans in a mountain of paperwork, especially when the brass wants a mission completed."

Merrilee jerked back, her throat burning. "What are you saying? That General Carson would find a way to keep Warm Springs from offering Claire treatment?"

"He could."

She clutched the chain holding the swing, the metal links digging into her palms. The longer therapy was postponed, the more likely Claire would never recover full use of her leg. "Claire's a little girl, Patrick, and the only place she can receive the therapy she needs is in Warm Springs."

"And General Carson believes you're the only person who can successfully complete this mission."

Trapped! Bile scorched a fiery path up Merrilee's throat. She didn't have a choice. Claire had to have her chance to regain the use of her leg, and the clinic in Warm Springs was her best shot. An odd mixture of relief and defeat slithered through her.

Merrilee nibbled on her lower lip. Aurora was too honorable a woman for this not to be on the up-and-up. What if, by helping Major Evans, Merrilee could prove the allegations wrong? She turned the notion over in her mind. Yes, she could do that, and when she turned the information over to Major Evans, he'd have to drop his suspicions against the older woman.

And give Claire her best hope at recovering the use of her leg. "When do I get started?"

The urge to smack the smug smile off the major's face made her fingers burn. "Immediately. And when you bring in the evidence and we make our arrest, the army will be more than happy to help Claire."

"I will provide whatever help our daughter is in need of."

Every nerve ending in Merrilee's body jolted awake at the rich, tenor voice rumbling against the wooden planks of the porch. The voice was unmistakable, even though it was a shade deeper, more mature than the last time she'd heard it a dozen years ago. The thick humid air suddenly grew thinner, sucking the breath out of her lungs. The sound of solid steps came closer, spreading out like ocean waves inside her before settling into a dull ache around the heart he'd left broken.

John Davenport. Her former husband.

The swing shifted behind her before Merrilee realized she had stood to her feet. Her thoughts were scrambled but she needed to say something. Anything. "What are you doing here?"

His bright blue eyes sliced through her like the fiery torches she'd seen at the bomber plant, cutting through the thick sheets of steel. But it was his answer that set her knees to trembling.

"I'm here to see my daughter."

The hard tangle of emotions wrestling around in John Davenport's belly surprised him. Confronting the Japanese on the beaches at Guadalcanal hadn't twisted his gut as much as the thought of meeting his eleven-year-old daughter for the very first time.

And if he was honest, his former wife. Steadying himself for battle, he leveled his sights on the woman standing before him.

Merrilee Daniels Davenport.

"John?" Merrilee's full mouth gaped open, her gloved hands clinching in a ladylike knot at her waist.

His name sounded like a gentle caress—almost as if she'd been waiting for him.

John's insides tightened. For a split second, he was nineteen again, and this spitfire of a girl belonged to him just like he'd belonged to her.

But working hard and trying to live right hadn't been enough for her or her father. Jacob Daniels had raised his daughter with all the manners and refinement of a true Southern lady. He'd hoped that one day Merrilee would join her life with that of a lawyer or a banker from the county's elite, not a poor sharecropper who had to scrimp and save for a month to get a marriage license. Jacob had forced him to walk away from Merrilee, and she hadn't said a word or done a thing to make him believe she wanted him to stay. But she had to have known she was with child, his child, by the time he'd sent the divorce papers. Why had she never told him?

Snatching his hat off his head, John nodded his head in a mocking bow, taking in the inviting front porch to the majestic house that had been known as the Daniels homestead for well over a hundred years. He turned his head, glancing out over the small groups of people mulling around in the yard. "I didn't know you'd be entertaining today."

"It's just a few friends here for the wedding."

A movement caught John's notice and he suddenly remembered they weren't alone. Outfitted in the blue woolen uniform of the Army Air Corps, the man stood just short of eye level. A glance back to the stripes on his sleeves added fuel to the bitterness settling low in John's stomach. A major, just the kind of man Jacob Daniels had always thought Merrilee should marry.

Well, the major could have her, John thought, ignoring the dull stab of pain just under his ribs. The only reason he'd come back to Marietta in the first place was to see his daughter.

It might be his only opportunity.

Lord, please give me the chance to know my baby girl before the navy sends me away.

John slipped his hand in his jacket pocket, his fingers sliding over the soft folds of paper. "When can I see my daughter?"

Merrilee blinked, then seeming to recover, tilted her head toward the man beside her. "Could you give us a moment, Patrick?"

"Are you sure?"

John's midsection unexpectedly clenched. No mistaking the concern in the man's voice or the tenderness in his touch when he reached for her elbow. Not that John blamed him. A man would have to be dead and in his grave not to notice Merrilee. She'd always been a beauty, even as a young girl of sixteen.

She'd been leaner then, more angles than curves, her upturned nose covered with a delicate garden of pinkish brown freckles from working her father's cotton fields, punishment for defying Jacob. It hadn't mattered to John how she'd come to be working beside him. He'd been so taken with her that he'd stumbled in introducing himself, but Merrilee had responded with a sweetness he'd rarely seen in his eighteen years. If only he'd known her father was Jacob Daniels, one of the richest men in Cobb County. And the man who held the lease to John's land.

A fool, that was what he'd been. A complete and total fool.

The only good part of the whole mess was their child. Claire.

John shifted his attention from his former wife to her companion. What if this man planned on marrying Merrilee, becoming Claire's stepfather? The thought didn't set well with him, but he'd have to be civil, find out everything he could about the man. It was the only way to keep both his wife and his daughter safe. *No, just Claire,* he corrected to himself.

John extended his hand. "John Davenport."

The man studied him for a long moment, then as if satisfied by what he saw, clasped John's hand. "Major Patrick Evans, Army Air Forces."

"Major Evans oversees the Bell Bomber Plant right down the street," Merrilee added.

Evans tightened his grip. "What about you, Davenport? You serve anywhere?"

Something about the man's attitude set John on edge. "Independent contractor for the navy, training the men of the Sixth Construction Battalion out of Hueneme. Shipped out with them."

"Almost a Seabee, huh?"

The touch of humor in Evans's voice grated on him. *Never let the enemy see you sweat.* Well, if Evans wanted a war, he'd give him one. John smiled as if he were in on the joke. "Must be nice having a stateside job far away from the fighting, Major."

Bull's-eye! The man tensed, glaring at John as if he'd fired the first round.

Merrilee's voice interrupted his thoughts. "The last I heard, you were heading for Australia."

She'd kept track of him while he was overseas? The thought of it was a surprise attack much worse than anything the Japanese had ever thrown at him. John lowered his gaze to meet hers, ambushed by the fleeting look of concern worrying the faint lines around her eyes in the moment. John shook his head. "Hawaii."

No sense mentioning his time in Guam. Or the military inquiry hanging over his head. The repercussions of helping one child make it through this war would be a small price to pay.

Merrilee nodded, a quiet sigh on her lips. Was it possible she'd been worried about him, personally, while he was overseas? No. She had a soft heart—she probably only felt the same sympathy for him that she would for any man coming back from war. Best if he stayed focused on his mission: getting to know their daughter. "Can we talk?"

Merrilee's chin bobbed in affirmation. "If you'll excuse us, Major."

The man's shoulders stiffened beneath the dark blue wool of his uniform coat. He obviously wasn't used to being dismissed. "I hope we can finish up our conversation—maybe later this afternoon?"

Merrilee rubbed her thumb across the tips of her fingers in tight circles. "I might still be busy, cleaning up after the wedding."

"Then in the morning over one of your fine breakfasts and a cup of joe." Putting his cap on, Evans lifted his hand to the brim in a mock salute. "Davenport."

"Evans."

The major walked down the porch stairs and across the yard, joining a small group of people John didn't recognize. John frowned as he watched the major chat and smile. He didn't like the man, not one bit.

"Would you like a glass of iced tea? Or maybe a piece of wedding cake?" Merrilee grasped the handle of the screen door, once again the society hostess her father had shaped from a very young age. "Folks have told me it's pretty good considering the rations I had on hand."

Part of him wanted to demand to see his daughter immediately—a meeting that had already been postponed for eleven years. But first he had to know if Merrilee's future included the pompous major. For Claire's sake. The wooden planks trembled beneath him as he marched near where she stood, whipping off his hat. "You're not marrying that guy, are you?"

The high-pitched crack of wood slamming against the door frame echoed across the porch as Merrilee marched toward him. Eyes darkened to the color of swirling waves tossed about by a raging storm glared at him, the bright spots high on her cheeks dull compared to the flash of fiery curls bouncing around her shoulders. Merrilee pulled up short of him, but not far enough for him to miss the faint scent of vanilla that teased long-forgotten memories of happier times. "Who do you think you are to voice any opinion on who I marry?"

John grimaced. She'd always done this—answered a question with a question—but he wouldn't let her get away with it this time. "Merrilee."

Her full lips thinned into a stubborn line, one perfectly shaped eyebrow cocked high in a dare.

Blast her! Couldn't she see that he was just looking out for Claire? Even their brief meeting had been enough to show John that Evans was the type of man who liked to maintain a firm grasp on the people in his life, who thrived on controlling the world around him and everyone in it. Little things like a bad grade or a burned dinner might set his temper into a rage.

John's fingers crushed the soft felt brim of his hat, swallowing against the knot of bile rising in his throat at the thought of his own stepfather. *If Evans so much as touches a hair on either of their heads, I'll beat him to within an inch of his life!*

But before John could interrogate her further, Merrilee beat him to the punch. "Why do you want to see Claire now, after all these years?"

He wasn't finished with the subject of Major Evans, but figured she might be more cooperative if he answered some questions himself. John shoved his hand back into his pocket, fished out the letter and held it out to Merrilee. "I got this from Claire a couple weeks ago."

Taking the letter, she skimmed over the childish handwriting on the envelope, a tiny line worrying the smooth skin between her eyes. "How did she know where to send this? Beau never mentioned having your address."

"You've heard from him?" Seemed his daughter had failed to mention Beau had come home to Marietta.

Merrilee's lips turned up into a soft smile, her dark reddish-brown lashes resting shyly against the curve of her cheek. "Who do you think got married this afternoon?"

"Beau!" Was she serious? It would be just like Merrilee to tease him like this. He knew Beau, had taken

Merrilee's nephew under his wing after they'd found him in their barn, half beaten to death by his low-life father. Beau had followed John into the Civilian Conservation Corps and when the papers that had ended his marriage to Merrilee were delivered, Beau had been the one to fish him out of the hole he'd crawled in. "I thought he didn't think too much of marriage."

"That was before he met Edie Michaels. I've got to admit, for a while there, I didn't know if they were going to fall in love or come to blows," Merrilee said with a soft chuckle. "But once they figured things out, Beau couldn't get that girl to the altar fast enough."

"Are they here? I'd like to meet the woman who hogtied your nephew."

She looked out over the yard, then shook her head. "You must have just missed them. They only have tonight for a honeymoon before Edie has to get back to work at the bomber plant."

Beau married. If anyone in this world deserved to find happiness with a wife and children, it was his friend. Merrilee grinned back at him, clearly pleased as punch about the married couple. Without really knowing how it happened, he felt his lips hook upward. Sharing a smile with Merrilee for the first time in years felt far too comfortable, as if their years apart were nothing more than the blink of an eye. He stepped back to give himself a moment to think. "Hopefully they can make a better go at it than we did."

The color drained out of Merrilee's face. She took a step back as if his words had struck her with the force of a fisted blow. John grimaced. The words had been aimed to hurt her, only now her reaction sliced through him like a bayonet. "Look, I shouldn't have said that."

"You were only speaking the truth."

"Right." But the truth had still hurt her, hadn't it? And John knew more than anybody how words could inflict pain. As a peace offering, he asked, "Why don't you tell me about Claire?"

Merrilee unfolded the letter, her slender fingers tracing the small tears along the worn edges of the paper. "Looks like it's been to the other side of the world and back."

"I only got it a couple weeks ago." Which was true, but he'd read it until he'd memorized each of his daughter's words. Getting that letter from Claire had been a treasure he hadn't expected or deserved.

"I guess this shouldn't surprise me. Claire has always asked questions about you."

"Really?" The thought of his daughter wanting to know him shed light into a place he'd long thought locked away for good. "What kind of questions?"

"You know. What do you look like? What kinds of things did you like to do? What cities have you been to? She particularly liked Beau's story of how the two of you had to hang off the side of Boulder Dam to do rock work." She hesitated, her eyes widening with understanding and the unmistakable shadow of a battle lost.

An uneasiness slid down his spine. "What is it?"

"Claire hasn't asked about you in a long time."

Why would his daughter suddenly stop asking questions about him? Had she given up on him just like her mother? "How long are we talking?"

Merrilee held out the letter. "Probably not long after she wrote this."

"That doesn't make sense." John shook his head. "Did something happen last spring?"

Merrilee jerked her head up. Soft lines arched in somber grief around her eyes and mouth, her pained stare meeting his, begging, pleading. "I don't think Claire's ready to meet you just now."

Evasiveness again. Irritation pricked John. "And why is that, Merrilee?"

"Mama?"

They turned in unison. The young girl was tall for her age, the perfect height to fit under his arm and rest her head on his chest. Strands of reddish-gold hair curled around her delicate face while the rest of her thick mane had been pulled back into a neat ponytail. Her eyes matched his former wife's, that blue-green storm of color the memory of which even now managed to keep him awake long into the night. Then her lips lifted into a tentative grin that resembled the one staring back at him in the mirror every morning, and John's heart tumbled over in his chest.

Claire. His baby girl.

Her eyes widened on him. He wanted to reach out to her, but the thought that he was a father—correction, this child's father—warred with his usual confidence. Give him a building to erect or a landing strip to dig out and he'd know just how to respond. Those things he'd been taught to do. But how could he be a good father when the only lessons he'd learned from his own father were brute force and abandonment?

Thump!

John's gaze shifted lower to the crutch pulled taut against her side as she dragged her right foot forward. His insides did a sickening flip, and for only the third time in his whole thirty years, he felt the burn of salty tears behind his eyes. He slammed them shut before he made a ninny out of himself, his prayers already lifting to Heaven.

Please, Lord, give me the wisdom to be the daddy my baby girl needs!

Chapter Two

Merrilee leaned forward toward Claire, then stopped herself. Her daughter had become terribly sensitive about her limited abilities since her illness. She hated being coddled.

John knelt down in front of their daughter. The slate-blue eyes that had sharpened their edges on Merrilee moments before had softened. Silver shards of light came alive as John's gaze floated over their daughter's face, drinking in every line and nuance as if quenching a thirst he hadn't realized he possessed. The harsh lines that had marred his still-handsome face faded, giving her a glimpse of the boy she had fallen so heart over head in love with all those years ago.

Merrilee watched the two of them—father and daughter, yet strangers.

Why did John have to show up now, when Claire still struggled with the paralysis in her right leg? When their home was days away from foreclosure? Shaking her head, she reminded herself that the timing didn't matter. For better or for worse, he was here now…and she was sure that once John found out the extent of their problems, he'd hightail it out of town just like he had twelve years ago. What mattered now was protecting her child at any cost. Stepping in front of her former husband, Merrilee took a deep breath and smiled at her daughter. "What is it, sweetheart?"

"I'd just wondered where you'd gone."

"I'm right here, same as usual." Merrilee smiled, but it felt tight against her lips. Polio had done more than paralyze Claire's leg; it had crippled her spirit, making her clingy in a way the old Claire had never been. "Unless I'm out in the kitchen, making more coffee for this bunch."

The wooden tip of the crutch scratched across the hardwood planks as Claire leaned against it, cocking her head to one side, her gaze intent on the man behind Merrilee. "I don't remember you at the wedding."

"Claire!"

"Well, I don't, Mama."

Merrilee glanced over her shoulder as John spoke. "That's because I didn't make it to the ceremony, but I'll bet it was lovely." He twisted the brim of his hat in a nervous circle that made something inside Merrilee soften before she caught herself.

"It was rather pretty," Claire answered, standing up a bit straighter than normal. "Though I don't understand why I couldn't walk up the aisle with the other bridesmaid."

Another disappointment for Claire. "Sweetheart, it was only Maggie, and she was the matron of honor."

Claire's lips puckered into a pout. "Then why couldn't I walk down the aisle like she did?"

Merrilee sighed inwardly. The excitement of being

asked to stand alongside Edie and Beau as they exchanged their wedding vows had given Claire something to fight for as she'd lain in sweat-soaked sheets, her fever climbing higher by the hour as polio ravaged her body. That had been before any of them had realized the extent of the damage to Claire's leg.

Would Claire ever understand that Merrilee had only been protecting her?

"I bet I know what happened."

Merrilee swung around to glare at John. When she met his gaze, his expression threw down a challenge that made her stomach flip-flop. He wanted her to trust him with their child. But how could she when she wasn't sure he wouldn't break Claire's heart?

"What do you mean?" Claire asked.

"Well, brides are a mighty particular bunch when it comes to their wedding day," John said, stepping around Merrilee and crouching down in front of Claire, the gray serge suit coat stretched tight against his wide shoulders. "Just ask your mama here."

Claire lifted her head to look at her. "Is that true, Mama?"

Where was John going with this? Merrilee nodded slightly. "I guess so."

"Did you know your mama was so peculiar as a bride that she let your daddy sit in jail for three days before she finally got up the nerve to tell anyone they were married?"

Heat danced up the back of Merrilee's neck. He'd have to bring that up, wouldn't he, not thinking she'd been barely seventeen years old and scared to death of what her father would do to the both of them. But then she'd never told him the truth of those three days, had she? "He survived."

"Just barely, from what I hear," he answered, his lips turned up in a wicked smile. "Like I said, brides are a peculiar breed."

"But why wouldn't Beau and Edie let me walk down the aisle?"

Merrilee blinked in surprise. Claire hadn't spoken to anyone outside of family and close friends since she'd come home from the hospital, yet she talked to John as if she'd known him all her life.

"Well," John started, his brow furrowed in thought. "I've been studying on that for the past few minutes and I don't know if you're aware of this, but you're a mighty pretty young lady."

Claire's lashes fluttered down to rest on the rose of her cheeks. "People say I'm the spitting image of my mama."

"Yes." John tilted his head back, his gaze stealing over Merrilee's face, appraising her eyes, her nose, the curve of her lips until her cheeks burned. "Yes, you are." He cleared his throat. "But no woman wants that kind of competition on their wedding day."

Claire shook her head, but the upturned bow of her lips was evidence John's comment pleased her. "But I'm crippled." She fisted her hand around the handle of her crutch.

Worry tightened in a knot at the base of Merrilee's throat. *Please, Lord, give him the right things to say. One wrong word, one careless glance might crush what's left of my girl's spirit.*

"What happened to your leg?"

So much for answering that prayer, Lord. All he'd had to do was tell Claire she was beautiful despite her leg, but no! He had to start in with his questions like always. Why couldn't he have just left them alone? Maybe Claire hadn't heard him—he had spoken in almost a whisper.

"I had polio."

His smile faded just a bit. "That's too bad, but that doesn't have anything to do with you being pretty, Claire. Real beauty comes from inside."

Claire tipped her head to glance at Merrilee. "That's what you're always telling me, isn't it, Mama?"

"Yes." Merrilee cupped the tight knot of hair at the crown of Claire's head and brushed her lips against her silky soft brow. That was what Merrilee told her daughter—and what she believed. But she knew that not everyone agreed. People could be cruel when it came to someone who was different, whose arms and legs refused to work, who need a wheelchair or a crutch to function. She didn't want that life for Claire.

"Your mama always was smart like that."

An uncomfortable weight settled on her chest at the praise. What would John say if he knew what she was planning to do to Aurora, the woman who'd raised him? "Just repeating what my daddy used to tell me."

John's terse nod caused her to let go of a frustrated sigh. Her father seemed to affect John like a burning match to gasoline. The conversations between the two men had always exploded out of control, with each maintaining they were right. Like two bulls let loose in the same cow pasture, jockeying for position within the herd. Neither John nor her father knew how much their hostile words hurt her. But she was a grown woman—she could handle being hurt. Claire was just a child.

And the wound John could cause Claire by leaving again might be too much for their young daughter to overcome.

Maybe once she'd healed, once she'd recovered the full use of her leg, Claire would be capable of dealing with her father. But until then, Merrilee had to do what was right for Claire. "I think you should go, John."

The last notes of his name hung in the thick spring air before Merrilee realized her mistake. Claire leaned forward on her crutch, almost stumbling to the floor. "My dad's name is John."

"Sweetheart, a lot of men have that name. It's very popular," Merrilee squeaked. Worry clamping down on the muscles in Merrilee's chest, making each breath a painful chore. *Please, Lord, for Claire's sake, don't let John tell her who he really is!*

"Your mom's right. It is a very common name," John agreed.

Relief and a faint sense of disappointment raced through Merrilee as she glanced down at him. The smile that had lit up his face dimmed somewhat, as if snuffed out by the truth of Claire's situation. If he'd only turn and walk away now, before the girl realized this man was her father, it would be best for all of them.

Then why did the thought of John leaving bother her so much?

"I think it's a nice name," Claire answered. "Don't you?"

John chuckled, but the sound held no humor. "I don't think I have much of a choice but to like it."

Claire's girlish giggle startled Merrilee slightly. It'd been what felt like a lifetime since her daughter had laughed and talked like this. Merrilee almost hated to end it. "Claire, would you do me a favor and check the refreshment table to see if I need to make more coffee?"

"But, Mama…"

"No ifs, ands or buts, young lady." Merrilee gave her what she hoped was her sternest look, one she used only to get Claire up and moving.

It must have worked. "Yes, Mama."

"It was nice meeting you, Claire." John held out his hand.

Claire slipped her hand into his and shook it. "Will you come back to see us again soon?"

John glanced over their daughter's head, his gaze zeroing in on Merrilee, determination apparent in his crisp words as he spoke. "I'll be here faster than you can shake a puppy's tail, Claire."

It was a warning if ever Merrilee had heard one.

Claire answered with another giggle. Gracious, it hadn't taken long for John to climb into her daughter's good graces. Well, at least, he hadn't spilled the beans and told her he was her father. It would make life easier when he had to report back to his unit and leave them behind. Again.

"Be careful going down that ramp, sweetheart," John called out to Claire as she neared the wooden platform Merrilee had spent the better part of a week working on when Claire first came home. "It's a bit unstable."

Claire shot him a sweet smile. "Yes, sir."

Merrilee waited until her daughter was out of earshot before turning on her heel, her hands fisted on her hips. "How did you do that?"

At least he had the decency to look surprised. "How did I do what?"

"Never mind." Merrilee shook her head. So what if John had made a tiny crack in the solemn shell Claire had encased herself in this past year? Merrilee's bigger problem was how to keep her daughter from getting hurt by this man. "How long before you head back to your unit?"

"I don't. I've been relieved of my duties."

An odd way of putting it, but then John had always had his own unique spin on words. "Thank you for not telling Claire who you are. You can see she's a different child from the one who wrote you that letter."

"Maybe, but let's get one thing straight. Our daughter is going to know I'm her father," John answered, his voice slashing any hopes she may have harbored that he would fade from their lives once more. "Whether you like it or not."

An hour later, John sank down onto the park bench, watching the late afternoon sun sink below the rooftops of the brick buildings lining Marietta Square. Bright pink and white azalea blooms bordered the dirt paths leading into the park, mocking him with their sunny disposition as he pushed his hat forward on his moist brow. His frayed thoughts rushed through his mind until all he could do was pray.

Why am I here, Lord?

A hint of freshly mowed grass teased him with memories of distant Sunday afternoons with his friend Peter

Oahu and Peter's family. After church services, they'd all head over to a nearby park, Peter and Grace swinging a picnic basket between them while their children bombarded John with noisy chatter that never failed to make him smile. From that very first Sunday, he'd been Uncle John to Michael and Lilly. They became the family he'd never had. A family in grief, now that Peter was gone, lost in the fighting at Belvedere.

Reaching into his pocket, John pulled Claire's letter free and unfolded it, a slight smile tugging at the corners of his mouth, remembering the mail call that had delivered his daughter's stark-white envelope into his hands. Thinking it was another masterpiece from the Oahu children, he'd torn it open. Only it wasn't a page out of the coloring book he'd given Michael and Lilly, but a note in a girlish scrawl, little hearts and flowers dancing around the borders, circling him with the news.

He had a child, a daughter—and she wanted to meet him. Shock had segued quickly into fascination for this tiny snip of humanity that was part of him. Part of the only woman he'd ever loved.

Merrilee.

John snatched his hat off his head, then raked his free hand against his scalp. It had been foolishness, marrying her, knowing full well who her daddy was, but John hadn't been able to help himself. Basking in Merrilee's sweet nature and strong faith, he'd been certain that building a marriage with her would be worth every minute of putting up with Jacob Daniels as a father-in-law. With her, he'd believed he could have the love and comfort of his own family.

If only Merrilee hadn't allowed her old man to destroy their marriage.

Now he had another chance at a family, by being a father to Claire. Sure, she wasn't ready for the news but John would give her time, let her get to know him, maybe even love him. Then, when the moment was right, he'd tell her the truth, that he was her father. And maybe then he could move forward with his life again.

But how much time would he have with Claire before his hearing date was scheduled? Was that why Merrilee had asked him how long he intended to stay? Had she heard about the charges he faced?

A childish sob scattered John's thoughts. Standing, he scanned the area, searching for the source of the plaintive cry when he noticed a little girl, several years younger than Claire, at the swing set. A fierce line of stubborn determination creased her forehead as she pumped her stubby legs, tilting the swing back and forth but gaining no height. John watched the child's frustrating dance a few seconds before cutting through the bushes dividing the two areas.

He glanced around. The child looked too young to be left on her own. Where was her mother?

"Mister?"

The lispy way the girl spoke catapulted John toward memories shelved away long ago. Lowering his gaze, he closely studied the child: the rounded face with its determined expression, a pair of bright blue eyes set a tad too wide apart, the flat nose. A mongoloid, though not as severe as his brother. John's heart sank as he twisted around, scouring the park for anyone who might claim this child.

"Mister!" the girl said with a bit of impatience.

John crouched down in front of her. Such a sweet face. Who would be so heartless as to abandon her? "Yes, ma'am?"

She giggled at that. "You're silly."

That coaxed a smile out of him. "Well, folks need to be silly every now and then, don't you think? Is there something I can do to help you?"

"I can't get this thing to work." The child pumped her short legs up and down. "See?"

"That's because you need a partner to help get you going." He glanced over at the seesaws where several boys and girls played. "Didn't any of the other kids want to swing with you?"

She didn't answer, only shook her head, the same tight expression he remembered his little brother had often worn flittering across her face before being replaced once again by her smile. "But that's okay. Grandma says it's their loss, not mine."

"Your grandma must love you very much."

The little girl's cheeks turned rosy. "Do you know she picked me out of all the babies in the pum'kin patch?"

John had to force down a gurgle of laughter. "She must have thought you were a very special little girl."

The child's giggle reminded him of Claire.

"Ellie!"

John followed the child's gaze as she turned toward the sidewalk. An older woman hurried toward them, her gray wool coat matching the no-nonsense bun gathered at the nape of her neck and the glasses that dangled from the tip of her slender nose. She rushed down the path, her sensible shoes turned reddish brown with dust. As she drew closer, the smile he'd had for Ellie stretched wider. "Ms. Aurora?"

The older woman slowed, the corners of her mouth turning up gradually until she couldn't seem to hold back her smile any longer. She didn't speak, only nodded. Leaving Ellie by the swing set, John walked over to her, feeling as shy as the boy this woman had taken in all those years ago. He'd been barely ten years old and his brother, Matthew, not even six, but Ms. 'Rora hadn't blinked an eye, taking them as if they were her very own, a mother in every sense of the word.

"John," she whispered, her watery gaze sliding over his face as if committing him to her memory.

A faint pang of guilt stirred John into action. "I think I found someone who belongs to you."

"You know my grandma?" The girl now stood in front of them, her gaze floating from one to the other.

"Ellie, this is John Davenport." Ms. Aurora took the young girl's outstretched hand. "He came to live with me when he was just a boy not much older than you."

The girl stared up at him, her rosebud of a mouth quirked to the side as if confused. "Did Grandma pick you out of the babies in the pum'kin patch, too?"

"No." John glanced over Ellie's head to the woman, her pale blue eyes twinkling at the memory. More like a police lineup. "Well, now that I think of it, maybe it was something like that."

"You'll have to tell the children about it sometime." The older woman winked at him. "I'm sure they all would enjoy hearing it."

"I'm sure." He wanted to share his story with Claire

when he got the opportunity, tell her about her uncle Mattie. Maybe even tell Merrilee, though he'd never had the nerve to talk about his brother in the short time they were married. They'd already had enough troubles with her father. Why add one more?

"Ellie?" Ms. Aurora glanced around. "Where's Billy?"

The child stepped from one foot to the other, the hem of her yellow cotton dress swaying like jonquils on the breeze. "He's not in trouble, is he?"

The woman turned her attention across the street to the storefronts. "It all depends on what he's up to now."

"Who's Billy?" John asked.

"He's Ellie's older brother. And for the moment, the bane of my existence."

The little girl smiled brightly up at John. "Grandma picked him out of the pum'kin patch, too."

"That's a mighty active pumpkin patch you've got there, Ms. Aurora," John replied, barely containing the chuckle that caught in his throat. "How many more did you pick to take home with you?"

The older woman glared at him for a brief second before tumbling into laughter. "Three, but they're at home with Mrs. Williams. Not quite ready for a trip into town." She bent down toward Ellie. "You want to play for a few more minutes while John and I rest a spell?"

"Yeah!" Ellie scooted out from under Ms. Aurora's arm. Two short steps later, she turned to John, her deep blue eyes wide with innocence. "Will you play with me later, Mr. John?"

He knelt down. Maybe one day, Claire would trust him as this little girl did, with a childlike innocence.

Maybe one day soon, he'd earn that trust. "You bet I will."

"Yeah!" the child repeated, then took off in the direction of the slides. John stood. School must have let out for the day judging by the number of kids now crowding into the swing sets and seesaws. What kinds of things did Claire like to do? Did she like exploring the woods behind her house or was she more of a bookworm like her mother? He grimaced as the memory of his daughter leaning on her crutch lanced through him.

"So did you talk to Merrilee?" Ms. Aurora sunk down into a nearby bench and settled her purse beside her. "She must have been as surprised as I was when you showed up on her doorstep."

"Things didn't go like I'd hoped."

"Do they ever?" She nodded to the space next to her.

"No," John dropped down in the seat beside her. "I guess not."

Aurora reached over and patted his hand, reminding him of when she would comfort him as a small boy. "At least you're back home."

Guilt flooded through him like a jolt of electricity at the thought of how long he'd been away. The truth was that losing Merrilee and his hope for the family they'd planned to build together had right near killed him. He couldn't return to Marietta, not after the last time when he'd shown up for the divorce hearing only to be told Merrilee had sent her father in her place. Jacob Daniels had crowed like a rooster at sunrise, thrilled to let him know that Merrilee had moved on with her life. She was extraordinarily happy. There hadn't seemed much sense in sticking around. He'd distanced himself from almost everything that had to do with Merrilee, including Aurora. The woman who'd been like a mother to him.

"I'm sorry, Ms. Aurora. I shouldn't have just left like that."

"You had a job you needed to get back to. Plus I figured God would bring you home when He was good and ready." She lifted her face to his, her mouth quivering into a watery smile. "And here you are."

"Thank you." John covered Aurora's hand with his. The woman dished out love like she did everything else in her life, in abundance. "Aren't you going to ask me why I've come back to Marietta after all this time?"

"That's your story to tell, son, and I figure you'll tell it when you're ready." The steel-colored bun at the nape of her neck bounced slightly. "So are you going to tell me what happened with Merrilee?"

With a glance to check on Ellie, John reached into his coat pocket for his daughter's letter, then handed it to Ms. Aurora. "I got this two weeks ago."

The older woman read over the sheet of paper then glanced over at him. "I don't understand."

"I didn't know I had a daughter until I received this letter. Merrilee never told me."

Ms. Aurora's mouth gaped open in disbelief. "That doesn't sound like her."

He had to admit, it didn't sound like the woman he'd known. But if life had taught him anything, it was that nothing ever stayed the same. "Nothing folks do surprises me anymore."

Aurora ignored his sarcastic remark. "But I know Merrilee. Are you sure she didn't write you?"

The only correspondence he'd received from his former wife in the months after he'd enlisted in the Civilian Conservation Corps was the letter from her father's lawyer, informing him about the divorce. "She wasn't one to keep up with correspondence."

The older woman chuckled softly. "Neither were you, son."

"I wrote." Sparse letters to Aurora, just to let her know he still lived. But to Merrilee, he'd written pages filled with plans for the farm they hoped to settle one day, news about his days with the intricate work of building dams and planning new roadways he'd discovered came so easily to him, confessions of the aching loneliness he felt every night when he returned to the bunkhouse alone. His alarm had grown every day when it felt as if everyone around him had received some letter or package from their sweethearts or wives except for him. John ran a hand across his brow, his palm coming away with a fine sheen of moisture. "I know one thing. I would have been back a long time ago if I'd known about Claire."

"I know you would have." She nudged him with her shoulder. "So did you meet her? Claire, that is."

"Yes, ma'am." The memory of those few moments when his compliments had turned his daughter's cheeks pink with girlish delight made him stretch taller. Paternal pride? "She's the most beautiful thing I've ever seen, Ms. Aurora."

"The spitting image of her mother."

"Yes," he whispered under his breath, his stomach muscles clenching. If anything, Merrilee had grown more beautiful in the past twelve years. Of all the emotions he'd expected to feel today, he'd been surprised there was no anger left in him, just a deep disappointment over what might have been. And as much as he hated to admit it, he still felt the urge to shield her from the likes of people like that bum he'd found her with on the porch. Logical he guessed, this need to protect the mother of his child, only it didn't feel rational or wise.

"How did it go?" Aurora gave him an encouraging smile.

"Okay, I guess." He hesitated. "For a first meeting."

Her gray brows drew together in confusion. "I don't understand."

Aurora wasn't the only one. What could be wrong with a child knowing their father? Except he wasn't sure how long he'd have with Claire before the navy settled his case. Was he being selfish for wanting to know his child, even if it was just for a little while? "Merrilee seems to think Claire isn't up to knowing the truth about who I am just yet."

Songbirds filled the brief silence between them. "She might have a point."

"What? I thought you'd be on my side."

"I never pick sides between people I love." Aurora glanced toward the playground where Ellie happily lifted a handful of sand and watched it sift through her fingers. "But Claire's not the same little girl she was before she contracted polio, and not just because her leg doesn't work the way it should. No, there's a heartsickness in that child that has nothing to do with her injury."

John pushed back, flattening his spine against the wooden slants of the bench. "You've spent time with Claire?"

"Merrilee used to bring her out to visit with me every so often but after Claire got sick, she didn't come out as much." The lines across the older woman's forehead deepened with disappointment. "I figured Merrilee just couldn't face seeing my Billy without wondering if Claire would end up with a limp like him."

Sounded like Merrilee was the one with the problem. "What has been done to help Claire?"

"From what I've heard, she's taken that child to every specialist in Atlanta and Claire's not any better."

John rubbed the back of his neck. The thought of his baby girl hurting felt like a knife to his chest. Whether she walked without the help of a crutch or cane again didn't matter but if Claire was still willing to try new treatments, he'd do everything possible to make them happen. "What about the treatments we did with Mattie? You know, swimming and stretching in the water. Do you think they might help, if we told her about them?"

Aurora's mouth drew into a straight line. "I don't know, son. Merrilee's not one to take help from anyone. In fact, some of the men from the church offered to build a ramp up to her front porch so that Claire wouldn't struggle so badly with those stairs but Merrilee told them no."

"She must have changed her mind because I saw a ramp when I was out there. It needed a little more work to make it sturdy, but other than that..." His mother's stricken look halted his train of thought. "What is it?"

She waved a bony finger at no one in particular. "If the ramp is there, you can be sure Merrilee built it herself."

That would explain the exposed nails. She probably

didn't have the strength to pound them into the boards completely. John blew out a harsh breath. "Good to know she's just as stubborn as always. Did anyone try to reason with her about letting people pitch in?"

"Beau tried, but Merrilee wouldn't hear of it."

"What about James?" John asked. "He always had some pull with his sister."

"James is in prison."

About time, John thought. He'd never taken a liking to Merrilee's oldest brother. At first, it had just been a gut feeling, but he had downright despised the man from the first time Beau had shown up on their doorstep sporting a bruised lip and a black eye courtesy of James Daniels. John had wanted to go after him, but Merrilee had begged him to leave James be and to focus on getting Beau out of that house instead. Beau had been safe from his father for years, but John was still glad to hear that the man was locked away. At least in prison, that piece of trash couldn't get anywhere near Merrilee or Claire.

All he had to worry about now was Major Evans.

He stared out over the activity of the playground. Two little girls hugged the border of the area, whispering back and forth between themselves, their peal of childish giggles causing an ache to settle around his heart. He'd missed so much already, almost all of Claire's girlhood. And if the navy didn't drop the charges pending against him, he'd miss the precious years he would have spent watching her mature into a young woman. He had to make the most of his time right now. But how did he get started? John needed a plan.

The idea that came to him was almost too simple. Merrilee might fuss a bit, but he'd made a living using a hammer and nails. And if that wasn't enough to keep Merrilee quiet, well, it didn't matter. He was Claire's father and it was his job to keep her safe. "Ms. Aurora, do you know where I can get hold of a good hammer and some nails?"

Her gray brows furrowed together. "What are you up to, John Davenport?"

He smiled at her, the tension in his shoulders relaxing for the first time in days. "Going to build my daughter a solid, sturdy ramp, whether Merrilee likes it or not."

Chapter Three

The gray shadows in the brief moments before the sun rose mirrored Merrilee's mood as she made her way across the backyard to the kitchen. A yawn snuck up on her, a tender ache weighing down the muscles in her arms and legs, her eyes burning from countless hours of staring at the ceiling in the inky darkness of night, her mind reliving every moment of her time with John.

Or was it my heart reminding me of what I've lost?

She pushed the silly notion aside. Whatever feelings she had for John Davenport should have petered out a long time ago. No, it was just his sudden reappearance that had her feeling things she'd shelved away years before. It meant nothing that her heart had somersaulted when he'd been with Claire, looking at her as if she were the most perfect precious thing on this earth. He was right, Merrilee agreed silently. Their daughter was the best thing that had come out of the disaster that had been their brief marriage.

The rich scent of brewed coffee wafted through the crisp morning air, spurring her forward. The last time someone else had beat her to the kitchen… Well, no one had ever beat her to the kitchen since her daddy had stood her up on a chair and told her she was the lady of the house when she was barely five.

Lantern light flickered through the screen door. Merrilee peered inside. "Maggie?"

Her niece lifted her head, her gaze glassy as she looked Merrilee over. "Why are you dressed like Rosie the Riveter this early in the morning?"

Merrilee glanced down at her roomy one-piece coverall. "I noticed the ramp to the porch was a little wobbly so I thought I'd work on it. What about you? You're up with the chickens this morning."

"I woke up feeling kind of sick to my stomach. Figured some dried toast would help." A cotton sheet held more color than Maggie's cheeks at the moment.

Pulling open the door, Merrilee stepped inside, then made a quick turn and headed straight for the small pantry just off the kitchen door. "Soda crackers are good for morning sickness, you know."

Maggie gave her a weak smile. "Did you feel this sick when you were expecting Claire?"

"How do you think I knew about the soda crackers?" Merrilee opened the tin and shook a few crackers onto a plate. Walking to the table, she set the dish in front of her niece and sunk down in the chair beside her. "Have you told Wesley?"

"Are you kidding?" Maggie gave the crackers a wary glance then pushed the plate away. "He's the one who told me! I had to make him pinky promise he wouldn't tell anyone about the baby until we talk with Dr. Adams this afternoon."

"So I take it he's excited by the news?"

"Just like a kid on Christmas morning, waiting to see what Santa's brought him to unwrap." Maggie's expression softened. "And he's been so sweet. I mean, he's always been wonderful but yesterday, he asked one of the ladies in the plant lunchroom to make me a pot of her homemade soup just because he knows how much I love it."

Sounded like something Wesley would do. The man was always looking for small ways to pamper his young wife, like the loving husband he was. The dull edge of some emotion—jealousy?—caught Merrilee by surprise. She was happy for her niece, really she was, but in moments like this, even with a houseful of people, Merrilee couldn't help feeling, well, a bit lonely.

"You two are going to make great parents," Merrilee finally said, lightly squeezing Maggie's fingers before letting them go. "It will be good to have a little one in the house again. Claire's growing up so fast."

"How was Claire last night? Did she keep you up late as usual?" Maggie broke off a piece of cracker and popped it into her mouth.

"No, she went down pretty early." Which was odd, Merrilee thought. Since the evening the virus had struck, Claire had fought sleep as if she feared what the darkness would bring. Dr. Adams had assured Merrilee her daughter's fear would pass, but it had been going on for a year now and only seemed to be getting worse. But last night, for the first time in ages, Claire had fallen asleep almost as soon as her head hit the pillow.

"She seemed in a better frame of mind last night," Maggie said, pushing away the plate of crumbs. "I figured she'd still be upset about you forcing her sit out the wedding procession."

Merrilee's head jerked up. "You make it sound like I tied her to a chair."

"Well, you did in a way." Maggie covered her aunt's hand with her own. "You've got to let Claire live, even if she risks falling. It's the only way she'll learn to pick herself up and try again."

Easy for Maggie to say. Her child wasn't crippled. "What if she does fall but can't get up? What if she gets hurt? She's already suffered enough, Maggie. I couldn't stand for her to suffer any more than she already has."

"I know." Her niece's shoulders lifted in a sigh. "I don't want to see her hurt any more than you do. But I can't stand seeing you in pain, either. You've got to give this situation with Claire over to the Lord."

"I have," Merrilee snapped, pulling her hands from Maggie's grasp and settling them in her lap. She'd lost count of the times she'd prayed, begging for God to intervene, to heal Claire. But God hadn't answered, at least not in any voice she understood. So until He did, she had to keep doing everything in her power to get Claire well again. "Sweetheart, I appreciate your concern, but let me deal with this, okay?"

Maggie slumped slightly back into her chair. "Fine."

An awkward silence fell across the kitchen. Finally, Merrilee stood and, grabbing a cup from the strainer, walked over to the coffeepot on the stove. The warmth radiating from the metal doing nothing to chase the chill clinging to her soul. Why did everyone feel they had the right to tell her what to do? Did they believe she'd made such a mess of her life that she couldn't figure things out for herself? Was that why God was so quiet, because she'd failed Him in some way?

"I meant to ask you," Maggie said quietly. "Who was that man you were talking to after the wedding? I didn't recognize him."

Merrilee cringed. Out of the frying pan, into the fire. "I talked to a lot of people yesterday."

"You couldn't miss this one. Good-looking, blond, wearing a gray suit. He looked to be in his early thirties."

Thirty-one next month, Merrilee corrected to herself, though John still had a boyish charm about him, at least where his daughter, and it seemed, her niece were concerned. "That was John."

"John? I don't believe I know anyone…" Maggie's brows tightened into a perfect line, then released over wide green eyes. "Wait a minute. You mean *your* John?"

Merrilee pressed her lips together. "He's not *my* anything."

"But he was once, and he's still Claire's father." Maggie crossed her arms over her waist, a pale rose faintly coloring her cheeks as if the news of John's arrival had cheered her in some way. "Why didn't you tell me about this last night?"

"Because I was busy washing dishes after the wedding reception," Merrilee said. "And paying bills and prepping for breakfast." And if she were completely honest with herself, the fewer people who knew John was in town, the easier it would be for her when he left.

And he would leave again.

"Okay, you were busy and couldn't tell your only niece that Claire's daddy had come for a visit."

"Well, put that way, I sound like a thoughtless ogre."

"As long as you understand that." Maggie gave her a lopsided smile. "So what did he want?"

Merrilee hesitated for a brief moment, wondering how much to tell her niece, then figured she might as well spill the whole story. She told Maggie about Claire finding her father's address in Beau's room and sending him a letter over a year ago, about how John had only recently received it and immediately come to Marietta, about how she'd begged John not to reveal himself to their daughter. Merrilee finished with, "Once John realized just how bad things were with her, he decided not to tell Claire who he is."

Maggie finally spoke. "You mean for now, right?"

"I don't know." Merrilee pressed a hand to her forehead. "I fully expect the man to be gone this morning."

"But he's come all the way across the country and he said he wanted to know Claire. That's a pretty strong incentive to stick around for a while."

John said he wanted to make a life with me, but that didn't keep him from leaving and breaking my heart. The mistakes she'd made with John were too painful, even now. Claire's heart was too fragile to take another disappointment. No, as her mother, Merrilee had to protect her daughter. "Maggie, the only way John Davenport is going to stick around Marietta is if someone nails his feet to the ground."

The two sat quietly for a moment, then Maggie leaned toward her and wrapped her arms around her. "I'm so sorry, Merrilee."

"Me, too." And she was, for Claire and her hopes for

a real father in her life. For herself and what could have been if John had stayed true to his vows.

A light tap at the kitchen door caused both women to look up.

"Who would be coming to call this early in the morning?" Maggie asked as she went to the door.

"It's not a telegram from the War Department, is it?" Merrilee turned in her chair and leaned across the table, anxiety pooling in the pit of her stomach. With two nephews still in battle, dread hung in the air at the thought of a missive from Western Union.

The light oak door blocked any view Merrilee might have had of the visitor. She waited, her hands fisted into tight knots in her lap, any words between her niece and the unknown visitor lost in the thumping of her heart in her ears.

But when Maggie peeked around the edge of the door at her, the impish grin and a hint of mischief that sparkled in her sea-green eyes put Merrilee on alert.

"John Davenport's here, and he's got a hammer and some penny nails with him."

Chapter Four

John, here?

But he was supposed to be gone, fled once he learned the depth of Claire's physical problems. The wooden legs of the chair scratched against the brick floor as she stood, then hesitated. "What does he want?"

"I don't know. Why don't you ask him yourself?" The words were innocent enough, but her niece's glance spoke volumes.

Coward!

Merrilee pursed her lips. Who was her niece calling a coward? The only time she'd backed away from a fight, she'd been five months pregnant and on bed rest. No, if John wanted a fight, she'd be happy to give him one. She rounded the table and walked to stand next to Maggie. "I'll just do that, then."

The question stuck in her throat as she looked at the man standing on the concrete slab just outside her kitchen. Wearing a white T-shirt and a pair of overalls that had seen better days, the broad expanse of John's muscular shoulders seemed to brush against the brick border on either side of the doorway. His hair was combed back neatly, shorter than he used to wear it, drawing attention to the granite cut of his jaw. She dropped her gaze, only to find herself staring at his hands, one holding a metal toolbox while the other held a rusted bucket, which contained the nails Maggie had mentioned.

Merrilee drew in a deep breath. What on earth was she doing, gawking like some lovesick schoolgirl? This man had walked out on her and Claire, and he'd do it again. She needed to send him away before he did any real damage. "What are you doing here, John?"

The dark blue of his eyes suddenly sparked with mayhem. "Good morning to you, too."

She braced herself against his crooked smile even as her toes curled inside her shoes. "Is it?"

"Merrilee!" Maggie whispered sharply beside her.

But John just chuckled, a deep throaty sound she still remembered in the mist of long sleepless nights. "Someone hasn't had her cup of coffee this morning. I know your daddy taught you better manners than that. Snapping at a person, particularly one who's here to help, isn't a very attractive quality in any woman, much less a Daniels."

She mashed her lips together in a painful line. Oh, her daddy had taught her plenty all right, mainly that she wasn't worth much if she didn't do his bidding. But Daddy had been dead almost five years now, and she could finally do as she pleased, even ask questions and demand replies. "You still didn't answer me."

Merrilee's jaw tightened as one side of his mouth curled upward in that same crooked grin she'd seen on her daughter's face for the past eleven years. It had hurt at first, watching the child she loved smile that smile, but all that remained now was a slight ache.

"I thought I'd work on that ramp you've got out front. It wobbles quite a bit whenever Claire uses it."

He'd been here long enough yesterday to see Claire struggle up and down the ramp? "I noticed that myself, which is why I planned on fixing it today."

"You?"

The way he said it, so condescending. Just like a man. "Yes, me," she snapped.

"Then you don't have to worry about it now." He tightened his grip around the handle of the pail, penny nails winking back at her. "I'll take care of it."

She didn't need any favors, particularly from this man. "That's all right. I can handle it."

John's gaze hardened for an instant before focusing on a point just over her shoulder. "She's always been this stubborn. Did you know that?"

"Family trait," Maggie answered with a chuckle. "Daddy says all the Daniels women are as stubborn as mule's teeth."

Merrilee shot her niece a venomous look. Traitor!

John's warm laughter brought her attention back to him. "Aren't you going to introduce me?"

She hadn't planned on it, but he'd left her no choice now. "John, I don't know if you remember Jeb's daughter, Maggie Hicks. Maggie, this is John Davenport."

"It's nice to finally meet you, John. I've heard so much about you."

Gracious gravy, what was Maggie trying to do? Stir up a pit of rattlesnakes? This meeting with John was already uncomfortable as it was.

But if John sensed the daggers she was shooting at her niece, he didn't show it. "How is your father doing?"

Maggie pushed in close behind Merrilee. "Good. He's still running his crop-dusting business out of his farm in Hiram."

"I remember when we cleared out that field on the north side of your house to make the runway." John nodded. "Good man, your dad."

Merrilee blinked. Had John truly said something nice about one of her male kin? The world must have fallen into mayhem. Or maybe John had finally changed his opinion on the matter.

She knew she had.

"Would you like a cup of coffee?"

Merrilee glared at her niece. Had pregnancy caused Maggie to take leave of her senses? Even now, the room seemed to shrink around her at just the thought of John sitting at her table after all these years.

"That's mighty nice of you, Maggie, but I'm already looking at half a day's work just getting the boards measured and cut for the ramp."

Why wouldn't he let that go? "The ramp is fine, John. Or it will be once I work on it."

"The wood is rotted. Claire could put the tip of her crutch down wrong and go right through the board," he answered matter-of-factly, his words clipped as he turned his dark blue glare on her. "She could get hurt."

Merrilee's stomach turned sour. She'd known the wood wasn't in the best condition but with building supplies rationed like sugar, she'd been forced to use what she had on hand. "At least let me help you pay for the boards."

His expression turned stormy, his jaw clenched so tight, she feared for a second the bones would shatter. "I don't need your daddy's money to do something for our daughter. Is that understood?"

She hesitated for a moment before nodding. What would John say if he knew the Daniels money was just a memory now, like the Charleston dance or silent pictures? Or that the only way she could acquire Claire's treatments was to spy on her friends and neighbors? A new fear lanced through Merrilee. What if he found out the truth—that she was about to lose the house he'd bought her—and decided Claire would be better off living with him?

"It was nice meeting you, Maggie."

"Nice to meet you, too."

John turned away from the door and headed across the yard, the morning dew clinging to the legs of his overalls, darkening the denim cuffs to pitch-black. As if he knew she was watching, he glanced over his shoulder, the harsh line of his mouth making her heart sink even more. If John chose to fight her on which of them was better suited to provide for their daughter, she'd give as good as she got.

Even if it broke her heart again.

"He's a handsome fellow, isn't he?"

In her musings, she'd forgotten her niece standing nearby. "Well, you know the old saying. Beauty is only skin deep, but ugly goes clean to the bone."

Maggie scoffed. "You didn't come off too pretty yourself this morning, drilling him like he was one of Mack's suspects down at the police station. He only wanted to do something any father would do for his child."

"Maybe, but why now? Why, after all these years, after all those letters I sent him despite never getting any reply, does he show up to make some claim on Claire now?"

"I don't know. But aren't you always the one who says God reveals His plans when we least expect it?"

"Yes," she answered grudgingly. That was before Claire had come down with the polio, before Merrilee had mortgaged her house to pay for Claire's treatments, before she'd had to barter her soul to the army for a cure to heal her daughter's leg that might not ever come.

No, if she could get Claire into Warm Springs, there was a chance her baby could be whole again.

"I just wonder where he got those new boards from."

"New boards?"

"For Claire's ramp. Weren't you listening?" Maggie chuckled as she walked back to the table. "Wesley's been talking about making a crib for the baby, but Mr. Drummond down at the hardware store says it would take an act of Congress to get enough wood in the near future."

"And John said he had new boards?"

Maggie nodded. "Yes."

Maggie was right—that didn't make any sense. So where would he have gotten new boards for Claire's ramp?

Only one place. Aurora's.

John held the four-by-four flush against the stud, the penny nail secured between his fingers, a light dusting of rust covering his thumb and forefinger. It had taken half the night to sand down the three old boards Aurora had had stashed in the barn, but he'd wanted them to look nice as well as be sturdy for Claire. A lot of work, maybe, but he'd do it again in a heartbeat. Anything for his little girl.

And he wouldn't take a penny for it, no matter what Merrilee thought.

He lifted the hammer and banged it down against the nail head. Why had Merrilee flung her family's money in his face? Was she cruising for a fight? Or had she learned about the deal he'd made with her father some twelve years before?

John grabbed another nail from the bucket. He'd been a fool back then, trying to negotiate with Jacob Daniels. But it was the only way he'd ever imagined he could give Merrilee the home she deserved. Now she was living in the Daniels's homestead, and he was on the outside looking in, hoping for a glimpse of his daughter.

The screen door squealed open, the soft thump of wood against wood causing John to stop what he was doing and look up. A smile lifted his lips as he regarded the young girl who had him so neatly twisted around her little finger. The blue-and-white-plaid dress she wore hit her a few inches about the knee—too short in his opinion, but then, he was her father. What would he know about dresses and such? "Well, hi there."

"You're back." A smile hovered around her lips, but didn't move up into her jade-colored eyes.

"I told you I would be."

"I just figured..." she started to say, taking a little

step closer, then hesitated, her gaze shifting to the hammer and nails. "What are you doing?"

It troubled him, this uncertainty on his little girl's face. Didn't Claire have any idea she was perfect just the way she was, limp and all? "I noticed this ramp was wobbling a little bit when I was here yesterday, and decided to fix it."

"You know how to build stuff?"

Was that a note of excitement in her voice? What would she do if he told her he'd helped build Boulder Dam? He checked himself in time, remembering that Beau had told her about their adventures there. As smart as Claire was, she'd probably put two and two together and figure out who he was. "Yes, for the most part."

"Who taught you how to do it?"

He leaned back against the railing and studied the wonder that was his daughter. "You're a nosy little monkey, aren't you?"

"Mama says you won't ever find out the answers if you don't ask the questions." She stretched her crutch out to the side and slid her heavily braced right leg forward, crumbling against the crutch as she tried to maintain her balance.

Part of him wanted to lift her up in his arms and promise she'd never have to use the cumbersome crutch and brace again, but that wouldn't be doing her any favors. No, the only way she'd grow strong was in the struggle. Mattie had taught him that.

But he could give her help. "Can I ask you something?"

"Okay."

"Is that crutch you're using comfortable when you walk?"

Dark red lashes hugged the upper slopes of her cheeks as she closed her eyes. "None of this stuff is comfortable."

Poor girl. He held out his hand. "Can I look at it for a minute?"

Her eyes flew open. "Why?"

Again with the questions. Just like her mother! "I think the reason it's more uncomfortable than usual is because you've grown a couple inches since you started using it."

"So it's too short for me?" She handed him her crutch.

"For now," he answered, studying the wooden arms. "But I'm going to unscrew these wing nuts and pull it out a bit to fit your height, and looky there." He slid the leg up a couple inches, then lined up the two holes before retightening the screw. "We've fixed the problem."

She took the crutch from him, shoving it under her left arm. "Hey, that is better."

John bowed his head slightly. "I aim to please, ma'am."

He watched as she hobbled around the porch. She moved across the floor better now, without as much of the limp he'd noticed yesterday at the wedding. Why hadn't one of the doctors Claire had been visiting for treatment noticed something as simple as lengthening her crutch? Why hadn't Merrilee?

"You know, Mama says I'm not going to need a ramp or crutch real soon," Claire said, her gaze sliding to the floor.

John frowned. He'd seen that look before reflected back at himself. Their daughter wasn't convinced of Merrilee's assurances, not for one second. But why? Had she given up hope? "When you don't need the ramp anymore, I'll come over here and tear it down."

A faint smile returned. "Really?"

"Then you'll have to help me pull out every last one of these nails and straighten them out so that we can build something new."

"Like a doghouse?"

He glanced around the yard. "Do you have a dog?"

Twin pigtails shook from side to side. "No. Mama says it's hard enough to feed a house full of people without having to worry about taking care of a dog, too." Holding her braced leg out in front of her, Claire climbed down her crutch until she fell a short distance to the step beside him.

"I'm impressed," John said. "Not everyone can do that."

A shadow fell over her face. "I've had lots of practice."

His poor baby girl. No telling how much longer she'd be struggling to regain the strength in her leg. Merrilee had sought treatment for Claire, but where and with whom? What if there is nothing else anyone could do? How could he help this precious girl understand she was loved, no matter how her body failed her? *Help my baby girl, Father. And if she's to remain like this, give her the strength to handle it.*

He watched Claire study the hammer and the other tools he'd brought to fix her ramp. Healing her might be out of his control, but he could teach her how to be more independent. "You want to help me out here?"

Claire's eyes widened. "How can I? I don't know how to do anything like that."

"It just takes a little practice, that's all."

"But," she started, her expression somber, "what if I mess up?"

"Honey, everybody makes mistakes when they try something new. That's how you learn." He twirled the hammer around in his hand until his fingers closed over the metal head, the handle stretched out to Claire. "And I figure if I can do it, someone as smart as you won't have a problem at all."

"You think so?"

He nodded. "You can do anything you put your mind to. Now, grasp the handle, like you're shaking someone's hand."

She slid her delicate fingers over the wood and tightened her grip around the base of the handle. "Like this?"

"Good, good." John made a note to himself to run by Drummond's Hardware Store and see if they had a smaller hammer he could buy for Claire.

"It's a little bit heavy." She lifted the head of the hammer toward her, eyeing the claw hook with some suspicion. "What does this end do?"

More questions. Inquisitive girl, his daughter. He found that the thought filled him with pride. "We'll use that end to pull the nails out once you're ready for this ramp to come down." Fishing a nail out of his pail, he handed it to her. "Now tap this into the wood right here, just enough to get it started."

Scrunching her eyebrows together, she made short

little raps with the hammer against the head until it was embedded into the wood. "I did it!"

The look of sheer joy on his daughter's face almost undid him. How could something so simple bring so much happiness to this child? And he'd helped her do it. Just like a father should. "You sure did!"

"Now what do I do?" Claire looked so adorably sweet, her green eyes sparkling with excitement, her lower lip caught between her teeth. There was so much he could teach her, like how to catch a fish or fly a kite or a million other things.

If he didn't end up in prison.

"Claire? What are you doing?"

He'd been so involved with Claire, just enjoying this moment with her, he hadn't heard the screen door open. Though she tried to hide it, Merrilee looked none too happy at the moment.

Chapter Five

They looked so perfect together, John teaching their daughter how to use a hammer. Enthusiasm had seemed to infuse Claire's whole being at learning this simple task, the sheer joy on her face reminding Merrilee of the happy, exuberant child Claire once was. A mischievous bundle of ribbons and bows who brought light into Merrilee's lifeless world.

"Look, Mama. John taught me how to use a hammer."

She ought to be angry with him. He knew she wasn't keen on him spending time with Claire. But she couldn't be, not when he'd drawn their daughter out of the gloom she'd been mired in this past year, even if just for a moment. This respite, no matter how short-lived, was worth her gratitude.

Taking a step forward, Merrilee crouched down on the top step, smoothing her skirts over her legs, the hem brushing the tops of her shoes. "Why don't you show me, Claire Bear?"

Her daughter's face lit up, the impish grin that had disappeared in recent months back and in full force, stretching all the way into her eyes as she reached for a nail. Merrilee's eyes began to burn with each drop of the hammer. How had John known that something so simple could bring Claire this much enjoyment? And why did John's success make her feel as if she'd failed her daughter once again?

"Good job, Claire," John said as the girl finished tapping the nail one last time. "I think you've practiced enough for right now. Don't you think so, Merrilee?"

She glanced over to John and found him studying her, his expression cautious. *Great, another person walking on eggshells around me.* Had she become some old crone that made folks want to tiptoe around her? All she wanted was answers to her questions. One question in particular.

What do I have to do to get Claire well?

"Merrilee?"

"Oh, yes." She leaned over to examine the dainty dents Claire had made in the pine board. "You did a great job, sweetheart. John must be a very good teacher."

The girl's smile grew even bigger, if that were possible. "He said that when I don't need the ramp anymore, we can tear it down and make a doghouse."

"A doghouse?" Merrilee exclaimed, her eyes narrowing in on John. They wouldn't have a roof over their own heads soon, much less one for a dog. If he'd promised Claire a puppy...

"No, you said we could make it into a doghouse, and I asked if you had a dog. Unless your mother agrees, there won't be one, understand?"

Ah, a little more of the old Claire coming out, that determination to get what she wanted, even if she had to wear you down. And John was having none of it. Good. She'd fought this battle alone for years, so it was nice to have someone else in her corner.

But for how long?

She needed to nail him down on a date for when he'd be leaving. For Claire's sake. And, she grudgingly admitted, for her own. "Darling, why don't you go out to the kitchen and bring John a glass of iced tea? He must be thirsty."

"Yes, ma'am!" The young girl pushed herself off the stairs, shoving her good leg beneath her, wobbling as she tried catch her balance. Merrilee reached out to her, but John caught her by the hand. Her head jerked up, but instead of a dark glare, she found herself tumbling into warm blue eyes holding a hint of compassion that caught her off guard. She got a sense that he somehow knew about the constant fears she had concerning Claire, the overwhelming guilt that kept her awake at night, the heartbreaking despair that drove her to her knees. Just believing he understood, even vaguely, brought Merrilee an unexplained comfort.

"I'll be right back." Claire slid the crutch under her left arm and hobbled along the dirt path, her gait more fluid than Merrilee had seen in weeks.

When their daughter's shadow disappeared around the corner of the house, John let go of her hand. "Sorry about that, but I had to make sure I'd adjusted her crutch to the proper height."

"What are you talking about?"

"You might not have noticed, but Claire had a growth spurt." He told her about their daughter's dress and the way she seemed to fumble with the crutch. "So I lengthened the crutch out and she seems to be moving better."

She hadn't noticed a thing. What kind of mother was she? John had been here two days—two days!—playing daddy and he'd already found a way to make their daughter more comfortable, not to mention how he'd drawn Claire out of the shell she'd encased herself in this past year. Why was he doing all this? So he could up and leave them again? No. Merrilee stood. "You grabbed my hand when she was about to fall."

"You think I would let her get hurt?"

She ignored his question. "She could have fallen."

"Would it have been so bad if she had?"

Whatever words she might have thought to say stuck in her throat. "How could you be so heartless?"

John stood then, his body taut. The color had drained from his face, giving her the impression her words had hit their mark. "No more heartless than telling her she'll get the use of her leg back when it might never happen."

He spoke not in anger or defensiveness, but a kindness that did nothing to lessen the sting of his statement. "You don't understand."

"Yes, I do. You only want what is best for her. I do, too."

"But you'd let her fall?"

"I'd never let her get hurt if I can help it. But we can't be there all the time, so she probably will fall down." John stretched his back out, his white T-shirt pulled tight against the bunched muscles of his chest. "But isn't it our responsibility to teach her how to get up again rather than catch her every time?"

"You make it sound so simple," she scoffed. "But

you try watching your child struggle, wondering if you could have done something different so that they didn't have to suffer through the rest of their lives. It's pretty difficult just to sit on the sidelines."

He glared at her with a mixture of compassion and frustration. "I spent almost eight years of my life living with Ms. Aurora, so I have quite a bit of understanding on the subject."

"That doesn't make you an expert, John."

He shook his head. "No, but a person doesn't forget living with people like that."

"I wouldn't know." It was one of the mysteries surrounding John; how an able-bodied child like him had not found a home with any of the farming families in the county, but had ended up living with Aurora and her family of unadopted children. One he'd never felt close enough to her to reveal.

Would she ever learn the truth about John's childhood? And why, after all this time, did she still care?

His stoic expression told her she'd have to wait a while longer. "Bottom line, Claire just wants to be treated like everyone else."

"But she's not like everyone else, now, is she? She needs help until she recovers the use of her leg."

"And if this is as good as she gets? What then?"

"Don't say that!" Merrilee snapped. Because giving way to those thoughts might make them real, and Merrilee couldn't bear it for their girl. For the rest of her life, Claire shouldn't have to put up with all the covert looks, all the whispers people didn't realize she could hear. Almost as if they'd thought Claire had brought this upon herself. Their daughter didn't deserve to be treated like she had less value than anyone else. Nobody did.

"Look—" John picked up a couple nails off the steps and threw them into his pail "—I know you're worried and you're scared for her. You've got every right to be. Whether you believe it or not, I'm concerned about her, too."

How could John feel anything close to the emotions she felt for Claire? He barely knew her. But studying his face, seeing the edges of worry already carving out tiny lines around his eyes and forehead, she couldn't deny the truth staring back at her. The amount of time he'd known about Claire didn't matter. He cared for their daughter. A dull ache settled against her ribs. Jealousy? Merrilee swallowed hard at the bitter thought. What kind of woman envied what her child had?

John must not have noticed her discomfort. "What do the doctors say?"

Merrilee hesitated. Could she trust him with this burden, trust him to love Claire despite what the future might hold? She shook the fear away. He was Claire's father and had the right to know the extent of the damage. Merrilee slid down to the stairs, fisting her hands into her skirts to keep them from shaking. "Recovering the use of the weakened muscles a year after the initial virus is very rare."

John slid down to the place next to her, his forearms resting against his haunches, his long fingers threading into a loose steeple. "You've got a second opinion?"

"And a third, and a fourth. They all have given up hope on her."

She could feel his gaze slide over her. "But you haven't."

Merrilee shook her head. "I can't. Not yet."

He reached over and covered her hand with his, the hard calluses gently scraping the tender skin of her knuckles, closing over her fingers in a warm clasp. "We're going to get her through this."

She wanted to grasp the certainty in his words and hold on for dear life. But how much could she depend on a man who had already left her once?

"Mr. John!"

The sharp cry jerked Merrilee's head up and drew her attention to the sight of the young boy limping up the drive, his denim overalls covered in a thick coating of dust from the way his useless foot dragged through the dirt.

"Billy?" John asked, standing.

Billy Warner, one of Aurora's children. He'd been in Claire's class in third grade, but hadn't come back after that, Aurora deciding to school him at home rather than continue making repeated trips to the principal's office. Merrilee smiled. The kid was a fighter, taking nothing from anybody. A necessary trait for a boy with a twisted spine.

But there was no fight in him today. Only an expression of pained fear in his eyes that drew Merrilee to her feet.

John vaulted off the steps and rushed down the path to where the boy had stopped to rest and catch his breath. "Billy, what is wrong?"

The boy glanced at her, then at John, his lower lip trembling slightly. "It's Ms. Aurora. She sick."

* * *

Aurora sick? Why, the woman had a constitution as strong as any battleship John had sailed on during his time in the Pacific! The kid had to be mistaken. "What happened?"

Billy's frantic eyes caught his, making John's stomach pitch. "She was making oatmeal like she always does in the mornings, but then she went all white like she'd seen a mouse or something. I got up to see if I could find it, you know, shoo it out of the house. That's when Ms. Aurora fell on the floor, right there in front of the stove."

The boy shook beneath his hands as John grasped his thin shoulders. "You didn't leave her like that, did you?"

Billy shook his head. "Dr. Adams is with her now. He told me to come and find you. Said she was asking for you."

Aurora had to be alert to ask for him, so that was a good sign. Poor Billy, though—watching the only mother he'd ever known collapse like that. It made John wonder how the other children were faring. He turned around to find Merrilee close behind him. "I hate to do this, but I've got to go."

"Let me get the truck and I'll drive you."

Merrilee, driving a truck? Her father would be rolling over in his grave at the thought of his daughter doing something as unseemly as operating a motor vehicle. The image made him smile slightly. "We'd appreciate it."

"I'll get my handbag and tell Claire where we're going."

"Why not bring Claire along? Y'all haven't been out

to the farm in a while and I could sure use the help with Ellie," Billy said.

"I don't know." Merrilee seemed to war with the idea, her lips pursing in thought. Then she glanced at him. "What do you think?"

John wasn't sure what it was, the idea of spending more time with Claire or the thought that Merrilee had sought his opinion that made his heart race. Right now, he didn't have time to sort it out. "I wish I had thought of it first."

"We'll meet y'all around front." She took off toward the side of the house, her skirts twirling around shapely legs. Even hurrying across the yard, she carried herself with the kind of grace he imagined came from years of practice. How considerate it had been of her to offer them a lift back to Aurora's, but then Merrilee had always been a kind soul. How had he forgotten that about her? Probably pushed it to the back of his heart along with all the other memories of her, he guessed. Be best for him if they stayed there.

"She's a nice lady, isn't she?"

John glanced down at the cow-eyed boy, and what felt like envy caused the muscles in his chest to tighten slightly. "You know Ms. Merrilee?"

The boy's blond hair fell into his eyes as he nodded. "She used to bring Claire out and visit us every couple days. Brought us watermelons in the summertime. All of us liked to see her and Claire coming."

Aurora had mentioned Merrilee's visits, but had they really been as often as twice to three times a week? Why? Aurora was his family; the farm, his boyhood home. Both were worlds away from the society into which Merrilee had been raised. Yes, the two women had taken to each other like peas in a pod when he'd introduced Merrilee to Aurora years ago, but he was surprised to hear they'd remained friends all these years. Was that why Aurora had told him she wouldn't take sides? Because she loved them both?

Twenty minutes later, John thought they might've made better time walking. A low rumble from the direction of the engine shook the entire body of Merrilee's truck as she pushed in the clutch to change gears. When she finally placed her hand back on the wheel, John watched the gearshift wiggle from side to side. Someone—Beau, her brothers, even that stuck-up major—ought to be shot for letting her out on the road with the truck in such poor condition. Didn't anyone worry she could break down and get stranded? Or worse?

He stole a glance at Merrilee, who didn't seem the least bit nervous about their transportation. "Don't you think it's time to get rid of this heap? Maybe get something that's less likely to break down every time you drive it?"

"I don't know if you've heard, but there's a war going on. Cars are hard to come by." Reddish-blond curls fell across her shoulders as she grabbed the gearshift and pushed it into third. "Besides, I've got bills to pay."

A Daniels struggling with bills? How could that be? She owned her house—he'd made sure of that himself. With the money Merrilee had inherited from her daddy and the rent she took in at the boardinghouse, she should be living high on the hog. "So what did you buy? A new dress from the window at Saul's?"

Her fingers tightened around the steering wheel. "The bills are from doctors mainly. But there's also utilities and food and clothing and..." She mashed her lips together. "Let's just say money's tight."

It couldn't be as bad as all that, not with all the assets her father had owned throughout the county before his death. But as John looked at her, he noticed little things. The frayed hem of her dress, the worn soles on her shoes. Even the black leather handbag perched next to her looked like it had seen better days. And what about Claire's dress? Had there been no money to replace it with another when she'd outgrown it?

John frowned. He should have considered the possibility. He'd assumed Merrilee had never done without, what with all the Daniels's money. Could he have miscalculated the situation? Had Jacob Daniels left Merrilee with no way to support herself and their daughter?

Merrilee may have kept Claire a secret, but he'd do right by them both now. "I've got a little money put back if you need it."

The brakes protested with a high-pitched squeal as Merrilee stomped down on the foot pedal. He gritted his teeth as the truck slid to a stop. "I'm perfectly capable of taking care of my daughter."

My daughter. A dig, he recognized. Merrilee's way of getting him to back off. Okay, he'd let the subject go for the moment. But one thing was for certain. The first second he could manage to sneak away, he would yank the distributor cap off the piece of junk and put this truck out of its misery.

Chapter Six

"When did you learn how to drive?"

"A while ago." Merrilee tried to relax her shoulders, but the front end of her truck veered left unless she kept a death grip on the steering wheel so she tightened her fingers until she thought they'd break.

Why had she slipped up and told him she had a mountain of bills? It wasn't any of his business how she spent her money, or how little of it she had left to spend. It just made her spitting mad when he went on about buying new dresses and such as if she had all the money in the world. Is that how he'd thought of her, as some flighty socialite, only good at wasting her daddy's money? What would John say if he knew she'd sewn most of her own clothing for years, using discarded feed sacks from Mr. Varner's grocery store?

"You always did want to learn."

Stay focused. Merrilee nodded. "And you tried to teach me, remember?"

"In that old Model T." John draped his arm across the back of the bench seat, his fingertips barely brushing against her shoulder before curling over the top of the seat. "When your dad found us in front of the church, I thought he was going to drag me out of that car and beat me to within an inch of my life."

"Instead, he took a sledgehammer to your headlights."

"Your old man did me a favor." He chuckled, the sound low and melodious, like a Bing Crosby tune. "Sold that piece of junk for scrap metal the next day."

A gentle breeze blew through the cab of the truck, leaving in its wake the sharp scent of John's lemon-lime aftershave. "You always were one to land on your feet."

"I didn't have much of a choice."

She'd never thought of him that way, not when John came across as so confident, as if he could take over the world if he chose to do so. She knew how lonely it was, trying to convince yourself and everyone else that you've got things under control when really you don't have any idea what to do. Merrilee had felt like that most of her life. Why hadn't she ever thought that John might feel the same way?

"Why didn't Jacob want you to drive? It wasn't like you were running any of his moonshine or something."

She scoffed. "If I could have turned a profit running corn mash, Daddy would have had me in a car the minute my feet could reach the pedals. But he thought it unladylike for a girl to drive." Or at least that was what he'd told her every time she'd brought the subject up. But Merrilee knew the truth. A car meant freedom, and that was the one thing Daddy had refused to give her. "After Claire was born, it seemed silly sitting around, waiting for one of my brothers to come take me to the grocery store or to one of Claire's doctor's appointments. So I convinced Jeb to teach me."

From the corner of her eye, she caught a brief glimpse of his smile. "I wouldn't want to have been in Jeb's shoes once your father found out."

"He never put up with much of Daddy's nonsense like James did," she answered, putting her arm straight out the window to signal a left-hand turn. "Daddy wasn't doing too well by then, so he didn't have the fight in him like he once did."

"How old was Claire when he passed?"

"Barely two. She didn't understand that her papaw had gone away."

"I'm sorry," he answered soberly.

She glanced at him. "Why? Daddy made your life miserable. So don't pretend you could stand him just because he died."

"I was thinking more about you. How hard losing him must have been for you."

Where was a hole when she wanted to crawl in one? Of course, John had figured she'd taken the death of her father hard—and she had. Because she'd never measured up in Jacob Daniels's eyes, had always been "just a foolish girl," not a person on equal footing with her brothers, and with his death she'd lost any chance of changing his mind. "I appreciate it, but that was a long time ago."

"Not so long ago that it can't still hurt."

Merrilee stole a glance at him in the rearview mirror. Was he talking about her losing her father or…

Had something in her manner told John how much she still grieved the end of their marriage? How, in the wee small hours of the morning, as she'd lain in her bed, she'd let herself go back to those last few weeks before he'd sent her the letter asking for a divorce? In the years since, she'd pored over every moment, every detail, wanting an answer and never getting one that made any sense until only one conclusion remained.

John had stopped loving her.

Her fingers tightened around the wheel. *This isn't about me and John, Lord. It's about Claire building a relationship with her father. Please protect my baby girl's heart.*

She nodded toward the two children huddled in the back of the truck bed. "Do you think they're okay back there?"

Her breath hitched when John turned toward her, rested his bent knee on the seat between them where it lightly brushed against her hip as he stared out the glass. "They seem to be having a good time. Still think we should have made Claire sit up front with us."

She couldn't help but laugh. "Now who's being the overprotective one?"

"Billy's been talking her ear off. What could the kid have to say to her that would take that long?"

Poor man. He really didn't have a clue about raising a daughter. "Don't you remember when you'd sneak over to the house and we'd sit out on the porch talking until Daddy finally chased you off with a broom?"

The startled look John gave her would have been funny if he wasn't so serious. "But you were older. Not to mention mature for your age."

Merrilee laughed. "Claire's only two years younger than I was when you started courting me."

"She's not—" he hesitated, and his handsome face contorted in a look of sheer horror for one brief moment "—boy crazy, is she?"

Despite her best intentions, her heart ached for him. She gave him what she hoped was a sympathetic smile. "Not yet, but she's already wanting to wear lipstick and get her hair cut like Maggie and Edie." Merrilee caught herself. "But that was before she got sick."

She felt his gaze resting on her as he leaned back against the truck door. "No wonder your daddy put me in jail after we got married. If someone took off with Claire, I don't think I could be that merciful."

No, she could imagine he wouldn't be, not to a boy who'd come to steal away their daughter. But then John had always been the protective kind, watching out for Aurora and her children, acting as the man of the house. Maybe that was one of the reasons she'd been so attracted to him in the first place; with John, she'd always been safe.

Until he'd left her; then her world never seemed safe again. Merrilee bent her arm upward to signal her turn as she slowed in front of Aurora's driveway. "Remind me to hide all the shotguns and shovels when Claire starts dating."

John laughed, his face relaxed. "On the job two days and already I'm sounding more and more like your daddy."

He was wrong, Merrilee thought, wrestling with the steering wheel. Whereas John wanted what was best for Claire, Daddy had only thought of himself.

Silence filled the cab as she spent the next several minutes maneuvering through a maze of deep gullies, the truck pitching from one side to the other. A cloud of fiery-red dust trailed behind them, and Merrilee wondered if it was too much for the kids. But the peals of childish laughter coming from the bed of the truck eased any fears she might have had that Claire was distressed.

As she drove the truck into the clearing, which served as a front yard, John leaned forward, his brows furrowed together in confusion. "What happened to this place?"

She wasn't sure what he was looking at, still too busy fighting the truck's jerky moves. "Haven't you seen it already? I thought you were staying here."

"I am." He leaned against the dashboard, his arms cushioning the ebb and flow of the truck's movements. "But we got home after dark last night, and I left before the sun came up this morning. This is the first time I've seen it in the light."

The shock in his voice jerked Merrilee's gaze toward the house, her foot slipping off the gas until the truck slowed to a stop alongside a newer sedan. The place didn't look much different from the last time she'd been here, but through John's eyes, Aurora's home most likely looked shabby, rundown. The brick-red barn she'd watched John paint the summer before he'd joined the Civilian Conservation Corps had faded to a pale shade of pink. There were brown rotted boards patchworked into the old roofing, and a hint of mildew hung in the air.

The house appeared sturdy enough; the ramp running alongside a set of stairs looked fairly new, though some gaping holes between the casements and the windows were in sore need of attention. Georgia-red clay and granite grew wild in the front yard that had once boasted thick Kentucky bluegrass and pansies in rich shades of purple and gold.

"How did it get this bad?" John whispered, glancing around the landscape as if it were foreign soil. "Aurora always grew some kind of flowers along the house just for the little ones."

The bleakness in his voice caused a knot to tighten in her throat. She'd been fifteen the first time John had brought her home to meet Aurora and Margie, his "little sister," as he'd proudly called her. Barely three years old, Margie had been too feeble to do anything but lay in bed, her arms and legs a tangled mess that looked more like a spider's web than anything human. But every day, Aurora pushed her cot out on the front porch and sang to the child, planting posies and marigolds that teased a rare smile from the girl and made her gray eyes sparkle.

The cool metal of the door handle bit into her palm. Fourteen years had passed since Margie's smile had faded into dust. *Why does life have to be so unfair, Lord? Why?*

As she had begun to expect, He didn't answer. All things were supposed to work together for those who love the Lord, but what was His purpose in all this?

At least, she could answer John's question. "Most of the younger men are overseas now, and when the women aren't at the plant pulling their shifts, they're at any number of places helping in the war effort. Besides, with the rations on building supplies, everyone's house needs a little work, and gardening anything but vegetables is a low priority."

He pulled on the door handle and pushed it open. "I'll have to see what I can do while I'm here."

While I'm here. So she'd been right. John had every intention of leaving Marietta again, but when? And what kind of damage would his departure do to Claire?

Merrilee opened the door and jumped out of the truck, staring out over the sparse yard. One thing was for certain. There'd be no excuse for the rundown condition of the house and yard if Aurora had access to rationed supplies through the black market. Her job of proving Major Evans wrong just got easier.

Sunshine bounced off the screened door as Dr. Adams, a stethoscope flung around his neck, stepped out on the porch. Wrapped around one trouser-clad leg clung a little girl with the palest blond hair Merrilee had ever seen, her face lit up with childish glee.

"Ellie, get off Dr. Adams's leg!" Billy ordered, holding out his hand to help Claire scoot off the tailgate of the truck. "He's not a seesaw."

Adams lifted his leg, sending the child off into another fit of giggles. "It's all right. She's just having a bit of fun."

"Some fun, huh?" John raced across the dirt yard, the worry that had clung to the lines around his eyes temporarily pushed aside. He charged up the stairs, swooping down to grasp the little girl, then lifted her over his head, sending the child over the edge into a full-belly laugh.

"She's a cute little thing, isn't she?" Claire hobbled over and curled into Merrilee's side.

"A handful is more like it," Billy said. "You know, she actually climbed up in the hayloft and couldn't get back down. We spent nearly an hour looking for her." He shook his head. "Always into something. That's what Ms. Aurora says."

"She sure does like Mr. John," Merrilee stated, wrapping her arm around her daughter.

Billy glanced over at Claire. "Didn't you know? He's our brother. He lived here, too, a long time ago, with his little brother."

Little brother? John had never mentioned any family except for the one he'd found with Ms. Aurora. That must be what Billy meant by little brother. Because if it wasn't, where was John's younger brother now?

"Merrilee?"

She looked up to the porch where Dr. Adams and John, with Ellie perched on one hip, waited. She'd have to put her questions aside.

For now.

Something had happened, John thought, holding the wriggling child as he watched Merrilee speak to Claire and Billy. There had been a shift, probably not perceptible to most, a new edge of dogged resolve in his former wife's expression. What had happened in the short seconds since he'd left her by the trunk? And why did it seem he was in her sights?

"Merrilee, I didn't know you were going to be here, but I'm glad you are," the doctor said, giving her a smile that hinted at a familiarity John found annoying. "Ms. Aurora's been asking for you." He glanced at John. "You must be her son John, right?"

"Yes."

Adams's gaze slid over him, examining him for any of the impairments he'd most likely seen in all of Aurora's other children, then frowned almost as if he were disappointed he'd found none. "She's been asking for you, too."

"How is she?"

He glanced down at Ellie. "It might be best if we talked inside."

At least he'd had the courtesy to consider Ellie, John thought. Folks didn't realize just how much a child with Down syndrome could understand, and Ellie was brighter than most. He leaned his forehead against the little girl's. "Mr. John needs to talk to the doctor for just a few minutes, okay?"

Her twin pigtails bounced in rhythm with her nodding head, her little hands already pushing John away. She scrambled down his leg, then hurried across the yard to where Billy and Claire stood, her infectious laughter matching a nearby blue jay note for note.

John turned back to the doctor. "Where are the other children?"

"There's more?" Merrilee asked, her eyes wide with surprise. "She only had Billy and Ellie last time I was here."

"There are three more in the parlor," Adams answered. "Two mongoloid boys and a girl who's blind."

"Who's with them?" John asked.

"Nobody right now, but I don't think they can get into much trouble just sitting there."

The man's attitude irked him. Didn't he realize that

they were still children who, despite their disabilities, could manage to find trouble just like any other child?

He opened his mouth to say so, but Merrilee cut him off. "Children are children, Robert. Let me go check to see that they're okay, and then we can talk about what's going on with Aurora."

John stole a quick glance at Merrilee. He didn't remember her being so comfortable around Aurora's when they were together, so why the big change?

Of course, she'd been barely a woman then, with a heart he'd sometimes suspected was too tender to handle his adopted family. Her attitude had obviously changed over the years, he thought as the screen door closed behind her. What other changes would he discover in the woman who'd once been his wife?

He turned back toward the doctor, but the man's expression was as hard as the granite peeking out under the crimson dirt in the front yard. Another set of giggles drew his attention across the front path to where Claire and Billy stood, swinging Ellie between them.

The screen door slammed shut behind him, and Merrilee came to stand next to him, lifting her face to look at him. "They're fine. The boys are playing with their toy trucks and the girl is sitting by the radio, listening to music."

"Thank you."

She lowered her gaze, but couldn't hide the faint blush that invaded her cheeks. He turned back to find Dr. Adams giving him a dubious look. John cleared his throat. "It might be best if we talked out here."

The doctor's shoulders lifted in a sigh. "I can't go into the details of Ms. Aurora's condition except to say that she needs complete rest. At least a month, maybe longer."

"That's not telling us much," Merrilee said, a slight bite to her words.

The doctor ignored her. "I've left her with a couple prescriptions. Make sure she takes them as directed."

Merrilee tensed beside him, finally wrapping her arms around her waist as if to keep her hands occupied. "Come on, Robert. Tell us what's wrong."

The man's lips pressed into a hard line. "You know I can't do that, Merrilee."

John felt a fight looming between the two, a battle that was part of a larger war.

He glanced down at the doctor. "Why can't you tell us what's wrong with her?"

Adams straightened to his full height, but still fell short of meeting John's eyes. "Because you're not legally Ms. Aurora's son, and as much as I'd like to help you, I'm forced to abide by the law."

"I see." Though truthfully, John didn't. How was he supposed to take care of Aurora if he didn't even know what was wrong or what signs he should look for if her condition was worsening? What if he waited too long to get help?

"Can you at least tell us if it's infectious?" Merrilee asked. "We've got a houseful of kids to worry about."

John hadn't even thought of that. All he needed was an epidemic running rampant through the house with no idea how to fight it. And what about Merrilee and Claire? Had he put them in harm's way by bringing them here?

Adams shook his head. "No, she's not infectious."

Merrilee gave a sigh of relief beside him. "Thank goodness."

But that still left them no closer to discovering what had caused Aurora to pass out. "I'm going to go talk to her," John announced.

Merrilee's hand stayed him, before she turned back to the doctor. "Could you at least stay until John has talked to her? He may have some questions for you afterward."

He shrugged. "I figured as much. I'll watch the children while y'all are upstairs with her."

"Thank you, Doctor." John held out his hand to the man. No matter the hard feelings that seemed to exist between Adams and Merrilee, he was grateful to the doctor for treating Aurora. "I appreciate it."

Merrilee said nothing, just stood at the door waiting. John opened it for her, then followed her inside. A fine layer of dust formed a film on the few pieces of furniture lining the hallway, brightly colored pictures scrawled in childish hands hanging on the walls like grand works of art. Crayons sat scattered on a table along the stairwell as if to give the tiny artists ample time to put on their final touches. A laundry basket sat in the corner, loaded down with colored balls, chipped building blocks and a sad-looking doll in a dress that had seen better days. Instead of coats and hats, baseball gloves hung from pegs alongside the door.

A perfect place for any kid to grow up.

Merrilee glanced over her shoulder as she took the first step. "Any ideas on how we're going to get Aurora to rest for the next month?"

John touched her shoulder, and she turned, stopping

on the stair above him. The position erased any distance
in their heights, her gaze level with his. This close, he
could count the thick auburn lashes that rimmed her
eyes, feel her warm breath sliding over his face in little
puffs, smell the light scent of warm bread and home she
always wore. A faint tug pulled at his heart, as if she'd
lanced an invisible string through him, holding them
together. But whatever had bound them lay in tattered
threads now.

He stepped back. "Why are you doing this?"

Confusion, and another emotion—nervousness?—
clouded her eyes. "She asked for me."

"Why is that? You never seemed to like this place
before."

Anger flashed bright green in her eyes. "People
change. Besides, I couldn't keep Ms. Aurora from her
granddaughter, now could I?"

Any questions he'd had died with her admission.
"Claire thinks Aurora is her grandma?"

The words hung in the space between them. Merrilee swayed toward him, her lips parted, her eyes wide
with shock and confusion. "Why did I tell you that?"

The urge to catch her and pull her against him pushed
him back a step. "Why wouldn't you?"

She shook her head, the action seeming to give her
time to regain her composure. "We should talk to Ms.
Aurora. Dr. Adams isn't going to wait all day."

"Right." John nodded, watching her turn and start
back up the stairs. He was glad that their conversation
had been forced to end. He was dealing with enough
already, and the more time he spent alone with Merrilee, the more questions he found that needed answers.

Chapter Seven

John rapped his knuckles lightly on the door. "Ms. Aurora?"

Merrilee stared down at the faded carpets, her gaze following a muddy trail of footprints that passed Aurora's doorway and continued on down the hall. Meticulous to a fault, it wasn't like the older woman to let the house get in such a state.

Like it wasn't her habit to blurt out personal secrets. Merrilee mashed her lips together. Keeping Claire's relationship with Aurora quiet had been the older woman's idea, not hers. She'd respected her wishes, though she'd never quite understood why Aurora was so adamant about it. Her mother-in-law, whether legally or not, had always been good to her and to Claire. Surely she would understand Merrilee's slip.

"Come in."

John opened the door, then stood to the side, allowing her to go inside first. Probably just wanted her to make sure Aurora was decent. But the courteous gesture still left her feeling funny, a little jittery inside and utterly feminine, as if she were the only woman in his world. What complete nonsense!

If only that were true.

Entering the room, she felt as if she had tumbled back in time. The same lacy curtains she'd helped Ms. Aurora sew when she first married John still dressed the windows, as did the faded bedspread they'd bought her their first Christmas together. But while the furnishings were the same, time had taken its toll. Age had turned the once white walls to a butter yellow, the bones of Aurora's favorite chair peeked out beneath the threadbare cloth, the once-plump cushions smashed into a thin line.

"John. Merrilee."

Aurora's whisper catapulted Merrilee's attention to the four-poster bed that dominated the room. Walking closer, her breath caught at how frail the woman looked, her long hair freed from its usual knot at the back of her head, the iron-gray strands stark against her snowy white pillowcase. Twin blue bruises under her eyes provide the only color on her pale face. Her breathing rushed out of her, as if she was ending a long day with the children.

Complete rest, the doctor had said. Merrilee bent down beside her. "Can I get you some water, Ms. Aurora? Maybe another blanket?"

"That quilt from the back of my chair would be nice."

"Yes, ma'am." Lifting the patchwork blanket, John unfolded it, his frown growing. He handed one end to Merrilee, his gaze meeting hers. The quilt was paper thin, not much warmer than a sheet. Merrilee made a mental note to check the blankets on the children's beds and go through her linen closet at home.

"I'm glad you're both here. I need to talk to you."

Merrilee stood at the edge of the bed, leaving John the place by his mother. Her hand looked frail in his as he traced the pale blue veins along her wrist. "What's wrong, Ms. Aurora?"

Aurora lifted her other hand and stroked John's cheek like Merrilee did whenever Claire woke up scared after another bad dream. The faint smile she gave them didn't reach her eyes. "My heart's been givin' me trouble for the past few months." She drew in a quick breath. "But I never passed out until today."

"Have you seen Dr. Adams about this before?" Merrilee asked, leaning over the railing, grasping the older woman's foot through the blankets. Even with the multiple layers, her toes felt like ice.

Ms. Aurora's eyes drifted around the room, settling anywhere but on them. "No."

"Why not?" John gently brushed a few rebellious strands of hair away from her face. "Why didn't you use some of the money I sent you?"

Her smile grew a bit wider. "That was earmarked, remember?"

Earmarked for what? She stole a glance at him, but his expression revealed nothing save the worry over this woman who'd raised him.

"Is there anything I can do for you, Mama?"

Aurora nodded, her eyelids drooping slightly. "The doctor says I need to stay in bed for a while, though I don't know how he figures to keep me here." She laughed softly. "I can't take care of the children lying around like this."

"You don't worry about it," John answered. "I'll take care of them."

She shook her head. "You've got to get those fields plowed and the crops planted before…" Her eyes met Merrilee's. "He can't do it alone."

Her insides began to tremble. Aurora couldn't ask that of her. It would be too cruel. She'd seen what John's desertion had done to Merrilee, had worn the tears she'd shed puddled on her blouse. "Can't we get someone to come in and take care of them for a little while? Maybe I could ask around the hospital?"

"I tried," the older woman started, stopping to take several deep breaths before continuing. "I even put an ad in the newspaper a couple months ago. Didn't get the first response."

"Their loss, if you ask me," John answered, shaking his head. "But don't worry about it, Ms. Aurora. I'll take care of everything."

This was the John she remembered, determined to take on the world for those he loved, even against impossible odds. And caring for five children with special needs and a sick elderly woman while putting a crop in the field was as close to impossible as it gets.

But she couldn't help, not while caring for the boardinghouse and getting Claire to her doctor's appointments. Only there wouldn't be any more doctor's appointments for the time being—there weren't any more treatments to be done, not until her girl was accepted into Warm Springs, and that would happen only if Merrilee could dig up information on Aurora's supposed black market activities.

I'd be like a fox in the henhouse.

But if Merrilee didn't do it, who would Major Evans send to conduct the investigation? Possibly someone with a predetermination of her guilt, who would hassle and prod Aurora unmercifully right when she was at her weakest. Then what would happen to the children? Would Adams finally prevail in getting them carted off to the sanitarium?

She couldn't let that happen. Instead, she'd investigate herself, and find evidence to exonerate her old friend. It should be obvious to anyone with a brain that if Aurora were supplying a local black market, she'd have the cash to buy a new blanket at least. Could the Lord be providing a way to help both Aurora and Claire out?

She'd have to shuffle things around at the boardinghouse, ask Maggie if she could handle the cooking, at least. But if Merrilee could kill two birds with one stone, she had to try. She swallowed past the worry knotted in her throat. "I'll be happy to help John out with the kids."

Had he heard her right? Had Merrilee just volunteered to help him with the children while Aurora healed? And why did the thought of him and Merrilee being under the same roof give him a sense of elation? John retreated from the thought. "I don't know about this."

"Son," Aurora admonished with a whisper, shaking her head.

"What is there to know?" Merrilee said, the jade-green daggers she shot at him pinning him to the mattress. "You need help running this farm and caring for Ms. Aurora and the kids. I want to help."

"What about your boardinghouse? Who's going to run your business while you're out here helping?"

A faint shadow passed over Merrilee's face but was gone just as quickly. "Maggie's been looking for something to do now that she's home waiting on the baby, and Donald already helps me out with the cooking. He'd love a chance to try his hand in the kitchen."

Jealousy nipped at his gut. "Who's Donald?"

"Maggie's grandfather-in-law." Merrilee turned her focus on his mother. "You remember him, don't you, Ms. Aurora?"

The first bit of color he'd seen in his mother's cheeks bloomed as she smiled faintly. "A very godly man, if memory serves me correctly. I believe he's a good choice to watch the boardinghouse."

John smirked. They made this sound too simple, but nothing between him and Merrilee had ever been that easy. "What about Claire?"

Merrilee stared at him as if she wasn't quite sure what he meant. "What about her?"

Exactly what he'd expected. She hadn't thought this situation through completely. "Where is she going to be while you're staying out here watching the kids?"

"You make it sound as if I'm moving out here."

Aurora shifted worried eyes from John to where Merrilee stood at the end of the bed. "I'm sorry if I didn't make things clear, but if you're going to help, you'll need to move in here, at least for a little while," she explained.

John wasn't sure, but Merrilee seemed to wobble before tightening her grip on the bedpost. "Why? I can be here before the kids wake up in the morning and I'll stay until after we get them in bed at night. I've got transportation."

He barked with laughter. "You mean that truck? That piece of junk is going to end up causing you and our daughter to get hurt."

She leaned toward him. "It's not that bad!"

Merrilee in a temper was exhilarating to behold, he thought, taking in the fiery-red flush bursting across her cheeks and the sharp edge of green shining from her eyes. She'd never been easily provoked, but when she was, it was a beautiful sight. The urge to tease her when she got like this was nearly irresistible. "If I had any sense, I'd take a sledgehammer to it."

A tiny gasp escaped the tightly drawn line of her lips before softening, the tense lines around her eyes and mouth relaxing, the color in her cheeks receding to a perfect shade of pink, causing his fingers to itch with the urge to reach out and touch. Her curls trembled around her shoulders as a wave of laughter broke through her. "Why do you always do that?"

He felt his lips twitch and joined her. "You're just an easy target sometimes, sweetheart."

"And taking a sledgehammer to the truck might increase its value at the scrap yard, right?"

He snorted, joining her in another round of laughter.

"Did I miss something?" Aurora looked from one to the other, a smile tickling her lips.

Still chuckling softly, Merrilee leaned forward and squeezed his mother's foot. "No, ma'am. Just an old joke between me and John."

"But you are going to work things out?"

The laughter stilled inside him. Could he make this situation work with Merrilee? The children and Aurora needed her to look after them just like they needed him to get a crop in the fields. And really, he needed Merrilee, too. Left alone to handle everything, there was every chance he'd let his mother down if he found himself called before the naval tribunal before the planting was finished. He couldn't do that to Aurora and the kids.

"We'll figure things out," John answered, giving Aurora's hand a gentle squeeze.

"Right now, we need to leave you alone so that you can get some rest." Merrilee tugged on the corner of the quilt, pulling the wrinkles free. "You have to get better and back on your feet."

"But you'll talk it through, won't you? 'Cause I need to know I can count on the both of you right now."

Anxiety plowed deep rivets around Aurora's mouth and eyes, sounding an alarm bell inside John. Fretting over this situation between him and Merrilee wasn't going to help his mother's recovery, particularly when her mind was already occupied with worries about the children and this year's crop. Whatever he had to do to make it work, he'd do it. Hopefully, Merrilee felt the same way.

"We'll go downstairs and work it out right now, Ms. Aurora."

Merrilee's voice trailed around the corner of the bed, coming to a halt right behind him. Warm fingers slid over his shoulders before coming to rest, her palms putting slight pressure on his taut muscles, sending little trails of heat across his chest before settling around his heart. "Isn't that right, John?"

Words clogged his throat and he coughed. "Yeah, we'll make a plan of action."

Aurora sunk down into her pillow, obviously satisfied with their answer. "Good, because everything in this life that's worth having is worth working for."

John wanted to ask her what she meant, but he didn't have a chance before her eyelids drooped closed. He leaned forward instead, pressing a kiss against her soft cheek like he used to when he was still just a boy. He stood then, releasing the hand that had guided him through those awful years after his father had abandoned him and his brother.

He would carry this burden for Aurora for as long as he could. The problem was, he didn't know how long he had until the navy brought charges against him, until he had his day in court. Hopefully, once that day arrived, he'd be able to convince a jury of his peers he was no more a traitor than FDR. But he had to prepare for the worst.

And that meant coming clean to Merrilee.

Chapter Eight

Dr. Adams stood staring up at them from the bottom of the stairs, medical bag in his hand with his suit coat thrown over the arm, a brown nondescript hat in the opposite hand.

All ready for a fast getaway.

Not a very Christian way to feel, Merrilee admitted, as she stepped down the last few stairs, but it was hard feeling anything remotely Christlike knowing the doctor's opinion on the children Aurora took in here. Like Claire. Why couldn't the man see past these children's physical infirmities to the wonderful little people God had made and care for them as he did everyone else in the county?

"Don't like Adams too much, do you?" John whispered close enough for only her to hear, his breath fanning against her ear, gently stirring the tiny hairs at the base of her neck. "At least we're in agreement on that."

How did he know that? Merrilee tried to keep the shock from registering on her face as the man in question approached them. "How did it go?"

"She's dozing," John answered from beside her, his

fingers resting possessively against her lower back. A slight flutter started in the pit of her stomach, increasing to a wild pitch when he pressed his palm against her spine.

Adams's eyebrow lifted into his hairline. Was John trying to start the gossip mills around town? Or was he simply being supportive in light of her obvious dislike of the doctor? She clamped her teeth down on her lower lip…but she didn't pull away from his touch.

"So—" Adams twirled his hat around in restless fingers "—I can bring the paperwork out in the morning so we can get the process started."

Oh, dear. "What kind of paperwork?" John asked, his voice restrained as he leaned a hair closer to the man.

"The hospital in Milledgeville will need a medical history on each of the children." Adams paused. "That is what you're planning to do with them, isn't it?"

"No." John bit the word out. One push in the wrong direction and Robert Adams wouldn't know what hit him.

The doctor turned to her. "You can't seriously think you can handle taming this wild crew, Merrilee."

This man had no idea what she could handle. Merrilee stiffened. "I don't know what you mean by that, Robert. The children have behaved beautifully, considering what they've been through today."

Adams opened his mouth to respond, but John cut him off. "We should move this discussion into the dining room." He nodded toward the parlor doorway. "Little ears."

"Why? It's not like they understand what we're talking about."

A stark second passed before John grabbed Adams by the arm and pulled him toward the door, his medical bag dangling from one hand while he clutched his hat in the other. "We've taken up enough of your time today, Dr. Adams. Just send me a bill and I'll settle up Ms. Aurora's accounts."

"She needs to be seen in my office at the first of next week."

Merrilee followed behind them, enjoying the sight of the doctor being manhandled out the door too much to sit back and let John have all the fun. "I'm sure we can find another physician to check her out."

At the door, John let go of the man's arm. Adams straightened, slamming his hat down on his head. "Are you firing me?"

John opened the door. "It looks that way."

Adams's face scrunched up into an angry ball. "You can't fire me."

"Sounds like he just did," Merrilee said, trying to give him as sweet a smile as she could muster. "Don't let us keep you."

The screen door slapped shut behind the doctor, his mumbled jangle of words growing fainter until finally stopping at the sound of his car door slamming shut.

Merrilee closed her eyes and took a deep breath. "Someone needs to wash that man's mouth out with soap."

John leaned back against the doorjamb. "I understand why you're not a fan."

She glanced toward the parlor, relieved to find the arched entranceway empty. "Remember, little ears."

He nodded toward an open room across the hall, the crooked smile he gave her sending her pulse thrumming through her veins. She told herself that it was just the thrill of firing Dr. Adams that made her heart pound, not the man walking in front of her. The situation called for her to be serious, not silly.

She followed him into the room, then stopped just inside the door, lifting her nose a fraction of an inch. "What is that smell?"

John continued on to the table where five medium-size bowls sat, thick syrupy lines crisscrossing between each place setting, converging at a half-filled mason jar. "Looks like they had a little oatmeal with their honey this morning."

She tried to lift her foot, but the sole of her shoe clung to the wooden surface as if magnetized. "The floor got a helping of the sticky stuff, too."

"Here, let me help." She expected a wet towel to clean off the bottom of her shoe, not the firm arm around her waist bracing her against his side or the work-calloused hand he held out to her. "I'm sorry about this."

"Poor things. The oatmeal probably burned while Billy took care of Aurora and he didn't know how to fix anything else." She lifted her foot, then stopped.

"What's wrong?"

"I don't want to track honey all over this floor."

He glanced down at the ground, his lips twitching slightly. "I don't think that's an issue."

Of course, it wasn't an issue to him. He'd probably never had to clean the sticky concoction after it had hardened. "I'm already going to have to get down on my hands and knees to mop this mess. If we let it set, it'll take your hammer and a chisel to get it up. The less territory I have to clean, the better my chances of taking care of it all before the situation becomes that bad."

"The voice of experience?"

She gave him a wry smile. "Claire was a very active toddler."

"I wished I'd seen that," he answered, a wistfulness in his voice.

She had wanted him there, too, more than anyone knew. Her prayers had been full of John; praying God would watch over him, would help her understand what had caused him to stop loving her. Instead, she'd endured years of silence, on earth and from above. Then Claire had fallen ill, and she'd focused her prayers on her daughter. But God's silence continued.

"Can we at least talk first?"

A few more minutes wasn't going to matter one way or the other. "I suppose."

Before her soiled foot could touch the ground, her legs were pushed from underneath her and she found herself being lifted into John's arms. Merrilee wriggled, but his limbs tightened around her, pulling her high on his chest. "What are you doing?"

His blue eyes stared at her with such innocence, she wondered if maybe she had missed something. "You didn't want to track honey all over the floor so I thought I'd help you to a chair."

"You didn't have to take me so seriously." She pushed against his shoulder, the muscles bunching and flexing beneath her palm, shooting sparks of awareness up her. She snatched it back. "Put me down!"

"That chair looks unscathed." Nodding to a high back across the room, he tightened his hold on her.

With a resigned sigh, Merrilee gave in to the need to steady herself and wrapped her arm around his shoulders. But there was nothing remotely safe in the way her insides sizzled like beads of oil on a hot frying pan or the heat that ran up her arm as her fingertips grazed the soft hairs at the nape of his neck. She balled up her fist to keep from repeating the movement.

John toed the chair out from under the table with his foot, then gently sat her down. A shiver ran up the length of her back at the loss of his warmth. These reactions to him wouldn't do, not when John already had one foot out the door. She admired the fact that he'd come back to do right by Claire, and yes, she still found him terribly attractive, but whatever they'd had between them had died years ago.

Hadn't it?

John pulled out the chair next to Merrilee, hoping that his heart rate would soon slow to normal after the delight of holding her in his arms. He scooted the chair back a few more inches, then sat down. "Now that I've fired Adams, you want to tell me what he did to cross you?"

She glanced at him for a brief second, then dropped her gaze to her lap, her fingers tightly knotted, rubbing the pad of her thumb over the top of the other. He recognized it as a habit she had whenever she was frustrated. "He was Claire's doctor."

"*Was* being the operative word here?"

That coaxed a slight smile out of her. "He doesn't think Claire has a chance of getting the use of her leg back."

"So? He's not the authority on the subject, is he?"

"No, but if you didn't notice, he's a prideful man." The gaze that met his was hard and unforgiving. "He's of the mind-set that if he can't fix someone, then they can't be fixed, so the only solution is to get them out of everyone's sight."

White-hot anger flashed through him, his fingers itching with the need to grasp that so-called physician by the neck. After that, he wasn't sure what he'd do, but it wouldn't be pleasant. "He wanted Claire to go to a sanitarium."

"Said I was letting her condition ruin my life, that it was time I accepted it and moved on." Strands of sunlight dancing through the window crowned her with a gold-red coronet around her head. "As if I could just abandon her."

John bunched his fists together, then loosened them, Aurora's words barreling through the red haze that had fogged his thoughts. *Always turn the other cheek.* Needing something to do with his hands, he leaned over and covered Merrilee's fingers with his. "Of course you couldn't."

Merrilee glanced up at him, her lovely green eyes holding him captive, the heartache he saw reflected back at him causing a knot to twist in his stomach. "How could he suggest such a thing? Doesn't Adams know that would break Claire's heart?"

"Probably not." John hadn't noticed this ribbon of

steel laced through her when they were married. Or maybe he hadn't given her the chance to ever display it. It wasn't just admirable, it was rare, made stronger by her love for their child. It must be something to be loved like that, protected against the Adamses of this world.

Was he any better than the doctor, showing up at Merrilee's doorstep, wanting to claim Claire as his child only to slink out of town when his hearing before the naval commission came up? He wanted time with his daughter, but would Merrilee give him that if she knew the truth?

Best he take what time he had left with Claire and put it to good use. "We need a plan to make this work."

Merrilee sat back in her chair, relaxing just a bit. "I agree."

Suspicion shot through him at her instant affirmation. "I wasn't expecting that answer."

Her perfectly shaped brows lifted slightly. "Why not?"

"Wasn't it you who always said God laughs when we make plans?"

"Maybe He does, but I've learned over the years that having a plan isn't necessarily a bad thing." She slipped her hand from beneath his. "Just don't plan everything down to the last detail, okay?"

That very quality of his was what had drawn the attention of the navy when they searched for men to train the new branch of Seabees. "My attention to detail helped us in Guam."

But Merrilee didn't seem impressed. She picked at the crumbs dusting the table, then brushed them into a bowl. "We're talking kids here, John. They're a lot tougher crowd."

John hesitated. Was that experience talking again? Maybe. "Anything else?"

"No, just as long as we agree to keep each other informed about what's going on with the children and with Ms. Aurora so if any decisions need to be made, we can offer advice to each other."

"Do those decisions include Claire?"

Merrilee mashed her lips into a tight line, then gave an affirmative jerk of her head. "For right now, at least."

A small concession, but enough for John at the moment. "Then I agree."

"Really?"

The surprise in her question should have irked him but it didn't. "Why wouldn't I?"

"I don't know." Her shoulder rose in a slight shrug. "I guess I figured you'd want more say where Claire is concerned."

Maybe one day soon, but not yet—not until he was cleared of the charges against him. And, John admitted to himself, when he'd regained his former wife's trust on the matter. "I'd never shove my opinions on you, Merrilee."

Her mouth relaxed into a slight smile. "I guess I just expected…"

She didn't have to complete her thought for John to understand. Jacob Daniels hadn't listened much to anyone except his crew of good ole boys who had agreed with everything the old man said. He'd certainly raised his daughter not to argue with his decrees or question his point of view. If he'd been able to prove to her that her daddy liked to interfere in their lives, John might still be married to the woman sitting beside him. Instead, it had always been clear to him that Merrilee believed her daddy could do no wrong. Only in the past two days had he noticed Merrilee questioning her father. "Well, this is a partnership. We'll listen to each other and try to make the best decision for all of us."

Merrilee seemed to consider that for a moment, then nodded. "Agreed. And even if we don't reach an understanding all the time, we present a united front to the kids."

"Sounds like that war slogan—united we stand, divided we fall."

"Exactly." She nodded. "Because kids can detect weakness and they'll pick it apart until they get what they want."

"Another lesson learned from Claire?"

Merrilee chuckled. "Sometimes, but mainly I got it from the kids I teach in Sunday school. If those parents knew some of the stories those kids told on them, they'd cringe."

"Okay, then, united we stand."

They talked for the next half hour, going over everything they could think of from what each should expect from the other to the children's routine, even settling on a new doctor for Aurora—one from Crawford Long Hospital that Merrilee had been impressed with from her visits with Claire.

John pushed back his chair and stood. "So when do you think you and Claire can be ready?"

Merrilee glanced up at him. "For what?"

A tide of apprehension rose up inside him. "To move in here."

She hesitated for a brief moment. "I don't know if that's such a good idea. Claire and I could go home every night after the children have had their baths and we've gotten them into bed."

"I was serious about the truck, Merri. Just the thought of you and Claire getting caught out in the dead of night in the middle of nowhere in that thing…" John ground his teeth together, his stomach turning at the idea of his family deserted on a lonely stretch of highway. "Besides, you heard Ms. Aurora. This is a twenty-four-hours-a-day, seven-days-a-week job."

"You're going to be here, aren't you?"

"Of course I'll be here. It's just…" What could he say? That the idea of having his family under one roof had been growing on him since they'd left Aurora's room? No, this was about the kids. Merrilee's comings and goings would only cause more confusion in their lives. "The kids need to have a woman around all the time, especially the girls. And I'm not sure what kind of arrangements to make for Ms. Aurora's care…." Heat raced up his neck. "You know what I mean."

She chuckled, a warm throaty sound that made his breath catch in his windpipe. "You're such a man, you know that? But you've got a point." The laughter tittered off. "What about Claire? How are we going to handle the whole situation with her? There's a good chance she'll find out who you really are."

"Would that be so bad?"

A tiny line formed between her brows. "I know you plan on leaving again."

John blinked. How had the woman figured that out? "It's only for a little while."

He could tell by her closed-off expression she didn't believe him. "Don't you think Claire has enough going on in her life without the added worry of when her father, who she's only just met, will walk back out that door?"

Blasted woman! "I'm coming back."

"How do I know that?"

If it calmed her fears, maybe it was time she knew about the plans he'd made, even though he'd not intended to tell her yet. "I bought the farm next door."

She gave him a look of utter disbelief. "Ms. Aurora bought that property."

John shook his head. "She made the payment for me, with my money. After I got Claire's letter, I contacted Ms. Aurora. She mentioned Mr. Todd was on the decline and that he'd offered to sell her his farm. He quoted a fair price, but she wasn't in the market for another farm. I figure it's close by if Ms. Aurora needs me, and I thought Claire might like coming out to visit sometimes."

"You bought a farm, just like you bought the homestead." She shook her head, the area around her eyes crinkled in confusion. "How did you manage it?"

"How did I manage it?" John mimicked. What did she think he'd done, robbed a bank? No, he'd worked from sunrise to dark, lived on barely anything, put away every dime he'd earned for a life he'd never found time to live. He'd bought the Daniels's property simply to right a wrong, to give Merrilee the home her father had never intended to leave her in his will. Beating Jacob Daniels at his own game was just icing on the cake.

"Forget it. It's none of my business."

But it seemed important for her to know how he'd raised the money. "After I bought the homestead and deeded it over to you, I started an account for Ms. Aurora, just in case she needed something for herself or the kids. I didn't have many expenses and figured she could use the extra cash. Only she didn't use it. She saved every penny I ever deposited in the bank. Guess she figured I'd need it one day."

"That was smart of her, and kind of you. Thank you." Gratitude filled her voice, but also…shame? Why would she feel that way? What could she possibly be ashamed of?

Unless she was embarrassed by him, needing to save every penny just so he could buy the type of property she'd been born to.

Was that the real reason she didn't want Claire to know the truth, because having a poor dirt farmer as a father didn't exactly reach the high standards of the upper-class Danielses?

John turned and paced, his boots echoing against the four walls. If she thought so badly of him, what would Merrilee do if she learned the truth, that by helping another child, he'd gotten himself brought up on charges that might ruin his chances of staying around to get to know his daughter?

"But you're still planning to leave?"

Not planning to, being forced to. Big difference. "Yes, but like I said, I'll be back."

"How long will you be gone this time?"

He'd never lied to her, but would Merrilee give him a chance to explain with Claire's heart on the line? He couldn't risk it. "I don't know."

She gave a slight nod, as if his answer had provided the resolution she needed. "Then maybe it's best if we wait until you come back before telling her. That way…"

"That way, if I don't come back, Claire will never know," he finished for her.

Merrilee dropped her chin to her chest, her eyes closed, her delicate shoulders slightly rounded as if defeated. "I'm just trying to protect her, John. That's all." A loud cry from the direction of the parlor drew her attention to the door. "We've left the kids alone too long as it is. Why don't you go upstairs and check on Ms. Aurora, okay?"

John watched her walk to the arched doorway, then hesitate before slipping first one shoe off and then the other. The boards in the hall floor barely creaked as she crept out of sight.

A shaft of pain shot up the side of his head, and he unclenched his jaw. Claire needed to know the truth about their relationship, sooner rather than later. He'd abide by Merrilee's wishes for the moment, if only to give her a reason to trust him. But it didn't mean he liked it, he thought, stacking the sticky bowls and spoons into a pile and heading to the kitchen.

Because he didn't like it. Not one bit.

Chapter Nine

The sun had partially sunk behind a grove of tall pines lining the front yard when Merrilee pulled up to the front of her house. Blackout curtains had already been drawn, slices of light escaping around the thick cloth, assuring her that life in the boardinghouse had gone on without her today. She tugged the keys out of the ignition, then sat back, resting her head against the glass window, the remaining heat of the day falling around her like the warm rags physical therapists wrapped around Claire's leg during her treatments.

Every bone, every muscle in her body cried out for a hot bath and her bed. She'd get used to coping with six children, seven if you counted Ms. Aurora. She had to. The only other option was the sanitarium. Yes, she'd get used to it sooner or later—but she wasn't there yet.

What would she have done without John? Merrilee closed her eyes and smiled. The man was a marvel! By the time she'd carried a platter of peanut butter and jelly sandwiches into the dining room, he'd made short work of the children's breakfast dishes, removing every speck of honey, every drop of oatmeal from the table.

The linens had also been replaced, the chairs scrubbed of all the debris. He'd even managed to give the wooden panels in the floor a shine that rivaled the sun. Probably should thank his military training for those cleaning skills. Or his time with the Civilian Conservation Corps.

She could already see how easy it would be to depend on him, to count on his presence and his help. But she couldn't let herself trust in him, not when he still intended to leave. What could be so important that it would take him away from Marietta? And why wouldn't he tell her?

A rapping of knuckles against the truck's window made Merrilee jump and she stared out into the waning light, the tension in her shoulders causing a dull ache at the base of her skull as she made out a face.

Oh, no, not him. Didn't the man crawl under a rock at night? She rolled the glass down slowly, reluctant to speak. "Major Evans."

He folded both arms against the door frame, looking like a tomcat who'd trapped a defenseless mouse. "You stood me up this morning."

As if it were a date or something. Please! She swallowed back a retort. "I'm sorry I missed our meeting. An emergency came up."

"I heard." Evans slid off his hat, his dark hair plastered to his head as if he'd used a whole can of rationed motor oil to keep every strand in place.

Merrilee mashed her lips tightly together. Only four people knew where she'd been, and three of them had spent all day at Aurora's farm. His source could only be Adams.

"Where's Claire? I thought she went with you."

It wasn't any of his business where her daughter was, but as he'd only find out anyway, she might as well tell him. "She stayed back at Ms. Aurora's." It'd been more than that; she'd begged to sleep over with the two younger girls. It was the first time in over a year Claire had asked for an outing like that. John hadn't made it easier for her to refuse, telling her she'd be able to pack faster without having to worry about Claire. How he'd convinced her, she'd never know.

Now she was glad Claire hadn't come home with her. Explaining Major Evans to her bright, curious daughter was one conversation she didn't want to have. "Doesn't Adams know about patient confidentiality?"

Evans shrugged. "I ran into him picking up a sandwich at the lunch counter and he was in a huff, not that I blame him. Those kids Aurora keeps, they give me the heebie-jeebies."

Bile rose up in her throat. She swallowed it back down. "Well, I'm sure there are a lot of folks around here who think you're pretty creepy, too."

He snorted. "I can only hope. So how is she?"

As if the man cared. "You mean Adams didn't give you a full report?"

"Oh, he did. I just wanted to hear your version."

Merrilee's stomach tightened. Adams refused to so much as tell her and John what was wrong with Aurora, but he could report it to Major Evans? "She's better this afternoon, but will need to be on bed rest for the next few weeks."

One side of Evans's mouth lifted in a crooked smile. "That makes your job a bit easier. It was a stroke of genius, you volunteering to watch over those mush heads of hers. Very smart, thinking on your feet like that."

A sick feeling settled in the pit of her stomach. "You're wasting your time investigating her."

His eyebrows furrowed together. "Now, why would you say that?"

"Adams didn't tell you?" Merrilee asked. Figured the doctor would reveal everything to the major except the information that might exonerate her. "Aurora's been feeling like this for months, but never called the doctor because she can't afford it, and if you saw her place…" she hesitated, the memory of John's expression causing a pang deep down inside "…you'd see it's run down and needs a lot of work."

"So? She could be hiding it. Plus you're forgetting she paid cash for that farm right next door to hers. Where did she get that money?"

"She purchased the farm for someone else."

"That's convenient," Evans scoffed. "Did she happen to tell you who this person could be?"

He was trolling for another suspect, not caring how much of a fool he made of himself. And that was what all this spy nonsense was, foolish.

But, she thought, if she told Evans John had bought the old Todd place, he'd look into it. Not that the major would find anything to tie her ex-husband to the black market ring the major was investigating. John had been in the Pacific serving his country for the past few years. But he might uncover the reasons John needed to leave Marietta again, and if he did, maybe she could get some answers. "John Davenport. He had a savings account that Ms. Aurora had access to and bought the place when it became available for a good price."

"What do you know about him?"

The cab of the truck grew uncomfortably. hot. "Why?"

"I need to find out as much as I can about this man. I mean, he's sent a known suspect in a black market operation large amounts of cash, not to mention he just shows up here in Marietta after, what? A dozen years? And you were married to him."

"That was a long time ago."

"Wait a minute." Evans hesitated, pointing his finger at her. "Didn't he buy your father's house and put it in your name?"

Merrilee bit the inside of her lip. This wasn't what she'd wanted when she'd told Evans the truth about Aurora's purchase. John didn't deserve Evans's pinpoint focus on every aspect of his life. "Yes, but…"

A wicked glow lit his eyes. "Where does an uneducated dirt farmer like Davenport get that kind of cash?"

The urge to smack the living daylights out of the major grew stronger with each passing second, but it wouldn't do any good. "John's always been a hard worker. Maybe he just scrimped and saved his money."

"And bought houses in a town he hasn't bothered to step foot in in twelve years?" The major shook his head. "I'm not buying it."

"Are you forgetting he was in the Pacific with the Seabees for the past few years?"

Evans chuckled. "He wouldn't be the first soldier we've caught making money off Uncle Sam."

What had she done? Was she so desperate for information about John that she'd hung him out to dry? "He's a good man, Patrick."

Evans grabbed his hat from the hood of the truck and put it on, tilting it at an awkward angle. "It'll be better for you if he's not. If we can find something on him that helps our case, then we'll be a lot more inclined to do a favor in return. Keep giving me information like that and Claire will be in Warm Springs before you know it."

John eased himself into the porch swing, the chains clanging softly as he finally settled in. The cool morning air caused gooseflesh to form across his bare forearms, but the temperature would rise quickly, especially when he started loading Merrilee and Claire's belongings into the truck for their trip back to Aurora's.

He drew in a deep breath, the faint hint of freshly plowed dirt teasing his senses, an excitement he'd long forgotten pulsing through his veins. His palms itched at the thought of plunging his hands into the soft, warm soil again. Maybe, if he got Aurora's fields planted in time, he could put some time in at his place, maybe even put in a small crop of his own. Nothing big; just a victory garden, some beans and tomatoes, vegetables Merrilee could can. Everything else would have to wait until after he knew how long his prison sentence would be.

John closed his eyes. *Lord, I only did what I felt was right. Please deliver me from the charges made against me if it be Your will.*

He barely opened his eyes at the sound of the house's door opening, watching Merrilee through a curtain of dark lashes. The sun had risen a fraction of an inch more, allowing color to seep slowly into the black-and-gray landscape. She stood in the doorway, the dark snood at the nape of her neck doing very little to hold in the rampant strands of golden-red hair from curling around her oval face. The dress she'd changed into yesterday for their trip to Aurora's had been traded in for a pair of neat overalls, not denim like his, but a mossy green that he imagined brought out the golden sparks that rimmed her irises. A white sweater hung around her shoulders.

The ruffles of her sweater swayed in a soft rhythm with each breath. "What did you do? Follow me home last night?"

John sat up. He'd considered it, worried that the piece of junk Merrilee called a truck might fall apart on her while she was only halfway home. But Ellie had had a bad dream, and Billy had snuck out to the barn sometime after lights out. "I thought we could get an early start, maybe get back before the kids are up and about."

"Have we got time for a cup of coffee first?"

After barely four hours of sleep, he wasn't sure he'd get through the day without it. "Please."

She pulled the edges of the sweater around her. "Be right back."

John settled back into the swing, the gentle twitter of a songbird waking along with the morning singing a lullaby in the trees behind him. A squirrel hurried across the lawn, his thin tail shaking furiously behind him as he threw himself against the trunk of a water oak and scurried into the branches. The faint glow of light disappeared around the corner of the house, and John could almost taste the cathead biscuits baking in the oven.

He could understand why Merrilee loved this place.

Good or bad, it was the home where she'd spent most of her life. At least Jacob had given his daughter a stable childhood. John's own parents had changed zip codes as often as most people changed clothes, bouncing from town to town, as if the doctor in the next city held out more hope than the last six. Mama had died, holding out hope for Matthew, and Dad chose to leave rather than face the heartache anymore.

The screen door squealed slightly as Merrilee shouldered it open, a swirl of steam rising from the two cups she held. The door slamming shut would wake up her whole house of boarders. John jumped up from the swing, aiming to catch the door for her, but she managed herself, hooking it with her foot and gently securing it in the door frame.

She handed him his coffee. "I've become quite the acrobat since opening the boardinghouse. Will probably hone some more skills out at Ms. Aurora's."

Teasing him, was she? "Well, until the circus comes to town, how about letting me help you out, okay? You could have been badly burned."

"You don't need to worry about me." She stared at him over the rim of her cup. "I can take care of myself."

Odd that the thought made him sad, when the girl he'd left behind had been so sheltered, she couldn't even drive a car. All she'd ever wanted was for old man Daniels to take note of her, to see her as more than a liability, as a daughter he could love.

John gulped down a mouthful of coffee. Jacob Daniels never knew what a treasure he had in this woman, how good Merrilee was to him. And Merrilee had never had a clue of just how special she was. Not a clue.

Had John ever bothered to tell her how wonderful she was, to show her?

No, he'd been too busy trying to farm the land her father had leased to him. And when the crop had failed, when there'd been no other way to support their dreams, he'd joined the Civilian Conservation Corps. Had scraped by on next to nothing so he could save their money and give Merrilee the home she deserved. Wasn't that enough to show her how much he valued her for who she was?

The question rattled him. Why did the answer matter so much to him? Even if he knew he'd be free to stay in Marietta and try again, what would be the point? Merrilee was the one who'd wanted the divorce, the one who had stopped loving him. It was hardly likely that she'd changed her mind about that. He shoved the thought to the back of his mind. "I didn't wake up everyone in the house, did I?"

She shook her head. "Most of the people living here have to get up early to get to their jobs over at the plant."

"And you?"

"Who do you think cooks for them all?" Merrilee chuckled, the soft morning sunlight unveiling a delicate pink blooming in her cheeks. "Do you think we can handle this? I mean…"

John had asked himself the same question at least a half a dozen times since they'd decided to work together to help Aurora out. Early this morning, staring up into the seemingly endless darkness, he realized the only hope of making this work was to be as honest as they could with each other. "Because our marriage didn't work out."

She sputtered on her coffee, coughing and choking. He patted her on her back, her shoulders delicate as butterfly's wings beneath his touch. He felt her breath almost as she drew it. "Right to the point, aren't you?"

Dropping his hand to his side, he took a step back to give her some distance. "And I want you to tell me exactly what you think, too. We need to be upfront about how we feel in uncertain situations, even if we don't agree."

She wrapped her hands around her cup, her eyes fixed on the liquid in her mug. Why did she seem to be hesitating over his suggestion? Was he not the only one who had something to hide?

Her head lifted, her chin notched a bit higher. "Then tell me how you came to live with Ms. Aurora."

Of course, John chided himself. Merrilee would want a show of good faith, a morsel to demonstrate he intended to live up to his word. At least her first question hadn't been about his reasons for leaving in a few weeks. He couldn't bear to tell her what a mess he'd made of his life, not yet anyway.

Maybe it was time she knew about Matthew anyway. "First time I met Ms. Aurora, she'd caught me stealing bread from old man Smith's grocery store."

Merrilee blinked. "Were you really that hungry?"

John felt the corner of his mouth tug up into a smile. Only one other person had ever questioned why he'd stuffed that loaf under his shirt, and she had taken him and his brother into her home. His gut tightened. How would Merrilee react? "It was the only thing Matthew would eat."

"That's your brother, isn't it? Billy mentioned him

yesterday," she said with a note of disappointment. Was that because John had never said a word about him? "Why would Matthew only eat bread?"

"Stubbornness, mainly. But I'd seen him swell up from just taking a bottle of milk when he was a baby, and I was afraid if he had another reaction like that, I wouldn't know what to do."

She nodded. "How old were you?"

"Ten. Mattie was five then. Mama had died the winter before from influenza and Dad… Well, he tried his best to find a job and settle down, but I guess two little boys were just too much for him," John said. His father had carted them off to every children's home around Atlanta, begging for someone to take them off his hands. Most were willing to take John, but simply shook their heads at Matthew, bundled up in an old hand wagon, his arms and legs drawn into his body at painful angles. John had refused to go without his brother. If he didn't watch out for Mattie, who would? In the end, it hadn't mattered.

"What happened to him?"

A dull ache lodged in his chest. "He got pneumonia when he was seven. We thought he was over the worst of it, but the doctor said Mattie's heart just gave out." He hesitated, the words sticking to the roof of his mouth, still difficult to say. "It's common in children with mongolism."

Chapter Ten

The world stilled around them for the briefest of moments. "Why didn't you tell me about Mattie before now?"

He searched his mind for reasons but came up blank. "I don't know. I guess I thought I was protecting you."

"From what?"

How could she ask? Surely she understood how cruel people could be. The taunts, the name-calling. John hadn't wanted that for her. "I didn't want you to be embarrassed by your husband's brother."

There, he had said it. But would she ever realize how much it had cost him to keep that secret from her? How many times he'd wanted to share a memory, talk about Mattie only to shove that notion away, afraid of how Merrilee's family might react? How they might take it out on her?

Her lips pursed together in a tight bow. "Is that the story you've been telling yourself all this time?"

"Excuse me?"

"Did you really think your brother would have embarrassed me?"

John stole another glance at her. Was she actually angry with him? "No, that's not what I meant."

"You want to know what I think?"

He was pretty sure he didn't, at least, not this time. But he had agreed—insisted, in fact—to full disclosure. Anything less would make a hard situation even more difficult. "What would that be?"

Her eyes met his, defiant and something else, not angry exactly. Something more like hurt. "That the only person you were worried your brother would embarrass was yourself."

John opened his mouth, then thought better of it. What was the point of arguing over something that happened years ago? But seeing the pain reflected in Merrilee's expression bothered him. Was she really that hurt he hadn't told her about Mattie? He'd thought he was doing her a favor, not unloading his problems on her, but obviously he'd been mistaken. Was he just as wrong in thinking he'd done it to protect her or was there some truth to what she'd said?

Was she right? Was I embarrassed by Mattie?

John gritted his back teeth together, a dull ache settling in at the base of his skull. The past few days hadn't gone as he'd hoped, but when did life ever go as planned? Within the house, a door clicked shut.

Merrilee must have heard it, too. "Maggie was in the kitchen getting some saltines to take back to her room."

"Morning sickness?"

Merrilee nodded, pressing her cup against her lips. "It's rough right now, but give it a few weeks and things are bound to be better."

John gave a brief nod. Was she only talking about

her niece or was she also referring to their situation? "If you'll show me your cases, I'll get them loaded into Aurora's car."

Merrilee hesitated, making him wonder if she was going to back out on their deal. Then she turned and walked quietly into the house.

How could he have kept that kind of secret from me?

Merrilee glared out the passenger's-side window, her arms crisscrossed tightly over her ribs, her body welded close to the door. Fresh patches of color whizzed by, announcing the arrival of spring, but she barely noticed. She'd almost reneged on her promise to help him, would have if Aurora and the kids didn't need her. Without this year's crop, they'd be hard-pressed to make it through the winter. She couldn't back out, not without explaining her reasons why.

She stole a glance over at him. What other secrets had John kept from her? Maybe Major Evans and his investigation would give her answers. A heaviness settled over her. Why was she so disappointed at the thought?

"I'm sorry."

Merrilee blinked, not sure if she'd heard John right. "What?"

A heavy sigh filled the cab of the truck. "Maybe you're right. Maybe I was a little ashamed of Mattie."

His pained expression vaporized whatever anger she felt. "You were a kid. We both were. And people, well, some aren't very kind when it comes to folks who are different."

Leaving one hand on the steering wheel, he looked at ease, but there was an underlying tension in his shoulders, a few tiny lines around his eyes that testified to the struggle going on underneath. "Is that why you're so determined to help Claire get well?"

She wanted to get mad at him, but there was no malice in his voice, just concern. Besides, he was right. That was what she wanted for Claire, yes, but also for her. "I don't want to talk about this right now."

"Why not?"

Really, why wouldn't the man just let the subject go? But then, he was Claire's father. He had a right to know. "I'm afraid she's going to give up trying."

"Why do you think that?"

The words came easier now. Maybe having someone to share the burden of the past twelve months would lighten her load. "It's been a year since Claire came down with polio and she still struggles."

John's lips flattened into a straight line. "Folks have been struggling since Adam and Eve bit into that apple."

"Yeah, but…" She hesitated. Really, baring one's soul was a little too much first thing in the morning. "Why Claire? She's only a kid."

"Just like the kids Ms. Aurora takes in?"

She nodded. "Exactly. I mean, why would God allow these kids to suffer like that?"

"Why wouldn't He?"

His words were like a punch to the stomach and for a moment, she couldn't breathe. Merrilee shook her head but didn't respond. God wouldn't deliberately choose to let children suffer, would He? "Why would you say something like that?"

He stole a glance at her, then turned his attention back to the road. "Because sometimes God uses those things in our lives that cause us the most pain to grow us in our faith."

Merrilee sank back into her seat. Was what John said true? Could Claire be growing in her relationship with the Lord through her bout with polio? She didn't see it, but then she'd felt alone, abandoned with no answers since she and Beau had raced Claire to the hospital that night.

"How will you feel if Claire always has a little limp?"

Merrilee's hands grasped the sides of her overalls, fisting her fingers into the stiff cotton. She might be foolish not to take the idea in account, but she refused to fill her thoughts with the negative possibilities. "If she still has problems walking after we've tried everything, then so be it. But I'm not giving up on her, not yet."

"Honey, I'm not giving up on her, either. She's a strong-willed girl just like her mama."

The crooked grin he flashed her made her heart flutter just a bit, causing her to stare straight ahead. "Still, I worry about her," Merrilee replied. "She may be strong, but she's extremely tired of all the doctor's visits and therapy sessions right now."

"Then let's give her a break."

"What?" She jerked her head around to glare at him.

"I'm not giving up on her, just saying a small break in the action may be just what she needs to catch her breath."

"I don't know," she answered, eyeing him cautiously. Was he sincere or just placating her after their rough start this morning? "I've been working on getting her into a new rehabilitation program."

"Is it her best shot?"

She nodded. Should she give him a notion of what they were up against, how every doctor and most of the physical therapists had given up hope of Claire ever recovering the use of her leg? No, Claire just needed the right therapies. Which was why Merrilee needed to get her daughter to the little town of Pine Mountain. "Yes, in Warm Springs."

"Isn't that where the president has a home?"

She nodded. "But it's also known for its work with polio victims. They say the mineral waters there have healing properties that particularly help those trying to regain the use of their limbs."

"Hmm. Odd that the president likes to go there, don't you think?"

She'd thought it was odd, too. President Roosevelt always seemed so full of vigor in the newspapers and speaking on the radio. "Maybe he knows someone who was stricken with polio and has a home in Warm Springs to support them. That sounds like something the president and Mrs. Roosevelt would do."

He nodded slightly, as if he sensed there was another part of the story not being told. "So what do we need to do to get Claire seen there?"

"I've put her on the waiting list."

A grimace came across his face. "Not too crazy about waiting."

Merrilee didn't have much patience when it came to waiting, either, particularly when in regards to Claire. Why else would she have made the deal with Major Evans? "It shouldn't be too bad. Maybe by the end of the summer."

"Then maybe a break before we get her into Warm

Springs might give her the energy she'll need to tackle the new treatments," John said, turning on the blinker.

"I don't know. It can't be good for her not to exercise her leg for that length of time."

"Oh, she'll exercise the leg, only we'll make it fun for her. Remember the lake on the back corner of Ms. Aurora's property?"

Of course she remembered that lake. It was where John had taken her on their first date, for a picnic that he'd put together himself. Afterward, he'd dug out a baseball and two mitts and taught her how to play catch.

Her best first date ever.

The only first date she'd ever gone on, she told herself. "Yes, I remember."

"Maybe we could take her out there, with the other kids, of course. Get her swimming a little, build up those muscles."

It was a plan. There was only one hitch. "Claire doesn't know how to swim."

"Then I'll teach her."

She tilted her head to the side to stare at him. "I don't remember you ever knowing how to swim."

His warm chuckle vibrated through her. "When I was assigned to a ship the Japs were trying to bomb out of the water, I thought it would be in my best interest to learn."

A wave of laughter rumbled up her throat. "Survival of the fittest, hmm?"

"Well, you know me. Always the optimist. Figured if anyone could make it to shore, it would be me."

Knowing John, she didn't doubt he would at least try. So why had he given up so quickly on their marriage? Had their union not been worth fighting for, at least, not to him?

What did it matter now? They'd been apart for more than a decade. The only reason John had come back to Marietta at all was to be part of his daughter's life. But all the reasoning in the world didn't silence the questions she had. Why did she feel that if he ever told her the truth behind the demise of their marriage, she might not be able to fight these feelings she'd buried away so long ago?

As the truck bumped through the clearing to Aurora's house, Merrilee noticed the black truck parked next to the barn. It looked vaguely familiar. Who would be visiting Aurora at this time of the morning?

"Do you know who it is?" John asked, slowing down to glare out of the windshield.

What if these were the people running the black market Evans had her investigating? Had they learned about Aurora's illness and come to close down her part of their operation? Merrilee's heart knocked against her ribs as she scanned the area. "I don't see any of the kids, but there's someone standing near the far edge of the front porch."

The truck jerked to a stop. Merrilee's body lunged forward, her eyes slamming shut, tensing as she continued to move toward the glass windshield. She hung there for a moment, her forward movement interrupted, John's arm a steel belt across her middle. The truck rocked backward, gently tossing her back into her seat before settling.

Seconds passed. The bench seat gave a little beneath

her as she felt John move toward her. "Are you okay, sweetheart?"

His breath whispered across her cheek, raising the sensitive hairs along the nape of her neck. She drew in a steadying breath, but the combined scents of clean soil, coffee and something purely John brought back mornings of waking up alongside him, causing her insides to jitter even more.

Time to stop this foolishness and find out who was waiting on the porch. She pressed herself back against the seat and away from the warmth of his arm still draped around her waist. "Nothing broken or banged up."

"Are you sure?"

His voice carried a note of concern, and for the briefest of moments, she almost gave in to the urge to stare up at him. Instead, she sat completely motionless, save the slight nod she gave him to answer his question. "Don't you think we should find out who is here?"

John let go of her then, retreating to his side of the truck. "Why don't you stay here, at least until I find out who they are?"

The man was sadly mistaken if he was under the delusion she wasn't going in with him. "It's probably just one of the neighbors. More than likely they heard Ms. Aurora was doing poorly and brought something for supper."

"It could be someone dropping off another kid for Ms. Aurora."

The matter-of-fact way he said it bothered Merrilee. Could people really be that cruel, leaving a poor defenseless child, *their* poor defenseless child, with a person they didn't know? Then she remembered that it could be worse. The reprobates could have left them out on the street to fend for themselves...the way John's father had. A disgust for the unknown man welled up inside her. Merrilee studied the vehicle. "The truck looks familiar."

"Probably someone from out of town. Ms. Aurora says it makes it easier for them to forget about what happened if there's not a chance of running into us in town."

Merrilee gave a vicious shake to her head. "It will take me dying before I could ever stop thinking about Claire Bear. You just don't stop caring about the people you love."

"You're right," he whispered, a sad smile playing along the corner of his mouth before he climbed out of the truck. "Would you stay here, just until I find out who this person is?"

Merrilee fell back against the seat as the door clicked shut. "'Stay here,' he says. Stay here, my foot," she muttered to herself. But despite his being so unreasonable, the feminine part of her thrilled at his protectiveness. She'd been so long on her own, she'd forgotten how it felt to have someone else watching out for her, ready to do battle for her. But was his protectiveness for her, or for the mother of his child?

Of course, he'd done it for Claire, not her. Her mood suddenly cooled, she climbed out of the truck and slammed the door shut.

The warm steel stung the tender flesh of her arms as she leaned along the railing of the truck bed, her gaze turned toward the porch. There was something familiar about the man standing there, the way he held himself erect as if his battle wasn't fought over in Europe or in the middle of the Pacific, but here in Marietta. Sunlight caught on the badge on his chest. Sheriff Mack Worthington. Had Ms. Aurora had another spell? Or was it one of the children this time? Merrilee ran around the truck and across the dirt yard, passing John along the way. "Is something wrong, Mack? Are the kids okay?"

"Ms. Merrilee, I didn't expect to see you here." The tall man lumbered across the porch, a smile plastered on his face as he stood at the top of the stairs. "I'm sorry I didn't make it to Beau and Edie's wedding the other day, but I was on duty. Heard it was pretty, though."

"Yes, it was," she answered breathlessly, pressing her hand against the stitch in her side. "But you didn't answer my question. Are the kids and Ms. Aurora okay?"

"As far as I know. Billy came down a little while ago and told me he couldn't open the door until Mr. John got back. Said he was under strict orders." Mack grinned. "Good kid, that Billy."

Merrilee smiled. The boy reminded her so much of John when he was not much older than Billy, taking on more responsibility than any child should. "Yes, he is."

John stepped up beside her, his breath steady, eyeing Mack as if he were public-enemy number one instead of a peace officer. "Is this a friend of yours?"

Was there a hint of jealousy to his question? That was ridiculous. Then why did the thought make her stomach flutter? "You remember Mack Worthington. He hung around with Beau back in high school. He's the sheriff now."

Mack came down one step and held out his hand. "And you are?"

He shook his hand. "John Davenport."

"John Davenport." Mack's jet-black eyebrows furrowed, then released, his pale blue eyes growing wide, his finger pointing at one, then the other. "I remember when you two—"

"—ran off and got married," Merrilee finished for him. Well, if there was anyone in town who didn't know of John's return, that would change before lunchtime. Time to get down to business and find out what brought the sheriff out here in the first place. "You still haven't told us what you're doing here."

"Oh, I needed to talk to Ms. Aurora. I overheard something this morning at the diner and thought she ought to know about it."

"Ms. Aurora's sick, Mack. She had a spell with her heart yesterday." Merrilee placed her hand on the sheriff's arm and lifted her gaze to meet his. "John and I are going to be taking care of the kids and the farm until she gets back on her feet. So whatever it is you heard, you can tell us."

Mack's mouth flattened into a harsh line. "You're probably going to be the ones who have to deal with this, then. Dr. Adams is talking about reporting Ms. Aurora to the state. If he does, they'll send a social worker from Atlanta out here to decide if the kids should be sent away."

Chapter Eleven

"But those are Ms. Aurora's children. The state can't just take them away."

Merrilee had said it so matter-of-factly, no one besides John would have recognized the slight tremor in her voice for what it was.

Sheer and unadulterated fear.

Well, she had a right to worry; they all did. "Ms. Aurora never legally adopts the kids under her care, just takes them. Since the parents don't want them, there are no questions asked. It's better than having the families send them away."

"But that's not fair. She loves those kids like they're her own." Pleading green eyes full of compassion stared up at him, begging him for some resolution to this problem.

Her sweet protectiveness toward these children no one but Aurora had ever cared for warmed John's heart. He'd been wrong not to tell Merrilee about Mattie, should have remembered it wasn't in her tender nature to be anything like her father. Maybe she'd been right. Maybe he had been protecting himself. But there were other concerns that needed his attention now. John met the sheriff's gaze. "Do you have any idea when he might be doing this?"

Mack shook his head. "Didn't hear that part, but I can do some digging around, see if I can come up with a day."

"I'd appreciate it," John answered.

"We both would," Merrilee added.

"Sure thing." Mack lifted his hat and placed it on his head. "I'd better get back to town before anyone misses me." He started down the steps, then turned back. "If you need anything, just let me know, okay?"

"Thank you, Mack."

Color rose in the sheriff's cheeks. A smile answered the one Merrilee had given him, only his held a hint of masculine appreciation. A lawman probably would have ranked higher than a dirt farmer with Jacob Daniels. Well, the man could pursue Merrilee later, out of his view. "Yes, thank you, Sheriff. If you'll excuse us now, the kids are probably hungry and we need to get started on the chores."

If Mack Worthington thought he was being rushed off, he didn't show it. He took the steps two at a time. "I'll see y'all later."

Merrilee waved to the man one last time as he got into his car. "He turned out to be a nice boy."

"A man doesn't like being referred to as a boy." Especially by a woman as beautiful as Merrilee.

"Well, Mack will always be that little boy who used to get into trouble with Beau." She gave one last look to the sheriff's departing car before turning toward the front door. "Give me about thirty minutes and I'll have breakfast ready."

"I'll check on the kids and Ms. Aurora." So Merrilee wasn't interested in the good sheriff. The knowledge brought a smile to his face, though why, he wasn't sure. Merrilee deserved to be loved by a good man, a man who appreciated a woman like her, kind and considerate, gracious to a fault. And beautiful—very beautiful. He swallowed past the hard knot in his throat.

He only wished it could have been him.

"After breakfast, maybe we could sit down and make a list of things to do to get ready, just in case we get a visit from the social worker," Merrilee said as she opened the door.

John shook his head slightly. He had to focus if he wanted to keep Aurora's family together, and that would mean keeping a nosy social worker at bay. No more daydreams of what could have been. Not now. Not ever.

Merrilee pushed open the kitchen door and stood, allowing her eyes a moment to adjust to the near darkness. A small lantern sat as the centerpiece on the table, a box of matches purposely left at the base. A soft scratch of wood against flint, the sharp smell of chemicals and a soft glow chased the darkness away.

Merrilee glanced around the space. Dish towels hung in a tidy row along the stove handle, an old but clean coffeepot resting in its place on the back burner. The cabinet tops were made of scarred wood and pale yellow curtains served as doors, the material so thin, the neatly arranged items on the shelves showed through.

A mason jar of bacon grease sat alongside the salt and pepper shakers near the stove.

None of these things had looked anywhere near this clean and tidy by the time she'd left last night. Clearly John had been hard at work.

How Aurora ever fit all the children she'd had over the years into this kitchen was astonishing. There'd just been six children last night, and she and John had eaten their dinner over the sink. And the mess! With all the elbows and hands flying around, by the end of the meal there seemed to be more food on the floor than in the kids' bellies. Today, she'd tackle that dining room so that by this evening, they could all sit together like a family should.

Merrilee sighed, a whisper of discontent sliding through her. She hadn't thought much about having more of a family than Claire, figured she had been blessed to even have her. But listening to the children bustle around the table, mopping up Ellie's spilled milk, even cutting up the twins' carrots had made her realize how much she enjoyed a bigger family, with plenty of children around the table. She wasn't old, just turned thirty, so the possibility for more children still existed. But conceiving them required a husband and marriage, and she wasn't sure she wanted to dip her toes in that pond again.

The image of John wiping Ellie's creamed-potato-covered hands floated through her thoughts. The man had jumped in and helped her and the others, pouring milk, refereeing disagreements. He had a knack with the kids, an understanding that he used with gentle authority. Even Claire had fallen victim to his charm, her

laughter a sweet memory Merrilee had locked away
in her heart after a year of grief. How would she react
when she learned John was her long-absent father?

All this woolgathering was just a waste of time.
She'd have to work fast if she was to take inventory of
the pantry and root cellar before everyone else in the
house woke up. John had brought in all the supplies
she needed to make dinner last night, but she wanted
to take a look for herself—and not just to help her plan
meals. The stock Aurora had or didn't have would give
Merrilee enough information to start her investigation.
She lifted the lantern from the center of the table and
slipped out the back door.

She hiked the lantern over her head, the early morning suddenly darker as she scanned the ground near
the back porch. An old weathered door sat at a slight
angle on the ground almost as if it had been discarded
there. Merrilee bent down and tugged, the coarse wood
scratching her fingers as the door lifted only slightly before slamming back into place. A length of rope around
the handle would give her leverage, but that would mean
she'd have to wait until she could get out to the barn.
Still, it was better than explaining to John how she got
a handful of splinters.

*We need to be completely honest with each other
for this to work.*

Her stomach tightened. All right, she'd agreed with
him—for the most part. But the country was at war,
keeping the home front safe was her patriotic duty and
her work had to be done in secret in order for it to be
effective. Surely John would understand her reasons
for keeping him in the dark about this. And he wasn't

without his secrets, too. Like what was taking him away from Marietta again, away from her and Claire.

What's sauce for the goose is sauce for the gander, right? Merrilee smirked. Even she wasn't buying that line. The truth was she couldn't tell him about her investigation, at least, not until Aurora was cleared. Maybe not even then.

"Ms. Merrilee?"

She jerked around. Billy stood in the doorway, his tousled hair falling over droopy eyelids, thumbprint bruises turning the pale skin under his eyes purple. "What are you doing out of bed?"

"Couldn't sleep." He leaned heavily on the broken stick he used as a cane. "Couldn't get my brain to stop thinking."

Poor thing. She'd had nights like that. "Would you like a glass of water?"

Nodding, he stepped back and held the door until she was safely inside. Aurora had done a fine job with Billy, with all of the kids. It would be a shame if Adams convinced the state to rob these children of the home she'd made for them here.

Wood scraped against the floor as Billy pulled a chair out, slumped down at the table and lay his tousled head against his arms. Poor kid looked as if he carried the weight of the world across his young shoulders. Merrilee lifted a glass from the dish drainer, filled it with water and walked over to where Billy sat.

"So you want to talk about it?" She pulled out the chair next to his and sat down, putting the glass in front of him. She needed to uncover what was bothering the boy. "Your leg's not hurting, is it?"

"No, it's just…" He hesitated, his hands wrapped around the glass. He shook his head again.

Merrilee understood. Some things were just too hard to talk about. Maybe a little time would help Billy be able to put his feelings into words. "Well, if you need someone to talk to, I'm here, okay?"

She stood then, but she could feel Billy's gaze following her around the room. She grabbed the empty coffeepot and headed for the sink. What kind of burden could Billy be carrying? And why was he so reluctant to talk about it?

Not that anyone had ever given these children a voice, save Aurora. Merrilee uncapped the pot, pulled the metal filter free and placed the container under the lip of the water pump.

"Is she going to be okay?"

The boy's question pulled Merrilee's thoughts away from her work. "Ms. Aurora?"

"She is going to be okay, isn't she?"

Merrilee grabbed a dish towel, dried her hands then leaned back against the counter. "She's going to be fine. She just needs a little rest, that's all."

"But I heard the doctor say it was her heart."

Oh, dear. Why hadn't Dr. Adams realized there were little ears listening? She crossed over to the table, then crouched down beside Billy, her gaze level with his. "You're right. It is her heart, but the doctor gave her some medicine to help her. That, along with some rest, should leave Ms. Aurora as good as new."

"Are you sure?" His voice held a note of wariness.

Merrilee didn't blame him. Doctors were only human, and made miscalculations just like everyone else. She'd learned that the hard way. She slipped her arm around his shoulders. "No, but John and I are going to do everything we can to give Ms. Aurora a chance to get better and back to taking care of you guys."

"But what if something happens to her?"

How could she answer that? She brushed his hair back off his face. "That's a hard question."

Billy's face scrunched in confusion. "I thought grown-ups knew all the answers."

She shook her head. "Not really."

He fell quiet for a moment. "Then I guess it's like Ms. Aurora always says. We've got to trust that God knows what He's doing and just keep praying on it."

Sounded like Aurora. But what happened when your prayers go unanswered? When everything going on around you didn't make sense?

"Could we pray about it?"

Merrilee blinked. "Now?"

"Ms. Aurora always says no time like the present." Billy reached for her hand, laced his fingers between hers and bowed his head. "You go first."

Her mouth suddenly dry, she licked her lips. "I'm a little rusty."

The boy tilted his head, one eyebrow cocked high on his forehead. "If you don't use it, you lose it."

Another one of Ms. Aurora's sayings, she guessed. She bowed her head; her eyes slammed shut. She might as well try, not that her words would be heard. God had stopped listening to her prayers a while back.

"Dear Lord, Billy and I come to You this morning to ask that You heal Ms. Aurora. Give her strength and rest in the coming days. And help Billy and the other children to have peace about the situation. In Christ's name—"

Billy gave her hand a squeeze and she glanced over at him. "I want to say my piece."

"Oh, okay." She lowered her head once more and waited.

"And, Lord, thank You for sending Ms. Merrilee and Mr. John to help us," the boy said so earnestly, tears began to burn behind the back of Merrilee's eyelids. "They didn't have to help us, but You brought them here, and I thank You. In Jesus's name, amen."

"Amen," she whispered and lifted her head.

"That was a fine prayer, Merrilee and Billy. From the heart, but to the point."

Her heart skipped a beat, then sped up. John stood in the kitchen door, one strap to his denim overalls hanging loose over his well-developed shoulder. Merrilee stood, holding on to the back of Billy's chair.

"Come on, sleepyhead." Merrilee helped the boy to his feet. "Go crawl into bed for another hour, okay?"

Billy nodded, his steps heavy as she walked him to the kitchen door. John gave the boy a concerned look, then lifted his gaze to hers, a tiny line carved between worried blue eyes. "I'll put him back to bed, okay?"

How many times in those early days, when Claire was just a baby, had she dreamed of moments like this? Of sharing the joys and the burdens of child rearing with John, of knowing what the other needed before any words were spoken? "I'll get the coffee going."

John nodded, took Merrilee's place behind Billy and walked him out of the kitchen. She stopped at the doorway and watched, John's long shadow filling up the hallway, his muscled arm draped around Billy's shoulders as they made their slow trek down the corridor. If they were still married, would she have borne John a son by now? He'd want one, of course. Every man that she'd ever known had. But John wasn't just any man.

And he wasn't her husband anymore. With a sigh, she turned and headed toward the sink.

Chapter Twelve

John leaned against the door frame, his arms crossed in front of him, enjoying the sight of Merrilee meticulously measuring out the coffee grounds and dumping them into the metal filter. The dusty-rose light of the new morning cast an ethereal glow around Merrilee's head, sparks of fire dancing along the reddish-gold strands every time she tried to blow the wayward curls off her brow. He'd always loved her hair, the way her curls framed her face, the silky softness that caressed his fingertips when he'd gently tilted her head to move in for a kiss.

John swallowed; his heart slammed against his ribs. What was he thinking? He was no better a candidate for Merrilee's hand than he had been twelve years ago. In fact, he was a worse marriage prospect now if the charges for helping the Oahus weren't dropped. He'd best remember that. "What was that all about?"

A spoonful of coffee rained down across the white countertop as she jumped. She pressed a hand to her chest. "I almost wasted a day's ration jumping like that."

"I'm sorry." The words came with more of an edge than he'd have liked. "I didn't mean to scare you."

"I guess I was thinking a little too hard." She grabbed a nearby dish towel and carefully dusted the grounds into her opened hand, then threw them in the pot. "Is Billy okay?"

John straightened, then crossed over to the cabinet where Aurora kept her cups and saucers. "Was asleep the moment his head hit the pillow."

"Good, I was worried about him."

"Is that why you were praying?"

Her whole body stiffened. "He asked me to. It must have worked. He's back in bed."

John lifted two cups out of the cupboard, perplexed. Praying, reaching out to God had always been second nature to Merrilee—as constant and certain as the rising and setting of the sun. When they were married, her faith had lifted him up, made him embark on his own walk with the Lord. But she had seemed uncomfortable praying, "rusty" she'd told Billy, as if she wasn't sure why she was even doing it. That didn't make sense. Had the burden of caring for Claire during this past year made her question her faith? Or was it something else? *Lord, use me to help Merrilee through this dark valley she seems to be in*.

"Has Aurora made any arrangements for the children if something happens to her?" Merrilee turned the knob on the stove, adjusting the flame before setting the pot on to percolate.

"No." He set the two cups side by side on the table. "She can't. She's not their legal guardian."

"How can that be?"

John scrubbed his jaw with this hand. Now came the tricky part—explaining. "Most families who have kids like Aurora's children admit them to a 'home,' an institution, but if they don't have the funds to do that..." He hesitated, his throat closing around the words. How could the emotions from that day—that moment he'd realized their father had abandoned them in the middle of Cooper's Drugstore—still elicit a response all these years later?

"They dump them on the street, Merrilee. Leave them to fend for themselves. And if the state finds out about the kids, that Aurora hasn't adopted them, they'll send those kids to the state institution."

"Milledgeville?" she whispered. "But how has she kept the children this long without having legal guardianship? Everyone in town knows she has kids out here. Hasn't anyone ever asked any questions?"

"Not when I was here. Most people assume Aurora's adopted all her kids, and she just lets them go on thinking that way."

Merrilee leaned back against the cabinet, her slender arms crossed in front of her, a thoughtful expression on her face. "How does she get the kids' ration books?"

Odd question, John thought. Must be the mothering instinct, that need to ensure that kids are being fed properly. "I don't know that she does. Probably makes do with what she has."

"That doesn't seem right. Those kids need to eat like everyone else does. How can they if she can't get their rations?"

This time, her honest concern for the children might be asking for trouble. "We have to be careful, Merri. We can't go demanding ration books for the kids, not when there's no legal reason for them to be here with us. Last thing we need is for the state to find out Aurora's taken in these kids without adopting them."

"But it's not fair, John. It's just not."

The urge to take her in his arms, whisper words of comfort, stroke her hair, almost overwhelmed him. He gripped the back of a chair. "You're right. If the children aren't getting ration books, then it's not fair. But I'd give up fairness to keep them safe and out of an institution, wouldn't you?"

"Yes, but…"

He interrupted her. "Trying to convince people to give these kids their fair share when they already think they belong in an institution is going to be nigh impossible."

"Nothing is impossible with God," she snapped, then blinked a couple times as if the words had surprised her.

Something most definitely had caused Merrilee to doubt God's faithfulness, but what? An idea niggled its way into his thoughts. Would it work? It had to. John walked over to where she stood. "You're right. But before you go at whoever, headlong, I think we need to pray about this, don't you?"

The low hum of coffee boiling saved her from a quick response. She turned the stove down and lifted the coffeepot. "Want some?"

Sidestepping the question. Well, he wasn't easily dissuaded. "Yes, please."

"I haven't gotten as far as the pantry yet so I don't know if there's any sugar or not. You always liked a couple spoonfuls in your coffee, didn't you?"

"Black is fine." The idea she still remembered how he took his coffee made his thoughts scatter into the four winds. What else did she remember about their short time together? His memories of their marriage had been all that had gotten him up in the morning those first few months after they'd parted. The need to come back to Marietta and prove he was every bit as good as any man her father had deemed worthy to court her had driven him to work harder. He'd scrimped and saved like a madman, hoping to show her all that he'd achieved for her…but his efforts were for nothing. At least, that was what Jacob Daniels had told him. Merrilee had forgotten him.

Or had she?

John watched Merrilee as she walked to the table, a graceful efficiency in her movements. Did it really matter now? Their marriage had ended years ago. They'd moved on, at least, she had. The only bond to remind them of what they had once shared was Claire. And while he wanted desperately to connect with his daughter, he didn't know how long he'd be able to stay with her.

But he could help Merrilee, bear her troubles even for a little while. Help her find her faith again. "You didn't answer my question. Don't you think we need to pray about the ration books?"

The lines of her mouth tightened as she poured first one cup, then the other full of coffee. "Prayer is always good."

Noncommittal, but a start. He pulled out the chair next to his, and waited for her to sit down before continuing. "Remember how old Otis Zimmerman used to pray over your daddy's fields before work started every morning?"

She smiled softly. "Mr. Zimmerman used to say the work wouldn't be as hard with the Lord on our side."

"He prayed for each one of us by name."

"He was a good man."

John nodded, wishing he could hear those words falling from her lips about him. "He's a good example to follow."

She laced her fingers around her cup. "I don't understand."

"Billy had a right to be worried. Even if Aurora recovers, she won't have much of a legal foot to stand on to keep the kids if the state gets involved." He drew in a deep breath, the scent of strong coffee filling the tight space of the kitchen. "It might take a lot of praying to keep this family together."

"And if God doesn't answer your prayers?" she whispered.

Was that it? Was Merrilee waiting for an answer God hadn't yet sent? "Then He has a better plan for the children than me or Aurora or anyone else might have."

A white cloud of steam from Merrilee's cup swirled toward the ceiling. "I don't see how an institution could be a better plan."

"Me, neither," he admitted. He could only pray it didn't come to that. "Anyway, I was hoping you would join me."

"I don't know, John. I mean, I appreciate what you're trying to do, really I do." She hesitated, a pained expression briefly shadowing her face. "But there's so much to do, with taking care of this place and the children, and not to mention keeping tabs on the boardinghouse. I won't have much time."

Disappointment slid through him. He'd been sure this was the way to help Merrilee, but he wouldn't force her. She had to come to this decision on her own. He could leave the door open for later if she changed her mind. "Well, if you'd ever like to join me, you're always welcome."

She gave him an aloof nod. "Could we talk about what we need to do to get ready for the state's visit? Maybe make a list we can knock out?"

"Sure."

"Let me get some paper and a pencil." She rose and hurried across the room to her purse.

John watched her as she dug through the contents. Well, if she was having a hard time praying at the moment, he'd have to do enough praying for the both of them, with prayers for Merrilee Daniels Davenport at the top of his list.

"Never thought I'd see the day you'd come back to Marietta."

John crouched back on his knees, his wide brim hat shielding his eyes from the midday sun as he looked over to his visitor. He scrubbed his dirty hands against the denim leg of his overalls, a smile tickling the corners of his mouth as he watched the younger man cut a path through the newly plowed rows. The white, thigh-length coat, starched shirt and plain black tie were as far removed from the tattered jeans and cotton T-shirts Beau wore in his days in the Civilian Conservation

Corps as night and day, but he wore both with an ease built of confidence and age.

"Never thought I'd see you hitched," John replied, "but wonders never cease."

Beau chortled. "How have you been?"

"I made it back home in one piece. How about you?"

"Spent some time enjoying the German's hospitality, but what's that saying? What doesn't kill me makes me stronger."

John nodded. He'd worried when he heard his nephew had been captured and sent to a German prison camp, but any concerns he'd had faded at the sight of the man standing in front of him. In fact, this Beau was in far better shape than the man John had loaded on an army bus years ago. Solid, more at peace than that boy. "Marriage seems to agree with you."

The corner of Beau's mouth lifted into a familiar crooked grin. "You said God had a woman just for me, and now that I've found her, I have no intention of ever letting her go."

Sounded like something he'd have said, but he'd been as green as a crab apple back then, naive and very much in love with his wife. Little did he know she'd already abandoned their home. John planted the shovel into the mound of dirt, leaned on it and stared at the man. At least Beau seemed happy. "Did your wife come with you?"

Beau shook his head. "She's at work. She's a draftsman over at the bomber plant."

A college girl. She'd keep Beau on his toes. "Sounds like a real peach. I'm happy for you."

"Thanks." Beau shoved his hands into the pockets of

his white coat. "I take it you got the letters I sent you. That's why you're here, right?"

"I only got one letter." John brushed the dirt from his hands, then pulled Claire's folded letter from his back pocket and handed it to Beau. "This."

Beau glanced over it, then shook his head. "That little sneak. I knew she wanted to hear everything she could about you, but I didn't think she would go through my stuff to get your address so she could write you herself."

"Did you know about Claire?"

"Not until I showed up at Merrilee's last spring. She's a great kid, John. Smart, always asking questions. The most determined little person I've ever met. Almost as bad as Merrilee." Beau looked up at him. "You didn't get anything from me? Judging from the postmark here, I'd guess I sent them off right after Claire mailed this to you."

Beau seemed awfully concerned over a couple letters. "Does it really matter? I'm here now."

"It's just…" Beau's mouth straightened into a sharp line before relaxing. "Maybe you're right. Anyway, I'll bet Claire loves having you here."

If only he could tell the child he was her father. "She doesn't know who I am."

"Why?" Before John could answer, Beau held up his hand. "Don't answer that. Merrilee, right?"

John drew in a deep breath. "She's afraid if Claire learns I'm her father that she won't be able to handle it when I have to leave again."

"Why would you leave? You just got back."

He didn't want to drag Beau into his mess, but it

didn't look like he could avoid it. "You remember Peter Oahu?"

"Yeah, he worked with us on the aqueducts out in California. The two of you were good friends."

"We were." A pang of loss speared through John at the thought of his old friend. "Anyway, right after you shipped out, Peter and his wife, Grace, received orders to report to the W.R.A. relocation center at Manzamar."

"But Peter was born in the United States, wasn't he?"

John nodded. "Both he and Grace were, but he still had a grandmother and uncles in Japan."

"That's rotten luck." A line formed between Beau's furrowed brows. "But what has that got to do with you?"

John probably sounded like he was stalling, but Beau needed all the facts to understand the situation. "Peter wanted to fight in the war, but he was declared unfit because of his heritage, until last year. He shipped out with the 442nd Combat Team last April."

"Probably needed all the warm bodies they could get by then." Beau grew quiet, clearly sensing that this story had an unhappy ending. "What happened?"

John didn't answer right away. It still hurt to say the words out loud. "He was killed in Belvedere."

"Oh, I'm so sorry, John."

He was, too. Peter had become almost a brother to him after Beau enlisted. The pain of his death clung to John like a death shroud. "Before he left, he asked me to take care of Grace. She was pregnant, and he wanted me to check in on her, see if she needed anything." He hesitated. "The shock of Peter's death sent her into labor. I barely had time to round up a doctor before the baby was born. A little boy."

"Peter would have been happy about another son," Beau said with quiet respect.

"The baby was born early, and Grace was too weak to nurse. The doctor said he needed some kind of home-made formula to stay alive, but it required canned milk, and that's rationed."

"And you did what you had to do to save Peter's son."

He knew Beau would understand. If only the home-land informant who'd reported him to the camp's commanding officer had had half a heart. "I'm to be called up in front of an investigative committee to face disciplinary action. I could end up in jail."

Beau sighed. "What does Merrilee say about all of this?"

John rubbed his palms down his denim-clad thighs. "She doesn't know."

His friend crossed his arms over his chest in a tense stance. "You've got to tell her, John. She deserves to know. And anyway, she'll understand."

Would she? John wasn't so sure. And this time, it wasn't just Merrilee he worried about. There was Claire to consider. "It's my mess, and I'll clean it up. Then I'll come back here and work the old Todd farm."

"You bought Mr. Todd out?"

John smiled. "Thought it would be a good place for Claire to come out on the weekends and spend time with me."

"And if you go to jail?"

He didn't want to think that far ahead. "Then I'll give it to her. She could sell it and take the money to go to college or something."

Beau's jaw tightened, then he shook his head. "I still think you should tell Merrilee. You owe it to her."

John's back stiffened, a spark of irritation flaring to life. Explaining everything to Merrilee would only complicate matters. Best to keep her in the dark until he had his day in front of the investigative committee. No sense leaving her or Claire open to scorn until then. "What are you doing here, Beau?"

The man glared at him for a long moment, then shook his head. "I convinced Dr. Adams not to report Aurora to the state, at least for right now."

An answer to prayer! John's muscles loosened slightly. "I appreciate you doing that."

"I don't know how long I can hold him off."

But at least it gave them some time. "It doesn't matter. Just thanks for doing it."

"One thing, John."

John glanced at Beau, his expression more serious than the day he left for basic training. "What is it?"

"You can tell Merrilee what's going on or not. That's your business," he answered with a sternness John had never heard from his former nephew in all the years they'd worked together. "But don't break my aunt's heart again."

John yanked the blade of the shovel out of the ground with a quick movement. "She's the one who filed for divorce."

"I know, and it doesn't make sense."

"What doesn't make sense? The woman divorced me." Even now, the words caused an ache to form around John's heart.

"But I'm not sure that's what she wanted." Beau grimaced, as if he'd spoken too much, then shook his head. "There've been certain things she's said since I've been home that make me think Merrilee still cares for you."

John scoffed. The only feeling his former wife had for him was a kind of wariness, and could he blame her? He constantly reminded her he would have to leave Marietta without giving her any reasons as to why. Was Merrilee holding him at arm's length for their daughter's sake or to protect her own heart?

No, Beau was probably reading more into the situation than he should. Merrilee's only interest in John now was as Claire's father. The thought only made the painful grip on his heart worse. John snatched his hat off his head, plowed a hand through his unruly hair then shoved it back on. "Don't you have better things to do than nosing around in other people's business?"

Dark auburn brows rose in an arch over dark eyes. "So that's how you're going to play this." Beau gave a decisive nod of his head. "Fine, then you can have your job back."

John blinked. Had the sun gotten to Beau? "What are you talking about?"

Beau grabbed the lapels of his coat and gave them an authoritative tug. "When you left to train Seabees, you made me promise that if I ever got back here, I would keep my eye on Merrilee. Make sure she was provided for, that she was safe."

John drew in a sharp breath. Yes, he remembered, but he hadn't figured on Beau having to make good on his promise. From what Jacob Daniels had told him when the judge granted the divorce, Merrilee would soon be settled with a new husband of her father's choosing, and in no time would have a fine house just off the square full of perfectly behaved children who would do the Daniels's legacy proud. Only she hadn't remarried, choosing instead to raise Claire alone. "What about it?"

"It goes without saying that I'll watch out for them until you get everything straightened out. But you'll be back. You wouldn't dare let Claire think she'd been abandoned by her daddy like you were. And once you're settled here, looking out for Merrilee and Claire should be on your shoulders again."

His friend knew him too well. "Why are you pushing this?"

Beau shifted his gaze over John's shoulder as if looking for the answer in the plowed fields. "I remember how torn up you were in those days after the divorce. I was angry Merrilee had hurt you like that." His gaze met John's. "But after I came back, after I spent some time with Merrilee, I knew she'd been hurt as much as you had. And when Edie and I found those letters at Dad's place, I knew he'd played a part in busting up the two of you."

"What are these letters you keep talking about?"

"They were from Merrilee to you. Dad somehow incepted them before they made it to the post office."

John nodded. He'd had his suspicions about James trying to separate him and Merrilee—the man always did his daddy's bidding. But he'd never had anything concrete against the man that he could take back to Merrilee. Not that she'd have believed him. She loved her brother and only believed the best about him.

Even at her husband's expense.

What did it matter now? "A few letters aren't going to make much of a difference, Beau."

"I'm not talking about one or two." The cockeyed smile the younger man gave him struck him as odd considering the conversation. "The woman sent you dozens of letters."

Dozens? It had to be a mistake. Surely one letter would have gotten through to him. "How many?"

"I lost count. It took me a week to find a box big enough to send them in."

His heart flip-flopped in his chest. If only he'd gotten just one! He could have lived off her words, held out hope that she'd be waiting for him once he'd saved up enough money, ready to build a home with him, raise a family. Jacob and his son had robbed them of that chance, all because of Jacob's ideas about his daughter's future. A husband with a good family name who would be a credit to the Daniels family, even if it meant a lifetime without love.

But Merrilee had refused to settle for anything less than love. How many times in their short courtship and marriage had she mentioned her happiness in finding him? Of discovering that death-till-you-part kind of love that would last all their days? He'd held those moments sacred.

How could he begin to hope for a future with Merrilee and Claire when a possible prison sentence hung over his head like a guillotine? Being so close to Merrilee, sharing her life for just this small amount of time, sparked emotions he had no business feeling now.

"Will you read the letters if they ever are delivered?"

No, what's done is done, John thought.

Only he found that even now, he wanted to know what she'd written, if there had been any hints at what was about to take place. If Merrilee had explained why she wanted the divorce, if she'd let him know that she was unhappy. John shook his head. "I haven't made up my mind yet."

Beau's face relaxed into a smile. "Good, at least you're keeping an open mind about it. And if the box is returned to me, I can bring it out Sunday morning when Edie and I come to sit with Ms. Aurora while you and Merrilee take the kids to church in our car."

Merrilee had mentioned something about church, but with only the truck to transport them, he hadn't seen how they could manage the trip to town and back safely. "Merrilee talk you out of your car for the day?"

Beau shook his head. "No, we offered. Edie mentioned it might be dangerous for the kids to ride that long in the back of the truck. Merrilee said she had to talk it over with you, but I don't know what needs to be talked about. I'm just loaning you our car."

But it was more than that to John. Merrilee hadn't plowed ahead without taking his opinion into consideration. The knowledge set off a blaze of warmth across his chest. "United we stand," she'd said, and it appeared she meant it. John held out his hand, took Beau's and gave it a hardy shake. "If Merrilee's okay with it, then we'll see you Sunday morning."

Early-morning sunlight sliced through a few straggly white clouds as John stepped off the porch the following Sunday morning, beads of perspiration bursting across his forehead. He blotted them away with a handkerchief. Too hot and humid this early in the spring, he noted. He could only pray that didn't mean a scorched crop come fall.

Shucking out of his coat, John glanced at his watch. They'd be walking in during the first hymn if Merrilee and the kids didn't get a move on.

The screen door slapped shut behind him, and he turned to find Billy, his britches barely stretching down to his knees, the edge of his suit coat frayed against the exposed skin of his wrist. The boy stuck a finger into the collar of the too-tight shirt and yanked. "I hate wearing suits."

Preaching to the choir, kid. Maybe if Billy had a suit that fit, he'd at least be comfortable. John made a note to talk to Merrilee about it. "Ms. Aurora always said that this is the Lord's day, and part of our worship is wearing our finest for Him."

Billy grimaced as he tugged on his sleeve. "You'd think the Lord would have better things to do than check out our clothes."

John couldn't disagree with him there. "Where are the other kids?"

"Ms. Merrilee is helping Ellie and Claire with their hair." Billy rolled his eyes. "Something about needing ribbons."

John pressed his lips together to keep from grinning. The boy may not yet appreciate the troubles his feminine counterparts undertook for their appearance, but give him a few years and those ribbons and curls would have his complete attention. Hopefully, he'd be there to guide Billy along, to give him advice. Maybe if he'd had a father to talk with, his life with Merrilee might have turned out differently.

But I have a Father, One who is always willing to listen when I come to Him.

The screen door squeaked open again, a little ball of pink and lace flying at him, plastering her warm little body against his leg, her giggles as soft and lyrical as Sweetwater Creek after a morning rain. "Mr. John! Ms. Merrilee put my hair up like a real lady!"

John bent down, untangled the girl's arms from around his legs and lifted Ellie to her feet. Her pale blond head shifted from side to side to display twin pigtails tied back with royal-blue lace. "My goodness, Ellie, you're pretty enough to eat."

A lopsided smile spread across Ellie's face, her blue eyes sparkled with girlish mischief, making John wonder. How can such a little bit of a girl find so much joy in a world that often viewed her as damaged? That was filled with people who called her names and treated her as less than a person because her eyes were set too far apart, her nose was too flat or her brain didn't work fast enough for their liking? He may never understand the kind of joy the little girl felt, but he would do everything in his power to protect Ellie from those who would steal it.

"What about me?"

John glanced over Ellie's blond head to where his daughter stood. The emerald-green dress perfectly matched Claire's eyes; the tiny cream-colored buttons looked like seed pearls buffed to a high gloss. Her reddish-gold hair had been pulled high on her head and tied with a bit of white lace, the long ponytail falling into curls against one slender shoulder.

A tight knot formed in his throat. What small bit of goodness had he ever done to deserve such a child? Nothing, but God had given him this blessing nevertheless. In a year, maybe two, he'd be forced to beat the boys off with a baseball bat.

"You're so pretty, Claire." Billy stared at his daughter, his mouth hung open, his cheeks flushed with color. The boy blinked as if pulling himself out of a trance. "For a girl, that is."

A delicate pink seeped into Claire's cheeks, and she lowered her gaze, a ghost of a smile playing on her lips. "Thank you."

Irritation speared through John. He might be beating the boys off sooner than he'd thought. Eyeing Billy one more time, he stepped around Ellie and walked to the bottom of the stairs, glancing up at his baby girl. "You're beautiful, Claire. The spitting image of your mother."

"I'll take that as a compliment."

The air in his lungs froze in place as Merrilee stepped out on the porch, shutting the door behind her. Her dress was patterned after Claire's, only in a pale lavender, fresh and sweet like newly bloomed lilacs. A black belt nipped in her trim waist while the pleated skirts fell modestly over the feminine curves of her hips and legs. She'd left her hair down, glorious waves of golden-red curls tumbling to her shoulders, a simple cream-colored hat perched at a stylish angle near her forehead, a wisp of opaque netting fluttering just over her eyes adding a bit of mystery.

Merrilee was beautiful, even more beautiful than he'd remembered. Not only because of her outer appearance, but also because of the lovely heart she carried on the inside, putting others' needs before her own feelings, like she had when she'd volunteered to help him with Ms. Aurora. The way she took care of Claire. A knot tightened around his heart.

What am I going to do about Merrilee, Lord?

John cleared his throat. "Are we ready to go?"

Merrilee nodded as she tugged on her gloves. "I've got the twins and Gail playing with Edie in the parlor, though I can't understand why Aurora doesn't feel like they're ready to sit through church."

"Ms. Aurora likes to give the new children a month to settle in," John answered. "Gail arrived a couple weeks ago, and the twins not too long after that."

Merrilee nodded. "That's understandable, I suppose. Then I guess we're ready."

"You heard the lady, kids. We're ready to go."

Ellie took off running toward the car while Billy and Claire drew up the rear, their crutches helping them make up ground quickly until Billy overtook the younger girl right as she reached for the handle. The boy grabbed it, pulled the door open then as if suddenly remembering his manners, took Claire's crutch from her and helped her into the backseat.

John frowned. He'd have to watch that boy, all right.

"Your grip on the railing gets any tighter and you'll break it in half."

John glanced back at Merrilee, his irritation growing as he noted the sparkle of laughter shining from her light green eyes. "You find the thought of that boy making goo-goo eyes at Claire funny?"

Merrilee's heels clicked softly against the wooden floor as she approached the stairs. "Oh, no. What's a hoot is watching your reactions to all of it! You look like you're ready to pounce on poor Billy for being nice."

John glanced back toward the car. "Maybe we should sit Ellie in the backseat between Claire and that boy."

Merrilee's laugher vibrated through him, and for a brief second, he couldn't think of anything except the feel of her hand pressed against his forearm. "We've got some time before they start making wedding plans."

His hand settled over hers of its own volition. "I don't know about that. I started planning how I would convince you to marry me when I was barely seventeen."

"I didn't know that."

Why in the world had he said that? And why did it bother him so much that she'd never guessed how in love with her he'd been even in those early days? Hadn't he told her? Maybe not. There were a lot of things he hadn't shared with her, particularly concerning her father and brother, but Merrilee had needed protecting, just like these kids and Aurora did. "It's nice of Beau and Edie to stay with Ms. Aurora and the little ones while we go to church."

Her disappointed sigh surprised him. "It seems my niece and nephew got together and made out a schedule. Maggie and Wesley are going to sit with Ms. Aurora next week."

John nodded, pressing a hand against her back as he guided her around several potholes in the yard. Merrilee had spent her youth fussing over her family, a problem that troubled John as he'd felt forced to stand by while her father and brother had taken advantage of her sweet nature. It was one of the few things they'd ever argued about, and a fight he'd never won. Maybe time had changed all that; maybe Maggie and Beau had grown up to appreciate their aunt better than their parents and grandparents ever had. "We had better get moving."

He hurried her into the car, noting with a bit of frustration that Billy had maneuvered his way into the seat next to Claire.

Merrilee must have noticed, too. "Billy, would you trade seats with Ellie please? She gets carsick if she's looking out the window."

"But I got here first," Billy whined.

"I know, but we can't have Ellie getting sick on us, now, can we?"

"I guess not." Billy didn't sound convinced, but he moved to sit behind the driver's seat.

Merrilee smiled up at John as he handed her into the car, her voice barely a whisper. "Does that work for you?"

He leaned down, lifting a corner of her dress and tucking it into the car. "That depends. Does Ellie really get carsick?"

She nodded. "Ms. Aurora thinks she'll grow out of it."

"Well, until then, let's use it to our advantage."

Her lips twitched. "You're hopeless, you know that?"

John didn't respond, his gaze on the deep red outline of her mouth. He was assailed by memories of her sweet lips against his. Did she still taste of sunshine and strawberries? He drew in a steadying breath, his lungs filled with the light scent of vanilla that clung to her like the finest perfume. It took all the strength he possessed to straighten and secure the car door.

John walked around the back of the car slowly to give himself a minute to pull himself together. He finally got into the driver's seat, determined to get this morning over without making a fool out of himself over Merrilee.

But he had a feeling Merrilee had called it right. He was utterly hopeless.

No one spoke until they reached the end of the driveway, not that he could have added much to any conversation. He was too distracted by his thoughts. Had he almost kissed Merrilee, right here in front of the children? How could he even consider such a thing? The woman hadn't told him about his child for almost twelve years!

Though in all fairness, he reminded himself, she could have written about Claire in those letters Beau had mailed.

But if she'd been so determined to let him know about Claire, why hadn't she shown up for their divorce hearing instead of sending her daddy to do her dirty work?

"Mr. John, you never told us what you're planting in Grandma Aurora's garden this year."

John glanced into his mirror to see Claire huddled close to her mother's seat, her arms hugging the headrest. "You call her Grandma?"

"What else would I call her?" Claire giggled. "She's my daddy's mama. What I mean is my daddy came to live with her when he was just a little boy so he grew up calling her mama."

He frowned. How much information about him had Aurora shared with his daughter? John glanced up at the mirror, and instead caught Merrilee studying him in his peripheral vision. Was she worried Claire might figure out the truth—that he was her father? "Why did your daddy come to stay with her?"

"I don't know. Grandma Aurora never told me."

Good, he thought.

"You know, Mr. John is one of Ms. Aurora's kids, too," Billy said.

Claire leaned closer, watching him. "Is that true, Mr. John?" Claire asked.

John stared at Billy in the rearview mirror. Last thing either he or Merrilee needed was for Claire to figure out on her own who he was. When the time came for Claire to know the truth, he wanted to be the one to tell her. Or if he ended up in prison, Merrilee could share it with her. But until then, he won't lie to her.

"Yes, I lived with Ms. Aurora when I was a kid."

"Why? What happened to your mama and daddy?"

Out of the corner of his eye, Merrilee turned in her seat. "Claire, John might not want to talk about this."

There was a sternness to her voice, but also something else, almost as if she wanted to protect him from Claire's inquisitive questions, queries that would lead to talk of his brother. He stole a quick glance at her, met her worried gaze briefly before she straightened in her seat and went back to staring out the window.

"I guess that makes us family," Claire said softly.

He glanced back at her in the mirror. "How do you figure that, squirt?"

"Well, you're Ms. Aurora's son, right? And my daddy's her son, too." Claire gave him a brilliant smile. "So that means we're related."

Family. John couldn't keep his lips pressed into a somber line, not while joy danced along his nerve endings, infusing him with a happiness he hadn't felt in a dozen years. The word conjured up all his hopes for the future. Claire's first date. Her graduation. Her wedding day. Milestones he would share with her, treasures he could take out and remember.

"You're right, Claire Bear. We are family."

Merrilee's affirmation slammed through him. Truth was he'd never envisioned raising a family without Merrilee, which was the reason why he'd never remarried. Or even dated, for that matter. His beautiful girl bride had been the only woman he'd ever wanted. He'd thought she'd discarded him for good years before, so to hear her claim him now as family meant more than he could say.

John stole a glance at her, her gloved hands folded neatly in her lap, a watery smile playing around the corner of her mouth. She seemed almost as if she were relieved Claire had taken another step in realizing the truth. But why? Had Beau been right? Did Merrilee still harbor some love for him even now, twelve years later?

And was he willing to risk his heart to find out?

He'd have to think about that. And pray. But in the meantime, why shouldn't he enjoy this moment he had with Merrilee, Claire and the other children? For the first time in his life, he had what he'd always wanted. A family.

Chapter Thirteen

What in the world was wrong with her this morning?

Merrilee closed the pages of her Bible and tried to concentrate on Pastor Williams's sermon. Maybe John hadn't noticed she'd held the hymn upside down, but his rich baritone, so lovely and unguarded, had caught her unawares, so much so that she'd stopped singing midway through the first verse. She'd also fumbled to the wrong chapter in the Bible, so touched was she by the reverence with which he turned the pages for Claire, then Billy.

So she'd decided to just listen to the sermon rather than follow along in her Bible, only concentrating proved almost impossible when she could look over to see Claire resting against John's solid shoulder, her arm threaded through his, as if she could think of no place better to be.

Claire had called him family. What was that old saying? Out of the mouths of babes. John had been thrilled, though he'd tried to hide it. Still, she'd known. His eyes had gone that stunning shade of blue that sent her pulse tripping and made her hands go moist under her gloves.

A look he used to wear every time she'd whisper "I love you," as if he couldn't quite believe his good fortune.

Well, now that Claire had adopted him into their family, there'd be no getting rid of him. Merrilee waited for the disappointment, but only felt relief filter through her. She didn't want to be rid of him—not now, not ever. But how much easier things would be if she could truly believe that he was here for good!

John may have bought a farm, but that didn't mean he wouldn't just pick up and leave again. He'd said as much. When he went away, she'd be left to pick up the pieces of their daughter's broken heart…and maybe a little bit of her own heart, too. The knot in her chest tightened.

Why did the man have to be so handsome? She'd almost fallen out of her high heels when she'd seen him this morning, the light gray, double-breasted suit fitting him to perfection. His skin had turned even more golden brown from the many hours in the field, the earthy smell of sunshine and freshly turned soil reminding her of happier times firmly planted in her memories.

"Are you okay?"

Merrilee blinked at Maggie's soft whisper beside her. Heat traveled up her neck and burst into flames in her cheeks. She tugged on her veil as she nodded, her eyes never straying from the pulpit. Maybe the little scrap of lace would hide her heated cheeks.

The soft thumping of Bibles closing summoned her out of her thoughts. She'd missed the whole service, wasn't even sure what the pastor had preached on. People rose to their feet around her, and she followed suit, bowing her head as Preacher Williams started to pray.

Oh, Lord, I'm so sorry. I came here intending to worship, to listen to Your word, but I couldn't get John out of my thoughts. What am I going to do about him? And Claire? What if he breaks my heart again? She waited, trying to still her thoughts, hoping the answer would flash through her heart. But there was only a quietness, a memory of her prayers with John that morning. He'd lifted up each child by name, poured out his hopes and dreams for them, for her, for Aurora and then gave each one of them over to God's care.

Everyone but himself.

Why was that? And why hadn't she thought about it before now? The urge to pray for John grew stronger with each passing moment.

"Now, if I can have your attention, I have an announcement to make." Pastor Williams held on to the edges of the lectern, his buoyant smile enough to lift any heavy spirit. His gaze settled on a young couple Merrilee didn't recognize in the front row. "My sister's daughter, Phyllis, is here today with her fiancé, Private First Class Ben Sanders. Phyllis didn't know when she arrived on Friday that Ben would be shipping out next week. We don't know when Ben will be coming home, but they've decided they would like for me to marry them before he reports for duty."

There were oohs and aahs around the sanctuary. Claire and Ellie sat at the edge of their seat as if hoping to get a look at the bride along with the rest of the congregation.

Billy sank back beside Merrilee. "Is this going to take long?"

Merrilee pressed a finger against her lips. Billy

crossed his arms over his chest and closed his eyes. John didn't need to worry about this young man stealing their daughter away anytime soon.

When she focused her attention back to the altar, the couple had come to stand before Pastor Williams. They both looked so young, barely out of their teens. Had the pastor explained the difficulties they would face— loneliness, hard work, wondering where the next meal would come from or how the next bill would be paid?

"Dearly beloved, we are gathered together in the presence of the Lord and these witnesses to join this man and this woman in holy matrimony."

Whatever worries she had for the couple slid away as she watched. The world around them seemed to have faded into the background, their eyes only for each other. A dull ache settled in Merrilee's chest. She remembered that feeling, that perfect moment when she'd looked up at John and saw their whole life unfolding before her. The unconditional love shining in his eyes had stolen every thought out of her head, save one: she would love John Davenport until she drew her last breath on this earth.

"If anyone has any reason why these two should not be joined together, speak now or forever hold your peace."

No one had been at her wedding to object, though if her father had been there, gunfire would likely have erupted. She and John had decided a justice of the peace just over the Tennessee line could be their only witness. Anyone else might try to stir up trouble.

When the couple turned toward each other to exchange their vows, Merrilee found herself staring into

John's blue eyes. Was he remembering their own make-shift wedding? The giddiness they'd felt when they'd left for Tennessee that morning, her bags packed and stored in the trunk of the borrowed car, the blue silk dress she'd picked to wear for the ceremony wrapped in tissue paper, sitting on top? The whole way there, they had talked of their hopes and dreams for their future: a small plot of land to build their own farm, at least four children—three boys and a girl that John could spoil.

"For richer or for poorer, to love and to cherish, in sickness and in health, till death do you part."

I do!

"Are they married yet?" Billy whispered loud enough to earn the scowl of Ms. Davis sitting in front of them.

Merrilee leaned down to talk to him, but Claire beat her to the punch. "Didn't you listen to the preacher this morning? They're making a marriage covenant."

How had she missed that particular lesson? At least her daughter had paid attention to the sermon. More than Merrilee could say for herself. She gave them what she hoped was her sternest look. Without another word, both children straightened and turned their attention back to the front of the church.

"Do you have the ring?"

Merrilee's hand went to her neck, her palm pressed against the thin band dangling on a chain beneath the collar of her dress. John hadn't had the money for a real wedding ring, so they had used a key ring Ms. Aurora had given him his first Christmas with her. It hadn't mattered that it'd turned her finger green, as long as it showed that she belonged to him.

"I want a pretty ring," Ellie exclaimed with a giggle.

John picked up the child and sat her in his lap. "Most females do."

A titter of laughter caught in the air, and several people glanced back at them with bemused smiles. But a few people, including Ms. Davis, gave the group a censoring frown that made Merrilee's temper flare.

The ceremony was drawing to an end. "Now a man shall leave his mother." Pastor Williams glanced from the groom to the bride. "And a woman leave her home, and the two shall be as one."

And a woman leave her home. The phrase doused whatever anger she felt. This had been the crux of every argument she'd ever had with John, this choice he'd given her between him and her family. Why did it have to be one or the other? Why hadn't he understood she could love both him and her father? She was supposed to honor her father, wasn't she?

Not at the expense of your husband's feelings.

The thought clung to her. Is that what she had done? Followed her daddy's advice rather than listen to John? Of course she had, and why wouldn't she? Didn't it say in the Bible to seek wise counsel? Who could have been any wiser than her daddy? She'd been so foolish to believe that for so long.

John had been wiser, she admitted to herself. He'd seen the problems she had with Jacob Daniels, had tried to warn her that her father's upstanding citizen persona was just a ruse to hide his lucrative moonshining business. She hadn't believed him, had even thought that John's accusations were just the result of jealousy over any relationship she shared with the father she'd wanted so desperately to please. That she had lived in the hope her father might one day see her worth as more than a worthless female had only frustrated John more.

"You may kiss your bride."

The couple shared a silly smile before the groom reached out and pulled his new wife into his embrace, his gaze caressing her upturned face before lowering his head to seal their vows with a kiss. The congregation burst into applause.

"Wasn't that the most romantic thing you've ever seen?" Claire turned to Merrilee, her expression one of girlish dreams. "It was just like a Clark Gable movie."

Billy smirked. "Forget the movie. I'd rather have popcorn. I'm starving."

"I hope my husband looks at me like that someday." Clare sighed. "Like I'm the most precious thing he's ever seen."

"Hopefully, that's a ways in the future," John said, a slight growl in his voice as he set Ellie on her feet and stood. He glanced down at Merrilee. "Why don't I take the kids outside and let them stretch their legs a bit? It will give you a few minutes to catch up with Maggie and what's going on at home."

"That would be lovely, thank you."

John retrieved the pair of crutches he'd laid down next to him and held them out to Billy and Claire. "Come on, kids."

Claire pulled herself up, using her free hand to straighten her skirts. "You know, Mama married my daddy when she was just seventeen."

Oh, dear. Claire had romance on her mind and that usually wound up with a new bunch of questions about her daddy. Maybe this was the time to tell her the truth, that John was her father. How would she handle the news?

"Well, don't you be getting any ideas. You've still got high school and college to look forward to."

Poor man, he'd have a tough time when Claire started flirting and going out on dates. And those poor boys who came courting! What kinds of torture would John put them through?

A warm hand came to rest on her shoulder and she tilted her head to find Maggie. "He seems very good with Claire."

"He is. With all of them, really. They adore him."

"And what about you?" A wicked grin floated across Maggie's lips.

Well, she wouldn't rise to the bait. "How are you feeling?"

"Coward," Maggie whispered before she sank back into the pew, her hand nestling protectively over her thickening waist. "I'm fine—feeling a lot better. The nausea has tapered off."

"So the saltines helped? You're eating more?"

Maggie slanted a glance at her. "By the time I have this baby, I won't be able to fit in the cockpit of my old crop duster."

"You'll figure out a way," Wesley said, draping an arm behind Maggie and pulling her close. He brushed a kiss against her temple. "And you'll be as beautiful as always."

Maggie leaned into her husband's embrace. "Thank you, dear."

A tiny fission of jealousy snaked through Merrilee, and she turned away, only to catch a glimpse of the newlyweds still standing at the altar, accepting handshakes and congratulations. Everywhere she turned, people seemed to be blissfully paired off. She didn't begrudge them their happiness; no, people deserved to find joy in their marriage. But what had she done to ruin her chances at a happily ever after of her own?

And a woman leave her home, and the two shall be as one.

Merrilee pushed the thought aside. "So what's going on at the house?"

"Nothing much," Maggie answered. "You know Sarah Jo and Rob moved out last week."

"No." She'd expected a small exodus of renters now that the bomber plant had gone from three shifts to two. With the war winding down, she was sure she could anticipate more of these sudden departures. Not exactly what she needed to hear with Claire's doctors' bills and the bank on the verge of foreclosing on her home. "I thought Rob transferred to the second shift."

Wesley shook his head. "Evans has been ordered to cut back on that shift, too. With the war being won over in Europe, I can't see this thing going on much longer. The plant might be only running one line by the end of the summer."

"Which means my renters will be moving out to find work." And Merrilee would have no way of paying off her bills.

"I wouldn't worry about it too much, Merrilee. They're bound to keep the plant open to be used for something," Maggie said.

"Hopefully. Anything else going on?"

They talked for a few more minutes, Maggie asking

where Merrilee kept certain items like floor wax and if she wanted her mail forwarded to Aurora's. They were still sifting through the details when a voice behind her caught Merrilee's attention.

"I've told Aurora those children had no business being in church. I mean, why bring them here when it's clear they don't understand anything anyway?"

Who would have the gall to speak that way about her children? Merrilee ignored the warning glance Maggie shot her, rose to her feet, and turned. Ah, Ms. Gladys Davis, she should have known. "Do you have a problem with my children, Ms. Davis?"

The older woman's gray eyes widened, her lips pursed in a strict line that irritated Merrilee to no end. "Look, Merrilee, I know you're just trying to help out Aurora. But that youngest girl with you today?" She lowered her voice to a whisper. "You must see that she couldn't have known what was going on. I mean, asking for a ring like that."

The woman had nerve, she'd give her that. Merrilee dug her fingers into the soft leather of her purse but kept her voice even. "Ms. Davis, Ellie is all of five years old. She just heard Pastor Williams ask for the ring and decided she'd like one, too, that's all—no different from how any other child might behave."

Ms. Davis leaned a step closer, closing the distance between them enough so that their conversation wouldn't be overheard. "Those children of Aurora's, they don't have the ability to understand the scriptures and such. It just confuses them."

Of all the arrogant—! Merrilee's fingers tingled, the urge to slap the smug little grin off the older woman's face so strong, her purse was in danger of having holes poked through it. *Forgive me for my unkind thoughts, Father. Keep my temper in check. Help me answer her with a gentle voice.*

Her lace veil fluttered softly as she drew in a steadying breath. It didn't matter what this—she struggled, each name she thought of worse than the last—woman thought; Aurora's kids needed to hear about the Lord just like anyone else. "Maybe you're right, Ms. Davis. Maybe they don't understand everything that's being taught in church. They're probably not the only ones in our community with that problem. But Ms. Aurora's kids do understand love, and what better example is there of love than God Himself?"

"Well, I don't know about that." Ms. Davis shifted her purse to her forearm as she stepped into the aisle. "I'm just going to put this little incident down to you being tired, taking care of those children and everything. I'm sure once you've returned home, you'll have a clearer head to think with."

The woman spoke as if the children's problems were contagious! Merrilee had to bite the inside of her cheek to keep from snapping back with a nasty retort.

"Old biddy, talking like that about those kids," Maggie snorted, slipping her arm around Merrilee's waist and pulling her close as Ms. Davis ambled down the aisle toward the door. "If I wasn't on the nest, I would have slugged it out with her right here in church."

"Good thing you're expecting, then. We wouldn't want the sheriff having to put you in jail."

Maggie shrugged. "Wouldn't be the first Daniels there."

A chuckle burst out of Merrilee. Her niece's son or daughter was very blessed to have such a great woman for a mother. "Anything else going on around the house?"

Maggie leaned in, her next words meant for only Merrilee's ears. "Major Evans came by yesterday afternoon. Said he needed to talk to you so I told him you were helping out at Ms. Aurora's."

Drat! Merrilee's palms broke out in a cold sweat. Time spent with John and the children had made her forget her real mission for being as Aurora's—to uncover evidence that would exonerate the older woman. If only she could stall the officer for a few more days, just until she secured enough information on Aurora to satisfy Evans.

What will John say when he learns I wasn't honest with him? Pain knifed through her heart.

"Was it okay to tell the major he could find you out at Ms. Aurora's?" Maggie's hand came to rest on her shoulder, her young face suddenly lined with concern.

Covering her niece's hand with her own, Merrilee forced herself to smile. She refused to burden her niece with her problems, not when Maggie had had such a rough start to her pregnancy. "Perfectly fine. In fact, I'm pretty sure I told the major where he could find me, but it must have slipped his mind. He probably wanted to tell me about the cutbacks at the plant himself."

That seemed to mollify Maggie's curiosity. "Oh, that makes sense."

Merrilee needed to get out of there before her niece came up with more difficult questions she wouldn't be able to answer. "Could you tell Pastor Williams that his niece and her husband are welcome to spend their honeymoon at the house? The third floor is empty since Edie moved out, and I know Pastor Williams doesn't have much room at his house. It'll give the newlyweds a little privacy."

Maggie studied her for a brief moment, then gave her a gentle smile. "I hope that I can be half the woman you are, Aunt Merrilee."

Merrilee felt herself go uncomfortably warm. If Maggie knew the truth, she'd know such compliments were unfounded. She slipped out of Maggie's grasp and shuffled down the length of the pew. "I'd better get going. John and the kids are probably starving by now."

"John and the kids. That has a natural ring to it, doesn't it?" Maggie teased. "Almost like you're married or something."

Merrilee chose to ignore her. "Go talk to the preacher before Ben and Phyllis leave."

Her niece stood at attention and snapped off a salute.

John leaned back into the porch swing, his long legs stretched out in front of him, his head pillowed in his hands, a satisfying yawn creeping over him. Sundays were a welcome haven for a farmer, a time to recharge and prepare for the week ahead. And he needed the break. Overused muscles in his back and legs ached from the miles through which he'd pushed the iron blade of Aurora's plow. A few more days and the first few buds would burst through the soil.

The warm afternoon breeze carried a hint of blossoming honeysuckle. Maybe later, he'd take the kids on a little treasure hunt and teach them the art of find-

ing just the perfect honeysuckle bush, show them how
to nip the ends of the flowers and draw the sweet nec-
tar to the tips of their tongues. He smiled. Ellie would
like that; they all would. Or maybe once the sun set, he
could show them how to catch lightning bugs with one
of Aurora's old mason jars.

But right now, his stomach was too full to even move.
Merrilee had always known her way around the kitchen
but she had outdone herself today. Just the spicy scent
of her homemade meatloaf had set his mouth to wa-
tering; ribbons of steam rose like misty clouds above
the bowls of creamed potatoes, green beans and fried
squash while a pan of her homemade biscuits had left
the kitchen smelling all yeasty and homey. He'd eaten
his fill along with the children while Merrilee had
pushed her food from one corner of her plate to the
other.

Bending his legs underneath him, John dropped
his arms to his sides and sat up. She hadn't been herself since they'd returned home from church. At first
he'd thought she was anxious to relieve Beau and Edie
of their duties so that they could get back to honey-
mooning, but even after they'd left, he'd caught Merrilee pounding the pot of cooked potatoes so hard,
he'd thought she would bust through the metal bottom.
Something had upset her after he'd taken the kids out,
of that he was certain. If she really meant what she'd
said—that united they'd stand—he needed to get to
the bottom of it.

"Mr. John, look at me!"

John stood up and walked to the railing, his attention
resting on the children huddled under the oak tree that

hugged the opposite corner of the porch. Ellie sat in the swing, her fingers tightly wound around the thick coils of rope dangling from a high-hanging limb, her plump legs pumping hard, each movement back and forth lifting her off the ground a little more. Her laughter hung in the air like that of a baby bird who'd just taken flight for the very first time. Claire and Billy stood nearby, their heads bobbing in time with Ellie's progress. "Now, you hang on, Miss Ellie. We don't want you falling out of the sky."

Billy waved back. "We're watching her."

"You always did like kids."

John swung his head around to find Merrilee standing in the doorway, her hands knotted in the skirt of the red-checkered apron she wore. "Maybe because I'm just a big kid myself."

"Maybe," she answered, but there was a mischievous glint in her eyes that made his heart contract. Whatever had been bothering her she'd put aside for the moment. "Personally, I always found you quite grown-up."

"Really? Even the time I took you to the lake and taught you how to play catch?" It had been their first date, and while he'd wanted to take her to the diner on the square and to a movie, his bank account couldn't have afforded it. So a picnic by the lake and a round of catch had had to do.

"I must have had a good time. I went out with you again."

John nodded. He'd been amazed when she'd agreed to go out with him again, never once voicing a complaint about the long walks they took around the outskirts of Aurora's land or fishing for bass at the lake in place of the more expensive, exciting dates other boys could have offered her. And many evenings had been spent on this very porch, curled together on the swing, making plans for their future. "Would you like to join me?"

She glanced back down the hallway as if something were pulling her inside. "I still have dishes to wash."

"It's not going to hurt them to soak awhile, and then I'll take care of them." He took hold of the swing's chains, steadying it for her. "After that dinner you cooked, the least I can do is finish the washup." He held his hand up against the protest he could see forming on her lips. "Aurora believes in everyone pitching in. It teaches the children to be more independent. You shouldn't have to do everything yourself."

"Oh." She picked at a loose thread in one corner of her apron. "I've never thought about it that way, but it makes sense."

What was making her so anxious? Was it the thought of sitting so close together, watching their daughter play with her friends as if they were an old married couple? The thought should have made him uncomfortable, too, but instead the lure of it was irresistible. John held out his hand to her. "We are going to leave the cooking to you, though. I haven't had such a good meal in I can't remember when."

That wasn't quite true. The pinto beans and corn bread may have been the only items in their cupboards, but Merrilee had turned them into a farewell feast never to be forgotten the night before he'd reported to the Civilian Conservation Corps.

Merrilee continued to stand at the door. "I wondered

if the kids would like it. Claire's always been a little picky, but she seems to be growing out of it."

"Kids go through that, grown-ups sometimes, too. Remember the first time you made me okra?"

The screen door banged softly shut as Merrilee took a half step toward him, a ghost of a smile playing along the corners of her mouth. "How in the world could I ever forget that ghastly look you gave me, like you'd rather starve than be forced to eat!"

The laughter in her eyes was doing strange things to his heart. "You would have, too, if you'd ever been forced to eat the pickled slime Mrs. Williams calls okra. It was like swallowing live earthworms."

"At least she tried to help. That's more than you can say for some folks." The humor faded from her expression slightly, just enough for John to notice.

Yes, something was definitely bothering Merrilee. "As Ms. Aurora always says, be thankful for those willing to help and pray for those who can't find it in their hearts to understand."

"Ms. Aurora is a lot more forgiving than me."

He didn't believe that, not for one second. But something had been lodged in Merrilee's craw since they'd left church, and he needed to figure it out. "Ms. Aurora is also a very wise woman."

Merrilee blinked, as if she wasn't sure where this conversation was going. "How's that?"

John swung the swing slightly forward. "She would have sat down five minutes ago."

The laugh he coaxed out of Merrilee filled the air around him like the most delicate music. "A few minutes of rest might do me some good," she conceded.

"Merrilee, even the Lord took a day off every week."

"That's hard to argue with." Her smile grew wider as she reached behind her and untied the apron, peeled it from her shoulders and slung it into a neat pile over the back of a nearby rocking chair. The fresh cottony white dress with blue trim she wore underneath complemented the lines of her lean curves. Her hair had been pulled back in a low ponytail at her nape, the reddish-blond curls rioting against the porcelain line of her neck. Her beauty didn't need powder or paints, though he did find himself staring at her full, deep red lips on more than one occasion. No, Merrilee's beauty came from within.

Beauty is only skin deep, but ugly goes clean to the bone.

A faint smile touched his lips. It had been one of Merrilee's favorite sayings when they'd been dating. He hadn't understood it at first, but the more he thought about it, the more time he spent with Merrilee, becoming familiar with her kindness and caring, the more he realized the powerful wisdom in those words.

The swing shifted slightly as she sat down, the skirt of her dress brushing against his pants leg, the faint scent of freshly baked bread and vanilla that she always carried with her filling his senses, making him wonder what might have been.

A peal of childish giggles dragged him away from his dangerous thoughts. He had no business dreaming about a life he couldn't have. A jury of his peers awaited him. Maybe a prison term, too.

But remembering those facts was almost impossible with Merrilee sitting beside him, her face aglow with tenderness as she watched the children play. "Ellie really loves to swing, doesn't she?"

"And play on the teeter-totter. But that takes two people, and I wanted Ellie to get a sense that she could do things on her own."

His skin prickled with gooseflesh when she shifted toward him, her warm breath soaking into the skin beneath the thin sleeve of his shirt. "So you hung that tire swing to teach her a lesson?"

"No," he admitted. "I saw her at the park that first day I came into town, and all she wanted to do was swing like the other kids. While I was digging up supplies to build the ramp at your house, I found an old tire and enough rope to make a pretty decent swing, and I couldn't resist." He shrugged a shoulder. "I'm just a sap for damsels in distress, I guess."

"I think it's kind of sweet." She nudged him with her shoulder. "But you always were thoughtful like that."

Her compliment washed over him. John cleared his throat. "I think swinging might be good exercise for Claire and Billy, too. Get the two of them working those muscles in their legs."

Merrilee's expression clouded over. "I don't know. Claire hasn't been on a swing since before the polio. It might be too much for her."

"Or it could be just what she needs. If we get her working on that swing, it's going to make our job that much easier when we get her in the lake. She will have built up some muscle and endurance."

"I don't know." Merrilee bit the corner of her lower lip. "Maybe I should contact the doctors at Warm Springs and ask them their opinion."

His jaw tightened into a hard knot. So she still ran around getting everyone's opinion on a subject rather than listening to his. Back during their marriage, she'd run home to Daddy, wanting to know how they should proceed with a problem or what crops to plant. The end result was always two against one, with him the odd man out.

Like he'd been most of his life.

"I'm sorry, John. Here you are, doing everything you can to get Claire up and walking again, and I go asking people who don't even know her for their opinion."

John jerked his head around to face her. There was a candor to her words, an earnestness, as if she was tired of playing the same old broken record and had exchanged it for a new one. Maybe he should meet her halfway. "I don't know. Maybe we should run the idea by her doctor, just to make sure we're not undoing all the hard work she's done."

Merrilee sagged into the swing. "I shouldn't be so worried about what everyone else thinks."

Was she talking about Claire's treatment or something else entirely? "Did something happen after I took the kids outside at church this morning?"

Her gaze drifted down to her hands knotted in a loose fist in her lap. "I had a run-in with Gladys Davis."

The name didn't sound familiar to him, but he'd been gone a long time. "Do I know her?"

Merrilee shook her head. "Her husband was one of the engineers who designed the bomber plant. They moved to Marietta so that he could oversee construction. When he died, Ms. Davis decided to stick around. She joined our church a couple years ago."

Didn't sound like Merrilee welcomed this woman into the community with open arms. Knowing his former wife, there had to be a very good reason as to why not. "I take it she's not on your hit parade?"

"Let's just say I love her as a sister in Christ, but I'm not sure I like her too much."

"That's not like you. You always find the good in everyone." *Even your despicable father,* he added silently to himself.

"Not this lady. Ms. Davis isn't very…understanding toward people who are different than herself." Merrilee shook her head slightly. "I shouldn't have been listening in on her conversation but I just couldn't ignore her when she started talking about our children."

Our children. A slip of the tongue, he knew, but it still didn't stop the warmth that flooded through his veins. This wasn't the time to assess his response, not with Merrilee so upset. "What did she say?"

Merrilee glanced over the railing, her expression softening as she watched the children play for a few moments, then relaxed back into her seat. "She said that the children shouldn't be allowed in church, said they were disruptive and…"

The tiny hairs on the back of his neck rose to attention. "And what?"

The stricken look she gave him made his gut twist. "That they were too damaged to understand anything about the Bible or the preaching, and we should just keep them at home."

John fisted his hand, then released it. It wasn't the first time someone had voiced their outdated opinions about Aurora's children, and it more than likely wouldn't be the last. Still the anger that flared through him burned as hot as it had the first time he'd heard James Daniels hurl those ugly names at Mattie.

Dimwit. Mush head. Retard.

He flexed his fist again, remembered the feel of James's face beneath it, the explosion of blood that had shot out of the other boy's broken nose, the pain that had shot up his arm with each new blow. But he hadn't stopped, not even when his own knuckles bled, until the boy's lips were too swollen to utter those filthy words again. Not the most Christian way of handling it, but it got the job done. James Daniels had steered clear of him and Mattie after that.

"What did you say?" He was almost afraid to ask, given her brother's response all those years ago, even though he knew Merrilee wasn't like that.

"Not much. What can you say to change someone's opinion when they've made their mind up like that?"

Truer words were never spoken, but it still didn't stop the vague sense of disappointment sliding through him. It never ceased to amaze him the cruelty of some people, particularly to those most fragile. "So does she expect us to stop bring the kids to services?"

"Nope." Merrilee clutched the bottom of the swing and with her feet, pushed off, the swing lilting forward gently. "She pretty much got the message we'd be there every Sunday morning bright and early. I told her that whether or not they knew the Bible, they knew love, and that there was no better place for them to find it than in God's house."

He crossed his arms over his chest to keep from reaching for her. "Really? You said that?"

"You think I'm going to let those kids miss church just because someone doesn't use the good sense the Lord gave them?" Her reddish-blond curls sparked into fiery flames as she shook her head. "Not on your life!"

"Why?" It was a simple question, self-explanatory, but John longed to hear her answer. They were partners, united, she'd said. And standing united with Aurora and her children would pit Merrilee against social conventions, against the very people she'd grown up with and admired. He knew she could be a crusader for those she believed in, but had Aurora's children made it onto that list? How far was she willing to go for these kids?

"That's why you didn't tell me about Mattie," she whispered, pain lancing her voice. "You thought I'd think less of you if I knew the truth about your brother."

"Of course I didn't. Where did you get that from?"

"Your questions over the past few minutes." The icy glare she shot him froze him to the spot. "It's almost like you couldn't believe I'd stand up for the kids."

His temper rose. How in the world could she twist his meaning? "I never said that."

"You didn't have to." She poked a finger into his chest. "Let's get one thing straight. I love to hear about Mattie. I would like to think I would have loved him because he was your brother and he meant the world to you."

John choked on the hard knot in his throat, his thoughts scrambled. Was she right? Had he kept Mattie from her, fearing Merrilee would wonder if he was as damaged as his brother?

The swing swayed as she stood. John reached out for

her hand, but grasped at air as she walked across the porch. "Merrilee, I'm sorry."

"Don't be sorry, John." She picked up the apron and laid it over her arm. "The truth is I might have backed down to Ms. Davis years ago, not because I agree with her but because I wouldn't have wanted to make a fuss or embarrass myself and my family by standing up for the kids. And that makes me ashamed."

The screen door slammed shut as Merrilee walked into the house.

Chapter Fourteen

"Lord, thank You for the beautiful weather You've given us over the past few days. It's been a blessing working this land You've provided for us."

John drew off his hat and slapped it against his leg, a cloud of red dust engulfing him like one of those misty fogs he'd seen roll into San Francisco Bay. The air was filled with the sweet fragrance of freshly plowed soil. He grabbed the handkerchief out of his pocket and swiped at the moisture beaded around his neck, satisfaction shifting through him as he glanced over the straight plowed rows—the last of Aurora's fields.

Tomorrow afternoon, he'd start work on his own farm. Growing things had always been in his blood; the idea of a few acres to call his own had been a dream he'd clung to for as far back as he could remember. A dream deferred until now—and maybe longer if the charges against him stuck. It didn't matter. God had blessed him with an extra dose of patience.

He could enjoy the fruits of his labor for the moment. Neat rows of turned dirt stood out like the stripes on the American flag, the Georgia clay just a shade lighter, a tad more orange than patriotic red. It had sliced easily under his plow, moist, ready to be planted. This afternoon, he would pick up his order of white, half-runner beans from the feed store and soak them overnight before planting this last field in the morning.

"You look thoroughly pleased with yourself."

His pulse quickened as he turned to watch Merrilee walking toward him, a mason jar of water in her hand. "I'd figured I'd have to leave this section unturned, especially after we got the corn and tomatoes planted early."

She glanced over the field, her lips curving up into a smile that reached her eyes. "You've always been good with the soil. Remember that year when nobody could get anything to grow? But you—you gave Daddy a bumper crop in beans that year."

Merrilee sure remembered a great deal about their time together. Probably for Claire's sake. He knew their daughter had wanted stories about her father. But even that knowledge couldn't dampen the satisfaction he felt in Merrilee's memories. John pointed to the jar in her hand. "Is that for me?"

"Oh—" she stammered, a delicate shade of pink blooming in her cheeks. "I noticed you forgot your water bucket this morning and thought you might be getting thirsty." She shoved the jar toward him. "Anyway, here."

"Thank you." He took the jar, uncapped the lid and brought it to his lips, the cold water sliding smoothly down his throat, the sweet earthy taste teasing his taste buds with memories of his childhood living in Aurora's house.

"I'll be leaving in a few minutes to take Claire into town, if that's all right with you."

John's gut tightened. She'd shied away from him since that evening on the front porch, avoiding him whenever possible, which wasn't easy in a house with nine people in it. But he'd still been aware of her, weeding out the flower beds while the children played nearby, reading to Claire and Billy as they sat side by side on the front porch swing, rocking Ellie after she thought everyone had gone to sleep. Watching her care for the children and Aurora had awoken a need he hadn't even known he'd had. "Maybe next time we could get Maggie to come out here and watch the kids so I could go with you."

That stubborn look she'd gotten whenever she had her mind-set settled across her features. "It might start tongues to wagging if you go into town with us, don't you think?"

Bullheaded, obstinate woman. "She's my daughter, too, Merri."

"Who doesn't know that little piece of information." She stepped closer, the light vanilla scent that clung to her invading his senses. "What kind of excuse would we give for you being there?"

"We could tell her the truth."

She didn't hesitate. "Are you still leaving?"

He slapped his hat against his thigh out of frustration and groaned. "It won't be forever. I am coming back."

John almost didn't hear her next words. Her whisper was so low, he almost thought he'd imagined it. But there was no denying the pain in her voice, the slight wistfulness that hung in her tone. "You didn't come back last time."

He shook his head. She wasn't making sense. It almost sounded as if she'd thought he had abandoned her, not the other way around. Why would she say such a thing?

Before he could ask her, Merrilee started back toward the house. "We need to get going."

He had questions he needed answers to, answers only Merrilee could give. "Wait."

She pivoted around halfway, facing the barn rather than meeting his gaze. "Our appointment is in a little less than an hour, John. If we don't leave in the next few minutes, we're going to be late."

Appointment? What was Merrilee up to? "Who are you meeting with?"

Her mouth formed a firm line. "That's my business."

And not yours! Well, he could be equally as hardheaded when it came to their daughter. "It became my business when you involved Claire."

White teeth slid against her lower lip, a sure sign she knew she'd lost this battle. "I have an appointment at the bank and thought I'd take Claire with me. Maybe get in some window shopping."

John nodded. Seemed innocent enough. Then why had Merrilee been so defensive about it? "Is Claire waiting in the truck for you?"

Merrilee shook her head. "I thought she was out here with you."

Their daughter didn't seem the type to wander off. "I haven't seen her. Maybe she's with Billy."

"We don't have time for this." Merrilee turned and marched across the yard. "Claire!"

He started off toward the house, going in the opposite direction as Merrilee. "Claire!"

John skimmed the tree line against the highway, his thoughts still scattered from his conversation with Merrilee. The more he thought about it, the more confused he felt. She was hiding something, but what? And why did it bother him so much? She had been the one to end their marriage. She had even ditched the court proceedings, sending her father to represent her when all John had wanted was a chance to talk to her, to work things out. Why should he expect her to be open with him now?

"Did you find her?" Merrilee hurried across the backyard toward him.

"No." A car flew down the road behind them. "She wouldn't have taken off for the boardinghouse, would she?"

Reddish-blond curls shimmered with golden sparks as she shook her head. "She's been happier here in the past few days than I've seen her in the past year. She's been kind of lonely."

"You mean since you took her out of school. She told me."

Merrilee straightened slightly as if preparing to do battle. "You make it sound like I wanted to."

Hadn't she? He'd just assumed, wrongly it appeared. "What happened?"

"She was having trouble getting around, then some of the kids started picking on her. I talked to Ms. Simmons, her teacher, who referred me to Principal Hard-ing, but they both agreed it would be best if Claire was taught at home while she was receiving treatment."

Anger flared in his gut. A country at war to assure their freedoms, yet instead of protecting their weakest citizens, they were deprived of their simple rights, like going to school.

But right now they had a daughter to find. "Come on." He pressed his fingers against Merrilee's elbow, ignoring the flares of warmth that shot up his arm as he steered her away from the house toward the barn.

"I didn't want to take her out of school, John," she continued. "I tried everything. I met with the school board. I even offered to come in and help out in her class if they thought it would do any good." Her shoulders fell slightly as if the starch had gone out of her. "They thought my being there would be detrimental to the other students."

John blew out a disgusted huff. That line of reasoning sounded familiar. "Still the same old group on the board?"

"Come to think of it, yes." She glanced up at him. "How did you know that?"

"'Cause that's the same line they gave Ms. Aurora when she tried to enroll me in school, except I believe in my case, they thought feeblemindedness was contagious."

"What did Ms. Aurora do? I mean, you obviously went to school. You're so well-read."

Another tidbit of information from his past he'd failed to tell her when they were married. But he'd been ashamed and a bit nervous about sharing it with her. What would the daughter of Jacob Daniels want with an uneducated misfit like himself? "She stopped beating her head against that wall and taught me at home."

"That's what I've been doing with Claire."

"You never mentioned that." Maybe because she already had so much on her plate with keeping the boardinghouse up, tending to the farmhouse and Aurora's children and caring for Claire. But knowing Merrilee, she'd probably thrown herself into teaching their daughter like she did everything else, with her whole heart.

"I figured Claire told you." She lifted her chin in that determined way John remembered so well. "I couldn't have Claire fall behind just because the school board doesn't have the common sense to get themselves out of a paper sack."

Ah, there was that feistiness he'd always admired in her! "What they need is some new blood, someone with fresh ideas about how to educate all of our children rather than force those who don't exactly meet everyone's standards to do without." He hesitated. "What they need is someone like you."

"Me? Are you kidding?" Her cheeks bloomed with color. Whether she'd admit it or not, she was honored by his suggestion, which pleased him to no end. "Those men would eat me for lunch."

"I doubt it. You're very determined when you put your mind to it."

When Merrilee didn't respond, he stole a glance at her. His heart caught in his throat at the excitement lighting her eyes. How he wished he could always draw out the life and laughter in her, that he could be the man Merrilee envisioned, a good man who met her family's expectations, not some throwaway kid who had just enough book learning to get by.

And a man who'd have to leave soon. To be honest, he had expected to hear from the navy by now. Who knew what would come out at the trial, or how long of a sentence he'd have to serve? Maybe it was better for him, and for Merrilee and Claire, if he stopped hoping for a future where he could be an important part of their lives again. A yawning emptiness filled him, taking with it what little joy the past few minutes had held.

But he could savor the here and now, couldn't he? Especially when he knew these moments would get him through whatever the navy threw at him.

"What's that?"

John followed the line of Merrilee's raised arm toward the end of the barn. He stared for a moment, wondering what exactly he was looking for, and then his eyes caught on a thin white cloud that floated around the corner of the barn before dissipating. A faint sweet scent he remembered from his younger days filled his lungs, and his stomach knotted in response.

"Is the barn on fire?"

John picked up his pace, gently pulling Merrilee closer, skirting the side of the barn as they hurried the last few feet. The only time Aurora had caught him out back behind the barn, she'd made sure he'd remember the punishment he'd gotten, and he had. His stomach flipped at the memory even now. But as Aurora had told him then, if you do the crime, you'd better be ready to face the consequences.

Then why did he have this sick feeling, as if punishing Claire would cause him physical pain?

Lord, I'm trusting You with this. Give us patience to deal with Claire and Billy fairly. And if Merrilee needs me, give me the wisdom to help her.

Merrilee pulled up short at the same moment he spied them—Billy and Claire huddled close together, their backs pressed against the barn wall as they sat. He tightened his grasp on her arm as she started forward.

"Wait," he whispered.

Her lips thinned, but she followed his instructions, her gaze glued to their daughter. Well, he'd need to confirm his suspicions before the two could be confronted with their misdeeds.

They didn't have to wait long. Seconds later, Claire raised a clumsily rolled cigarette to her lips and inhaled.

Her daughter, smoking?

"Claire!" Merrilee sucked in a deep breath, the buzzing in her head growing louder, her eyes stinging from smoke and disappointment. She coughed as the smoke smothered her lungs, physical evidence of what her heart didn't want to believe.

When had Claire slipped out of her control?

She wanted to believe that Claire was still basically a good kid, but she could no longer deny the problems that simmered beneath her daughter's quiet surface. Where had the Claire who laughed so often and loved with such joy gone? Had the polio damaged not only her leg but her spirit?

Lord, I just want my girl back.

"Where did you find the rabbit tobacco?"

John's question, his voice filled with just the right amount of authority, cut through her worried thoughts.

He stood so calmly, but his blue eyes bored into first one, then the other child.

She should probably take over the interrogation. It was her responsibility to correct Claire, to steer her toward making the right decisions. But John was Claire's father and he seemed to be doing a pretty good job of it.

"Billy?" John prodded.

The boy glanced up through a tumble of blond hair. "Ms. Aurora keeps it in the barn for when Ellie gets the croup."

Did Billy really think she'd fall for a cockamamy story like that? Why didn't he just confess the truth? "You expect me to believe that Ms. Aurora lets a five-year-old smoke?"

John's voice rumbled close to her ear, his breath warm against her cheek, awakening tiny sparks of awareness. "Probably a remedy she picked up from her grandma. She was part Cherokee."

She turned and found herself staring up into blue eyes the color of the sky after a violent storm, clear and calm. A safe place to rest from this jangle of emotions. "So it won't hurt them?"

"Well, smoking too much of it at one time can make you sick as a dog." He gave her a determined grin. "Which makes for a pretty good punishment when you think about it."

"You want to let them smoke until they get sick from it?"

He gave their two culprits a stern look. "Can you think of a better way to keep them from smoking again?"

Merrilee grimaced. No, she couldn't, but she didn't

know if she could stomach watching their daughter put that filthy thing to her lips again and again.

"I can handle this if you want me to."

Why was he asking permission to discipline the children? They were in this together, weren't they? United we stand. But this was more than that. This was his first time faced with Claire misbehaving, the first time he'd have to punish her, but he was willing to step up to do what he felt would be the right thing to help Claire in the long run. She nodded. "All right—I trust you. And I can see that it hurts you more than it hurts them."

He grimaced, and Merrilee found herself undone by the understanding mingled with apprehension in his eyes. No matter his faults, John made an excellent father. If only he wasn't determined to go away again. Maybe if he'd decided to stay, they could have mended some of the fences between them, become friends again over time. But she'd never know now.

John crouched down in front of the unrepentant pair and picked up something off the ground. Four more cigarettes. "Plan on doing a lot of smoking with these?"

Claire's chin shot up a notch even though her face had gone very pale. "Maybe not today."

Merrilee's mouth dropped open, then slammed shut. What had happened to her baby? "Claire Marie!"

John shot her a warning glance before turning his attention back to the children. "Why wait? Now is as good a time as any." He handed another cigarette each to both Billy and Claire.

"What?" The boy swallowed hard, his pale freckles darkened into ink dots against his pasty complexion.

"You must have thought you were going to smoke

them all today." John plucked a box of matches off the ground next to Claire and opened it. "You wouldn't have rolled them if you didn't."

She hadn't even caught that detail, but he was right. Why would they make all those cigarettes if they didn't plan to smoke them?

"Mama?" Claire threw her a desperate look.

John glanced back at her, waiting for her response. *United we stand.* "I agree with John. We can't have you wasting Ms. Aurora's medicine."

"What about your appointment?"

"I can reschedule my appointment at the bank," Merrilee replied.

Claire gasped, as if she'd thought the appointment was another trip to the doctor, but it was the approval in John's eyes that had Merrilee's heart beating out of control. This was silly. All she'd done was agree with the man, in keeping with the promise she'd made to stand united with him in front of the children. But she couldn't help thinking it was more than that—that an understanding had been forged between them. She felt lighter, as if the heavy responsibility of raising Claire alone had shifted to include John.

But they should do this together. Merrilee held out her hand. "Can I see that box of matches?"

He handed her the box without hesitation. *He trusts me to follow through,* she realized. She slid the lid open and extracted a match, struck it against the side of the box then bent down to light the fresh cigarette in Billy's mouth.

Fifteen minutes later, both children lay slumped against the side of the barn, Claire's hand tight against her mouth while Billy wrapped his arms protectively around his waist.

John leaned over toward her. "You think they've had enough?"

Merrilee nodded. "I've heard of green around the gills, but I've never actually seen it."

"Not even with your brother, James?" he whispered.

That John could tease her right now made her smile. "He probably thought it would cut into his profit margin if he drank his own mash."

He cleared his throat, but she caught a hint of his smile before he grew solemn.

"I don't feel so good," Claire moaned against her hand.

Billy drew in a shaky breath, a light sheen of perspiration breaking out around his mouth. "Me, neither."

Merrilee stepped forward. "Okay, go on into the house and get washed up," she instructed. "We'll be up there in a few minutes to check on you."

They stood slowly, bouncing into each other, their shoulders pressed against the barn wall until they finally found their balance. Claire kept her hand tightly against her mouth, her eyes watery as she hurried toward the house with Billy close behind her until he slowed, hobbled off to the tree line and heaved.

Poor kids. It really was a harsh way to learn a lesson. "Do you think they'll ever smoke again?"

"I didn't. Ms. Aurora caught me out here with a couple cigars once and made me smoke them both." His crooked smile made her stomach flutter. "I haven't ever been as sick in my life."

"I was wondering how you came up with such a devious punishment."

He shrugged, touching his hand to her lower back and prodding her forward. "I figure if it kept me off smoking this long, it might be worth using again."

Merrilee relaxed against his fingers. It felt good to be able to share this responsibility with him. Better than good—it felt right. "You handled them very well. Probably better than I would have."

"I doubt it. You've done a great job with Claire. She's a fine girl."

She snorted. "You do realize she was one of the two out here taking a smoke?"

The hand at her lower back circled her waist and brought her flush to his side. The memories of how it had always felt to be so neatly tucked up under his arm flooded through her with such force, she couldn't resist the urge to snuggle closer. She'd always felt safe in John's arms, so sure of herself and of him. It was one of the reasons she'd married him—the confidence he gave her. He'd believed she could do anything in this world and with him, she'd thought she could.

Strong fingers gently settled beneath her chin and tilted her head back until her eyes met his. "Everybody makes mistakes. It's how they learn to make the right choices."

They'd been almost children themselves when they'd married, barely adults when they'd parted. What lessons had she learned? What mistakes had she made? Staring up at John, the answer came to her quickly as if it had been lingering just outside of her thoughts.

And a man shall leave his mother, and a woman leave her home and the two shall be as one.

Pain lanced through her. That was the problem—she'd never left her home, not really. She'd always hung on her father's every word, hoping for the day when he would love her like he did his sons.

John had offered her everything she wanted; to be respected and protected. To be honored for herself. Most important, to be loved. But she'd let her family drive wedges between them time and time again. Was it really so surprising that he'd decided he'd had enough?

"Merri, are you okay?"

She hummed noncommittally. Life hadn't been the same since the day she'd opened the front door to her daddy's house and accepted the envelope that had ended her marriage and destroyed her world. Only God had pulled her through then, let her climb up in His lap and rail at what she'd lost.

Lord, I've prayed and prayed. Why can't I feel You anymore?

Faith is not a feeling. Preacher Williams's words drifted through her. Is that what she'd been doing, relying on goose bumps and shivers rather than a living, breathing belief in God's character, focused more on how she felt than trusting in the Lord?

Oh, Lord, forgive me. Please forgive me for failing You.

Something shifted inside her, loosened. Her lungs filled with the sweet fragrance of fresh earth and budding trees. And John.

"Are you sure you're all right? I've never seen you this quiet."

Merrilee glanced up at him. The brim of his hat shielded his eyes, but his mouth had tightened into a fine line, his voice deep with concern. He worried about her? Even after everything she'd done to destroy their marriage? Hope sparked into a tiny flame.

She lifted her hand to his face, the short stubble a pleasant sensation against her tender palm as she cupped his cheek. "You're a very wise man, John Davenport."

The hard line of his mouth softened, the corners turning up in a hint of a smile, a flush of color climbing in his cheeks. "I don't know about that."

He'd never known how to take a compliment, maybe because he'd received so few in his life. "Well, you are."

"Thank you," he whispered, his voice catching on the words. He shifted closer until only a few inches separated them. His eyes came into focus, the warmth and longing she found there setting her heart on a frantic pace. Her toes tingled, longed to rise up to their very tips and close the distance between them.

But what about the things that really mattered, the issues that had torn them apart? The thought nailed her feet to the ground. He'd already told her he planned to leave again. Why? What was he hiding from her?

And what about herself? Guilt lay in the pit of her stomach like a piece of granite. She hadn't exactly been on the level with John about her reasons for helping Ms. Aurora. How would John respond if he learned the truth, that she'd spent the past years spying on her neighbors and friends? Would he see it as her patriotic duty or a breach of loyalty and trust?

She took a step back, away from the protection his arms afforded, the warmth his embrace held. A slight chill ran through her as she moved another step away. "I ought to call the bank and apologize for missing my appointment. Hopefully, we didn't inconvenience them too much." Words tumbled from her mouth, but she didn't care, just knew she had to make a quick retreat before John said something, did something that would entice her to stay.

"Merri."

She pretended not to hear him, though her throat thickened at the worry in his voice, as she hurried across the side yard and up the porch stairs.

Chapter Fifteen

Why had Merrilee pulled away from him?

John pondered the question as he relaxed on the porch swing, his arms crossed over his chest, his legs stretched out in front of him, the light scent of clean air and budding grass lingering on the night air. She'd been supportive of the way he'd handled Claire and Billy, stood beside him. In that moment, he'd felt like a real father, partnered with Merrilee to raise their daughter. United as one.

Married.

He let the swing coast to a stop. Taking her into his arms had been meant to comfort her, to chase away the disappointment over their daughter's behavior, to convince her that she was a better mother than she gave herself credit for. John scoffed. Who was he kidding? Comforting her was just an excuse. Holding Merrilee had been in his thoughts since the very first day he'd shown up at the Daniels's homestead with Claire's letter.

Why had he even allowed his thoughts to stray? He'd come back to Marietta with one objective in mind: to know his daughter. Not get tangled up with Merrilee again. But he couldn't deny how right she'd felt nestled against his chest, the sheer joy of just being in her company. Maybe after serving his time, once he got settled in over at the Todd place, he could court her properly, see if they could build something solid, something that could last a lifetime.

First, he had to settle things with the navy.

The front door squealed softly, the lantern light from the hallway peeking around the corners as the shadow of a child stepped out on the porch, her movements slow and deliberate to prevent the long nightgown from tangling between her lanky legs.

John frowned. What was Claire doing out of bed? He watched her for a moment as she hobbled over to the railing and grabbed the banister to steady herself against her crutch. She lifted her face toward the sky, moonlight cascading over her girlish features, so much like her mother's that his breath caught on the surge of love that rolled through him. How could one tiny girl have wrapped him so tightly around her pinky in just a few days?

"Dear Lord," Claire said. "I'm sorry about today."

A tenderness he didn't know was possible flooded through him. Claire spoke to God so easily, not hesitating to lay out her heart before Him. Just like her mother did back during their marriage. He used to tease her that dinner would be cold by the time she finished talking with the Lord, but that didn't do anything to shorten her prayers. Why was Merrilee keeping her distance from Him now?

He sat back into the swing and waited until Claire

was finished before he spoke. "Having trouble sleeping?"

"I…um…" She shifted her grip on the railing, taking the weight off her affected side. "I didn't know anyone was out here."

"I spend a few minutes out here every night before I turn in. For some odd reason, I always feel closer to the Lord when I'm outdoors."

"Really?" Claire took a wobbly step toward him. "My cousin Maggie says she feels closer to God when she's up in the air flying, but Mama says He's with us wherever we are."

John tightened his grip on the swing's chains after Claire hobbled another step. No wonder Merrilee was in such a hurry to get Claire into Warm Springs. It killed him not to help her. "Your mother's right. He's always with us, no matter where we are or what we're doing."

"I was afraid of that."

The forlorn note in her voice troubled John. What could be tumbling around in her head? "Why?"

She shook her head. "Nothing."

John wasn't buying it. Obviously something troubled her, and it was his job to coax her into telling him so he could chase away her fears. "You want to sit out here with me for a little while?"

She nodded, the lantern light revealing a grim determination printed on her face as she limped the last few steps to the swing. She sat down beside him and drew up her legs, covering them with the train of her nightgown, her tiny toes peeking out from under the hem. "So you're not mad at me anymore?"

Her question caused his heart to ache. "I was never mad at you, Claire Bear."

"But you made me and Billy smoke all those nasty cigarettes he'd found. Made me sick as a dog."

"Will you ever smoke again?"

"No!"

Which meant he'd gotten the point across. "I could have told you and Billy how sick you'd feel, but you might not have taken my word for it. So your mama and I had to let you find out for yourself."

"Oh." She smoothed the white cotton over her knees, as if she were considering that for a moment. "How did you know we'd get sick?"

Confession time. He leaned toward her, the faint scent of soap and little girl tightening her hold on his heart. "Ms. Aurora caught me with a few cigars when I was about your age." He tapped the tip of her nose. "I was in bed for two days."

She chuckled weakly. "I should have told Billy to just leave me alone when he found me."

His daughter made it sound as if she'd been hiding. "What were you doing behind the barn?"

Claire lowered her head, pale shards of lantern light turning her golden red curls into a fiery hue, the long strands forming a curtain around her face. "I thought Mama was taking me to the doctor again, and I didn't want to go."

"Why not?"

The night went still—the only noise an old barn owl hooting off in the distance. John studied Claire in the dim light, waiting for an answer. How would he ever be able to get her to trust him?

Finally, she whispered, "I'm not getting better anyway."

He'd hit upon a bigger problem than misbehavior. "I don't know if I'd say that. Maybe you just need a little more time to work with your leg, make it strong again."

"That lady in the Bible didn't have to wait. My Sunday school teacher said she just had to touch the hem of Jesus's robe and she was better."

"She believed that Jesus could heal her."

"And He did, right then and there."

Claire's despair was beginning to make sense. He draped his arm over the back of the swing and leaned toward her. "And you think that the Lord's not going to heal you because it hasn't happened yet."

She lifted her head, the light catching on the tears lining her face. "I've prayed and prayed, but I still can't jump rope or swing on the swing set or go to school like all my other friends do."

"Honey…" He put his arm around her and brought her close, her head coming to rest against his chest. She felt so small in his arms, this little girl who had turned his entire life upside down. "Just because you're not completely better doesn't mean God's given up on healing you."

Claire hiccuped. "It doesn't?"

"No." He smoothed a tangle of hair down her back. "Sometimes it just takes a little bit of time."

"How much time?" She tilted her head back, watching him.

He brushed a thumb across the rose of her cheeks, her tears clinging to his fingers. "I don't know, but God does. And He won't be rushed. He does everything in His own time."

Claire lifted her head from his chest, her mouth twitching into a grimace. "I don't like to wait."

John mashed his lips together to keep from smiling. Patience hadn't been his or Merrilee's strong suit, either. "Maybe that's what the Lord is trying to teach you in all of this, to be patient and wait upon Him."

"I'm not sure I like that."

Yes, Claire was her parents' daughter through and through. "Me, neither."

She rested back against the swing and glanced up at him. "You know, I didn't like you too much this afternoon."

He hadn't expected her to. But it didn't stop the ache her words caused deep in his chest. "How about now?"

"I understand why you did it. Mama says that God loves us so much, He lets us face the consequences of our actions even though it hurts Him."

The words pricked, but he pushed them away to reexamine later. Right now, his only purpose was to be with Claire. "Darling, your mother loves you just like that, too."

"What about you? Do you love me?"

If she had asked him anything else, he might have found the strength to change the subject. But he knew what it was like to wonder if you were capable of being loved, had wondered for years if his father ever thought about him even in passing. No, he couldn't deny his little girl. He pushed a long strand of her hair behind her ear. "Yes, Claire. I love you very much."

A wondrous smile split Claire's face as she flung herself against his side, her childish arms barely wrapped around his waist, her head resting against his chest as if it had been her favorite pillow since the day she was born. A surge of protectiveness and unconditional love roared through him, and without thinking, he dropped a kiss in her curls.

"I love you, too, Daddy."

Daddy?

"Please don't be mad," Claire whispered, burying herself deeper against his chest.

Mad? He felt like a man in a maternity ward waiting room, willing the doctor to come out with news of his child's birth. Only his daughter was here, holding on to him for dear life. John hugged her closer, burying his face in her hair. "You're the reason I'm here, Claire Bear. But how did you know?"

"Cousin Beau had a picture of the two of you from when you were working out West in his address book. He didn't seem much interested in it so I took it. I put it back later, I promise." Her voice broke. "I just wanted to know what you looked like."

John could barely move Claire back enough so that he could look at her, her arms were so tightly wound around him. "So you've known from the first?"

"No. I snuck back in Beau's room after he left with Edie and found the picture again." She gave him a watery smile. The Davenport smile. "That's when I knew."

He and Merrilee would have to keep on eye on this snooping little thing. "Why didn't you tell us?"

"I don't know. Maybe I was a little afraid that you wouldn't want to be my daddy. Because of my leg." She drew herself up, her little body tense against him.

He brushed a kiss against her forehead, then leaned over on one hip, pulled the creased envelope from its resting place in his back pocket and handed it to her. "I've loved you since the minute I got this."

"My letter?"

"And I've grown to love you more every moment since."

Claire worried her bottom lip. "But my leg?"

John tightened his arms around her, resting his chin against her baby-soft hair. Only time would ease her anxieties, but until it did, he'd be there to reassure her. "No matter what happens, whether you're unable to walk without a crutch or hobble around for the rest of your days, I will always love you and the beautiful woman you become."

His heart lodged in his throat when she rested against him. This snip of a girl—part him, part Merrilee—had trusted him with her heart. He would do everything in his power to keep it safe.

"You're going to stay?"

He wanted to—the Lord knew that was his prayer. But whether he did or not was up to the United States Navy. He wouldn't lie to his daughter, no matter how much the truth hurt. "I have to go away for a little while, but I'll be back. I promise you."

"Will you be gone long?"

"I don't know, but no matter how long it takes, I'm coming back, Claire. And then I'm not going to leave again."

A luminous smile broke out on her face, and John couldn't help but be thankful she didn't require any further explanation.

"Good, because when you get back, I have something I want you to do for me."

He didn't like the sound of that. What was Claire up to? But there was nothing he'd refuse her. "Anything."

"When you get back from wherever it is you have to go," Claire started, her head tilted back, her eyes alive with excitement, "I want you and me and Mama to live together like a real family."

Merrilee pressed herself up against the wall next to the front door, her shaky hand fisted against her roiling stomach to keep the nausea at bay. She'd come looking for Claire after finding her bed empty, never figuring to find her out on the porch conversing with John.

I love you, too, Daddy.

Tears thickened her throat, and she struggled to swallow. Their daughter finally knew the truth. Instead of the worry she'd felt since John had shown up on her doorstep, relief flooded through her and, oddly, tenderness.

John had been so good with Claire this afternoon and tonight, strong but compassionate. He'd listened to her air her worries, helped her confront her fears. Loved her unconditionally. He was a man totally smitten, and a wonderful father.

"Nothing good ever came from listening in on another person's conversation, young lady."

Merrilee jerked her head in the direction of the stairwell where Ms. Aurora, her lean fingers gripping the banister, stood on the bottom step. Merrilee hurried over to her. "What are you doing up?"

"I checked in on the twins, then figured I'd warm

me up a cup of milk." Her chest rose in a deep breath. "Lying in bed all the time isn't as restful as everyone thinks it is."

"Maybe not, but you heard the doctor. You need to take it easy."

"Well, I can rest just as easy sitting at my kitchen table as I can upstairs with covers pulled up to my chin." Aurora glanced to the door and nodded. "What going on out there?"

Another jealous pang went through her. "Claire's outside talking with John."

The look Aurora gave her made Merrilee realize how silly she was being. "Does that bother you?"

She shook her head. Maybe she could shake the miserable feeling away through force of will. "No, Claire needs her daddy, and John…" She paused. "A person would have to be blind to not see how much that man loves her."

"Maybe it's time y'all told her the truth."

"She figured it out on her own. She found an old picture of John in Beau's dresser drawer along with his address book and kept it."

A soft chuckle rose from Aurora. "The little spy. Maybe the Allies should enlist her help."

"I don't think so." The words came out harsher than she'd have liked, but Aurora's comment had hit too close to the mark. One spy in the family was already one too many.

"I'm glad she knows. John deserves a chance to know his daughter as her father."

There wasn't any censure in her words, but Merrilee felt it nevertheless. She dropped her chin down, her gaze focused on her soft cotton slippers. "I wrote and told John about the baby before the divorce. A letter every day for months."

"Oh, dear. I know you did." Aurora's frail arm snaked around her waist and drew her close, her white head rested against hers. "Those were the letters Beau found in his father's house last year, weren't they?"

Merrilee jerked her head up, but the older woman's stare stopped her questions as they formed on her lips. "Let's go fix us both a cup of warm milk."

Merrilee nodded, grabbed the lantern from the hall table and followed the older woman down the narrow passageway to the back of the house. It was only when they'd reached the privacy of the kitchen that Merrilee felt ready to speak again. "Beau was supposed to keep that quiet."

Aurora headed straight to the icebox. "Maybe he didn't say anything."

With a frown, Merrilee walked over to the cabinet where the mugs were stored and opened it. Who else could it be? She went through a mental file of possible suspects, her mind shifting through any connections until she found one. "Edith Watson."

A low chuckle filled the room. "The most gossipy postmistress the United States has ever known. She overheard Edie and Beau talking."

"So much for loose lips sinking ships." Merrilee smirked as she pulled down two mugs.

"Probably. She's a nice enough woman. Just lets her tongue get the best of her at times." Aurora grabbed the glass container of milk and walked to the stove. "But enough about Edith. Has John ever mentioned receiving the letters?"

"No." And she'd given up hope of him ever getting them. It had been a year after all. Merrilee crossed over to the table and set the cups down. What would it have mattered anyway? But she couldn't push away the memory of this afternoon, of John pulling her in his arms, holding her close. She tried to convince herself that he'd only sought to comfort her after the whole mess with Claire and the cigarettes, to let her know that she was a good mother. But if that were the case, then why had his irises darkened to that indescribable blue when he'd lifted her face to meet his gaze? Why had his hands trembled slightly as he'd held her, as if she were extraordinarily precious?

The soft clang of metal against metal drew Merrilee's attention back to the stove. Ms. Aurora lifted a tablespoon from a small pot, milky white drops making a watery trail across the countertop as she turned off the gas. "Then they'll get here in God's own timing."

If she were someone like Aurora, it would make sense to be overly optimistic, but Merrilee knew better. "A year seems like plenty of time to me."

"Ye of little faith," Aurora muttered in a gravelly voice. "He just received Claire's letter a few weeks ago. Just when she needed him the most."

"What's that supposed to mean?"

"Oh, don't get all in an uproar, young lady. All I'm saying is that who better to understand a child dealing with physical difficulties like Claire than a man who championed his disabled brother?"

Merrilee stood quietly for a moment. Why would

God bring John back into the picture now if he'd already made plans to desert them again? But this line of conversation did open the door on another subject she was curious about. "Why didn't you tell me about Mattie?"

"It wasn't my story to tell." Aurora wrapped a dish towel around the pot handle, lifted it from the stove and carried it to the table. "It was John's."

Merrilee pulled out a chair for Aurora, then sat down. "What was Mattie like?"

A soft smile transformed the older woman's face as she sank down beside Merrilee. "Sweet as sugar. His arms and legs were all gnarled up by the time I brought them home—that's what happens after years of being kept in a crib, I guess—but Mattie always had a smile on his face. And he thought the world of John." Steam rose from the iron pot as she poured milk into one mug, then the other. "Mattie couldn't talk, but anytime John came in the room, his brother would follow him with his eyes."

Merrilee understood. John had had that same effect on her from the first time she'd seen him, standing so tall and handsome between rows of ripe cotton. She hadn't wanted to look at anything else ever again. "John said Mattie died the winter after they came to live here."

"Mattie couldn't draw a deep breath, so when he got the pneumonia…" Aurora's voice caught as if the memory of the loss was still fresh in her mind. "John refused to leave him. He was only ten, but he stayed right by Mattie's bed, bathing his face with cold water when the fever shot up, talking to him when he passed from this life into the next. I'd never seen that kind of love from such a little fellow. Figured that once he gave someone his heart, he loved them for keeps."

Aurora's words tore through Merrilee like buckshot, leaving a gaping hole through that innermost part of her, that place where she still held out hope John could love her again. Merrilee slid her hands around the mug, the warmth doing nothing to chase the chill settled deep in her bones. "I must have been the exception to the rule."

"What do you mean?"

Merrilee kept her eyes on the cloud of steam rising from her cup. "John was the one who wanted the divorce, not me."

"I don't believe that for a minute." Aurora shook her head, her voice strengthening with conviction. "I saw the way my son looked at you, Merrilee. When you were around, that boy was as happy as a puppy with two tails."

Wasn't that how she always felt around him, as if she'd had a stomach full of firecrackers and each time he came around, another one sparked into life? But if he'd felt the same way, then why had he wanted to end their marriage?

"I don't like to speak ill of the dead, but your daddy never favored John. Whoever heard of putting a man in jail for getting married? And keeping him there for three days was just plain mean."

Merrilee shook her head. "Ms. Aurora, that was my fault. I couldn't get to the jail to get the police to release him."

The older woman leaned into the high-back chair. "What do you mean you couldn't get to the jail?"

Merrilee swallowed. She'd never planned to tell anyone what had happened once her father had gotten her home. But what did it matter now? "Daddy locked me in the root cellar."

"For three days?" When she nodded, the older woman frowned. "It makes sense. Jacob went traipsing off to Chattanooga to find the justice of the peace who married the two of you. Guess he figured if he got hold of the license before it was filed, that would be the end of that. He wouldn't have wanted you able to get in his way."

And if he'd succeeded in his plan, they wouldn't have been officially married in the eyes of the law. "How do you know all of this?"

She drew in a weary breath. "A few months ago, I got a letter from Jimbo Haynes. He wanted to know if I had John's address because he needed to apologize."

Merrilee blinked. Jimbo had been one of her brother's lapdogs, doing James's bidding in exchange for the corn mash that numbed the pain of losing his wife and baby. "Why would he need to apologize to John?"

"I think it's part of a program he's in to keep him off drinking. Anyway, I wrote him back and told him John was off in the Pacific, but if he needed to talk, I was there." She took a long sip. "James must have told him about following you and John up to Chattanooga."

"But Daddy didn't convince Judge Reynolds to destroy our marriage license. He had to have accepted that I'd married John. He even set us up in our first home."

The challenge in Aurora's gaze sent a chill down Merrilee's spine. "Set you up on the worst plug of land he owned. Rocks wouldn't grow there, much less cotton or vegetables, but John coaxed a crop out of those fields until the rains washed him out. Didn't you ever wonder why all those letters were found at James's house, even the ones that you mailed from your daddy's house? And how did the one letter from John that demanded a divorce manage to get through when all the others didn't?"

"It didn't come through the mail—it was delivered by a lawyer." The memories of that morning, the fear that had coursed through her when Mr. Jacobson had stated he was there on John's behalf. Horrific scenarios had played out in her mind, flashes of John, his body battered and beaten against the jagged rocks as he worked building Boulder Dam. She'd snatched the envelope from the man's hand and torn it open, relief and shock warring within her as she read the words, once, twice, until finally, the realization had sunk in. John wanted a divorce. The wooden floor had reached up to meet her, her arms automatically curving around her swollen belly, protecting the life she and John had created together. Shadows and light had drifted by her over the next few days, but one voice had penetrated the unbearable pain that enveloped her.

Daddy's going to take care of this, baby girl.

"John would have never sent a lawyer," Aurora said softly.

"He would have come himself," Merrilee whispered, her eyes slamming shut, unshed tears like fire behind her closed lids. What had her father done? Why had he robbed her of the husband she loved, of the father of her child? And how had she missed what he was up to, sneaking around behind her back, watching their every movement in hopes of discovering a way to destroy her and John's marriage?

Spying on them just like she'd been spying on Aurora and all the others.

The truth gripped her heart in an unyielding vise. Like father, like daughter. How many lives had she ruined with the bits of information she'd passed on to Major Evans? She couldn't pretend she'd hurt those people for the greater good. How many leads had turned out to be rabbit trails, scampering down a dead-end path, with no prize at the end and only devastation left behind?

"Do you still love my son?"

The denial came quickly to her lips, then died. She needed the truth. "Yes, I always have."

Aurora reached over, clasped her hand and gave her an encouraging squeeze. "Then you need to figure out a way to convince him of that."

The older woman made it sound so easy, but Merrilee knew John had a stubborn streak almost as wide as her own. Was it too late for them, or was there hope? "I'll think about it."

"And we'll pray. God's already at work here."

"How do you see that?"

She patted her hand. "That letter Claire sent out a year ago reached him, didn't it?"

Merrilee couldn't argue with her reasoning. Claire's letter had traveled from one side of the world and back before being delivered to John, bringing him back to Marietta.

So what happens now, Lord?

One thing Merrilee knew for sure—no carrot Evans

dangled in front of her was worth turning into the bitter person her father had become in his later years. She turned to the woman who was as close to a mother as she'd ever had. "Aurora, I know this is out of left field, and you may not want me anywhere near John after you hear me out, but I've got to level with you. Major Evans sent me here to find out if you're trading in the black market."

Chapter Sixteen

Claire ducked her head inside the kitchen two mornings later where Merrilee and Aurora sat at the table, enjoying a cup of coffee. "Daddy wanted me to tell you someone's coming up the drive."

Merrilee stood. "It's a bit early for visitors."

"Probably just the sheriff," Aurora assured her as she lifted her cup for another sip. "Mack likes to keep an eye on us, seeing how we're a ways off the road."

"And maybe join us for breakfast?" Merrilee walked around the corner of the table, set her cup and saucer in the sink then leaned back against the counter. "I swear he ate so many meals at the boardinghouse, I should have asked for his ration books."

"Nothing wrong with providing a meal for someone who's watching over our community."

"No, but I get the feeling he's lonely."

The older woman leaned back in her chair as if she were thinking on the matter. "Yes, it must be very lonely being left behind while everyone else around you goes off to fight."

"Yes, I guess so." Merrilee grabbed a clean dish

towel off the countertop with one hand while the other worked the water pump. What she would give to be like Aurora, thinking the war only existed over in Germany or in the Pacific, never realizing that there was a battle being fought right here at home? Was Mack part of this secret war like she was, staking out loved ones and old friends, scrutinizing every move to test their loyalty? She'd have to ask him when the fighting was finally over and the boys came home at last.

The loud bark of high-pitched screams jerked Merrilee around, the wet, soapy dish towel hanging from her clenched fist. "That sounds like the children."

"I'm sure it's nothing serious." Despite her words, Aurora rose in a one quick urgent movement, the faint lines around her eyes and mouth sharpened into deep valleys, her complexion pale.

Merrilee dropped the dish towel into the sink, then hurried toward the kitchen door. "Those kids had better have a good reason for causing such a ruckus. Scaring a body like that."

"Now, don't be too hard on them," Aurora called out behind her. "I'm sure there's a perfectly good reason for all the noise."

Merrilee nodded, but only to keep the older woman from investigating the situation herself. The children knew enough about Aurora's illness to know not to go around screaming their heads off like that.

She had barely taken two steps out into the hallway when two strong hands reached for her, pulling her against a muscled chest that felt made for resting her head against. She drew in a breath of air full of the sweet smell of fresh earth, sunshine and John's unique scent. If only they could stay like this forever.

But questions barged into her thoughts. She lifted her head, but before she could form the first words, he lowered his face, his mouth seeking hers in a kiss that robbed her of her senses and scrambled her thoughts.

Merrilee lifted her arms up, her hands pressed against the firm expansion of his chest, snaking their way over sinewy shoulders, her fingertips tingling as she twined her arms around his neck, her fingers buried in his short hair. She heard a whimper when he ended the kiss and started to step back, to put some distance between them, but John only tightened his arms around her, bringing her even closer to him if that was possible.

"Merri."

The whisper of her name against her mouth felt like coming home. Here, with this man, was where she belonged.

"Well, it's about time," Aurora said, a humorous tone in her voice. "I'd begun to think you two had forgotten how to do that."

Heat torched Merrilee's face even as John loosened his hold, though his hands rested comfortably on her waist as if threatening to pull her in for another kiss at any second.

If only he would!

"I'm sorry, Ms. Aurora. I guess I just let the moment get away from me." John gave his mother an unrepentant grin that made Merrilee's heart gallop. "The Germans have surrendered! The war in Europe is over!"

"Praise the Lord!" Tears filled the older woman's

eyes, her mouth turned up in a watery smile. "All those boys are finally coming home!"

John brought Merrilee flush against his side and offered Aurora his other arm, kissing the top of her gray head as she curled into him. "Some of them will be, I guess, but we've still got a fight with the Japanese."

There was something in his tone, a hesitancy that caught Merrilee off guard. Was it fighting the Japanese that bothered him or something more, something personal?

What was she thinking? Of course, John wanted the war to be over, for their country and the world to be at peace. This was a day to celebrate, not nitpick every little thing.

Another thought burst across her mind. With the war won in Europe, her stint as a homeland informant was drawing to a close.

Thank You, Lord!

"You look happy."

Merrilee tilted her head back to look up at John, the tenderness in his gaze causing her heart to flutter wildly. Maybe they did have a future together once John returned from wherever it was he had to go. They could live on the old Todd place, make it into the productive farm they'd always dreamed of having. Aurora would be next door so they could keep an eye on her and the children.

Her smile widened even more. Claire would have the father she'd always longed for and maybe a little brother or sister, too.

Gracious gravy! She'd planned their entire lives based on a kiss or two. "Where are the children?"

"Out on the front porch with Mack. He said he had something for us in his car."

"Probably just another box of rations from the church." Merrilee's mouth quirked up at the corner. "I hope Mrs. Williams didn't get any ideas and send a jar of her pickled okra."

"She didn't."

Merrilee pivoted around, Mack moving down the hall toward them, the children following closely behind the lawman. The sheriff held in his arms not the box of canned goods she had anticipated, but a bundle of coarse, rat-tail blankets too dirty to even think of placing on any of the beds. Who would think to give such an unusable gift?

Then the bundle moved.

John must have noticed, too. "If that's a dog, Sheriff," he started, his arm slung over Merrilee's shoulders, "you'd be better off just turning around and going right back out that door."

"It's not a dog, Daddy," Claire replied, peeking over the sheriff's arm, trying to pull the covers back while Billy hung behind them, holding Ellie and the other children back. "It's a baby."

Merrilee glanced up at John, hoping he'd read her silent plea to not discuss this in front of the children.

He must have read the message in her expression because he shooed the kids back down the hall and onto the porch, firmly shutting the door behind them.

The soft sucking noises coming from the blankets caused a sharp ache in the pit of Merrilee's stomach. She jerked her attention back to the sheriff. "Why would anyone give up their child just because they're not perfect?"

Mack glanced down at the blankets, his expression one of tender resignation. "Merrilee…"

Aurora's frail arm came around her waist, offering comfort. "Sweetheart, these people are in pain. All their hopes and dreams for this baby are gone because society won't accept a deviation as anything other than something wicked, something best disposed of."

Tears crowded Merrilee's throat. How could anyone believe that the life God had given this child, even with its imperfections, was anything less than a blessing?

"This baby will be loved, just like every other child brought into my home," Aurora continued, her free hand settling over the blankets. "Because he or she has a purpose in this life. God says so in His Word."

Merrilee nodded. Yes, each child had a purpose, like Ellie and her way of seeing joy in everything. Or Billy and his gentle concern for Aurora. The twins with their uncompromising love and Gail with her graceful acceptance. Yes, even Claire in her determination to find her father. They'd all taught her so much about herself, about the person she wanted to be.

What would this baby teach her?

Merrilee cleared the knot from her throat and held her arms out. "So what do we have? A boy or a girl?"

"Girl." Mack shifted the baby in his arms, cradling her head in one strong palm before settling the child into Merrilee's waiting arms. Even with the blankets, the infant weighed less than a sack of sugar. "Born about a month early. Mama's just a kid herself."

"And the father?"

"Army guy. Killed just before Christmas," Mack answered solemnly.

"Poor thing." Aurora started unraveling the covers.

"The girl was aiming on raising it, but…" Mack hesitated. "It's better this way."

How is it better, Lord? Merrilee's heart shouted. How would being thrown away by your family ever be the best for the child? The front door clicked open and John ducked inside, the sounds of the children playing in the distance a welcome relief from the agonizing direction of her thoughts.

She watched John walk down the hallway, his steps confident, his expression alight with acceptance. Aurora had taught him that, by loving him when the person who should have cared for him and Mattie—their father—had dumped them on a street corner to fend for themselves. But unlike this baby, John had been old enough to understand, to feel the pain of his father's rejection. No wonder he kept things close to the chest. But how could she get him to understand nothing he could say or do would change the love she had for him?

"So what have we got here?" John asked, pulling up alongside her.

"A little girl," Aurora answered, still peeling back the blankets. "Are you sure she's in here, Mack?"

Color infused the sheriff's face. "I wasn't sure what to do so I wrapped her in all the blankets I had. Didn't want such a little thing to catch something."

"You did fine, Mack." John patted the sheriff on the back. "Premature babies tend to lose their body heat quickly. A few extra blankets probably kept her toasty warm."

Merrilee glanced over at John. How could he know that? Was Aurora in the habit of receiving preterm babies when John lived here?

The older woman finally turned back the last fold. Two perfectly formed legs jutted out of the bindings, ten dainty little toes curled against tiny flawless feet. Pink dimpled thighs, ten delicate fingers on hands already grasping. Merrilee lifted her gaze to the baby's face and froze. Where she'd expected a tiny bow of the mouth, the baby girl's top lip was drawn back, leaving a gaping hole that extended up under her nose.

"Cleft palate," Aurora diagnosed.

"What's that?" Merrilee asked, tightening her hold on the baby.

"It's when the space between the roof of the mouth and the nose doesn't close up properly before the baby's born," John answered, his eyes focused on the child's face. He glanced up at Aurora. "You think Dr. Tripp might be able to fix her up?"

"I don't know, but it's never stopped me from asking."

"Who's Dr. Tripp?" Merrilee asked.

John gave her a brief smile. "An old beau of Aurora's. He's a doctor over at Henrietta Egleston Hospital for Children. He helps Aurora with the children at times." He glanced back at Mack. "If we can get the local doctor to sign off on the case."

"You don't have to worry about that. Both Adams and Lovinggood were busy with an emergency last night so Mrs. Williams helped with the delivery. Says the child is as healthy as a horse except for…" He grimaced. "I didn't tell Adams about the problem, just that the mother didn't want her. He told me to take the baby down to Crawford Long, said they'd know where to place her." The lawman glanced down at the baby, a tender expression on his face. "But I just couldn't do it."

"Now, wait a minute," John interrupted. "We haven't made the decision about whether we should take on another child yet, especially a newborn."

Merrilee held the infant a bit closer, her heart catching in her chest at the very thought of sending this little girlish bundle away. John couldn't mean to reject this child, he just couldn't. "John Davenport, if you think that we're going to turn this child out…"

John replied as his fingers gently slipped under her chin and lifted her face to his. "I'm out in the field all day long and Aurora is still recovering. You're already taking care of so much with the house and the kids. I didn't want you to feel overwhelmed. Or obligated."

Silly man. But it was sweet for him to think of her needs, very sweet. "I've run a boardinghouse for the past three years. This will be a piece of cake compared to that."

"Are you sure about this? I can help you out in the evenings, but it's still a lot of work." Concern laced his voice, but his eye shone with hope.

Her heart did a little flip. *United, John and I will stand, together.* "True, but if it wasn't hard work, it wouldn't be worth doing, now would it?"

A spark of joy set fire to the blue in his eyes as he reached up to gently stroke the baby's cheek, faint surprise softening his face when the infant turned her head, her misshaped lips seeking his roaming fingers.

He jerked his head up and met Merrilee's gaze. "Why did she do that?"

Maybe the man didn't know everything about babies after all. It was going to be fun teaching him. "She may be hungry." Merrilee tilted her head toward Aurora. "Do you have any baby bottles?"

The older woman nodded. "I crated them up along with a bassinet and some clothes after the twins outgrew them. They're upstairs in the attic."

"I'll help you bring them down, Ms. Aurora," John offered.

"No, Merrilee's going to need help getting out all the ingredients for the baby formula. You can take care of that." Aurora gave them a prim smile. "I'm sure the sheriff here wouldn't mind pulling that crate down out of the attic."

Mack laid his hat on the oak bench. "Anything to help out, Ms. Aurora."

"Good," the older woman answered. "Then we need to get in business before this little one is howling for a bottle and a clean diaper." Tugging the tall sheriff by the arm, Aurora started for the stairwell, a little more kick in her step than in the past few weeks since she'd taken ill.

"Aurora looks more chipper than she did earlier this morning," Merrilee commented as she tucked the ends of the coarse quilt around the infant. First moment she had free, she would hunt down the softest blanket in the house.

"It's not just her. She taught all of her kids early on that there's something about making a difference in another person's life that can give you joy. Even when there's risk involved."

Risks? A tremor of some unknown emotion slid down Merrilee's spine. What risks were there? She could understand that there were hardships. Feeding the number of children Aurora had over the years had to have put a strangle on her wallet. Maybe Aurora worried about the state intervening more than she'd let on. Was that the risk she faced?

A tiny whimper came from the blankets, letting Merrilee know that their reprieve was over. "She's going to start wailing if we don't feed her soon."

"We'll handle this," John answered, his hand firm against Merrilee's back as he steered them down the hall toward the kitchen. "Remember, two are better than one."

A small bubble of happiness burst inside her chest at his mention of the Bible verse. No, she wasn't alone anymore. She had John.

"Here, sit down." John hurried in front of Merrilee and the baby, yanked the chair out from under the kitchen table then waited as she lowered the two of them down into the seat. The vision of Merrilee holding this little girl, the sound of the nonsensical words she cooed at the infant, had almost made his knees buckle out from under him.

Maybe he was still wobbly from those kisses.

He'd only meant to hug her, to celebrate the ending of this unmerciful war then step away. He'd been kidding himself to think he could stop there. The feel of Merrilee wrapped in his arms, that teasing scent of vanilla and woman that clung to his senses even in his sleep had been more than he could bear. It felt so natural to hold her close, as if he'd finally found his way back home after a long and unfulfilling journey that had stolen away years of time he should have been able to spend with the one person in this world he'd believed he could be certain of.

Merrilee.

How did she feel about him? Beau felt certain Merrilee still had feelings for him, but was it enough to build a life on? Could they forgive each other the mistakes they'd made in their youth and find a way to make a home together like they'd once hoped to do?

"I've been racking my brain trying to remember how to make baby formula, but I'm forgetting something." She bounced the fussy infant slightly, her hand gently patting the baby's back. "Does Aurora have the recipe?"

The future would have to wait. John hurried across the kitchen and flung back the curtain hiding long rows of shelved food supplies. "Don't worry. If I don't remember all the ingredients, I'm sure Aurora has got a copy of it around here somewhere."

Merrilee's soft snort had him turning around in his tracks. "What's so funny?"

"You." Her lips twitched with laughter. "Not much can shake you to your core. I never thought I'd see you this befuddled over a baby."

"And here I thought I was being so levelheaded," he teased.

Another giggle broke across the room. "Come over here and sit down."

Worry welled up inside him. "Are you sure? I don't want her going hungry."

"She's asleep. She must have had a little bubble that was bothering her," Merrilee whispered, her fingers lightly brushing the silky strands of pale hair that dusted the top of the tiny girl's head.

Was this how she had been with Claire, this need to touch and glance over the infant's tiny body and face as if to impress every dimple, every inch of pink skin into her memory? John hooked the chair next to her, pulled it out and sat down. "I guess Claire was a little bit bigger when she was born."

"No, she was born almost a month early." Her mouth turned up in a soft smile. "Maggie used to tease her about being a little half-baked."

A month early? Panic rose in his throat. "Was she okay?"

Her smile slipped a little as if the memory of those first days with Claire held more hurt than happiness. "We weren't sure if she was going to make it at first. She was just so tiny, and I couldn't get her to nurse." A pale shade of pink blossomed in her cheeks as she ducked her head. "I felt like such a failure, not being able to feed my own baby."

"Hey, that kind of thing happens." John reached out and cupped her cheek, his thumb gently stroking back and forth across her lips as if to quiet the words. "You shouldn't have been so hard on yourself."

"I know that now." She leaned a bit closer to him. "I guess I just always..."

"You feel like you missed something because you didn't get to nurse her."

"Silly, huh?" She rolled her eyes, but John could tell it truly bothered her. Just like it troubled him to think of Merrilee going through the worry and pain of those dark days alone. "You'd never know by looking at her now that she was a runt." Merrilee leaned down over the baby. "Just like this little sweetheart."

If only he'd have been there! He could have held Merrilee close, encouraged her during those dark days, given her his strength to lean on even in his own heartache. And he could have given her his love.

Instead, he'd been kept away, left without even an inkling of what Merrilee was going through, all because Jacob Daniels didn't believe him good enough for his only daughter, disregarding Merrilee's feelings on the matter as she was only a "female." How had the man treated Claire? "Guess Jacob was disappointed with a granddaughter."

Merrilee snorted. "Daddy and his old-fashioned ideas."

"That a son had more value than a daughter?"

"I don't know." She cocked her head to the side and gave him an impish grin. "Daddy never did like Jeb too much, either."

John blinked. Her father's treatment had brought Merrilee more tears than he cared to remember, but she'd always defended him. Until now. "How was Jacob with Claire? He didn't make her feel…"

"Like she wasn't good enough, the way he did with me?" She shook her head. "Claire had her grandfather wound around her little finger from the moment she was born."

"Really?"

"I know, it shocked me, too. But he was kinder, more gentle after Claire came along. I think it was because he was afraid he might lose us both during the birth."

John's gut clinched. Merrilee, in danger? He'd just assumed she'd sailed through the pregnancy like she had everything else in life. "Is that why Jacob wanted you to move back in the main house? Because you were expecting?"

"After Mama died in childbirth, I guess Daddy worried about me being all by myself in case something went wrong." The baby made a little smacking noise in her sleep that instantly drew Merrilee's attention. She folded her pinky finger and touched the knuckle to the child's bottom lip. Tiny hands grasped Merrilee's fist and drew the offered finger into her mouth. "Good thing, too. The doctor put me on bed rest when I was barely five months along."

Five months. John did a quick calculation and frowned as the realization hit him. That was why she hadn't shown up the day of their divorce hearing. She'd been confined to her bed to save their child. All this heartache they'd undergone—they'd both have been spared it if he'd been there, if he'd never left. Instead, he'd thought it best to leave and make a better living, instead of staying and sticking out the hard times with her. It would have been tough, going to her father, asking for an extension on their loan. But it would have been worth the shame to have spent the past twelve years with her and Claire.

"Here." The wooden legs of the chair scratched against the floor as Merrilee stood and held out the squirming pile of blankets to him.

The woman couldn't be serious! John sucked in a lungful of air. "But...I... Why?"

She smiled at his flustered state as she lowered the baby to him. "You're frowning, and everyone knows that you can't frown with one of God's little blessings resting in your arms."

He made a quick semicircle before she deposited the baby in his arms. "What if she cries?"

"You mean *when* she cries, because she will. We'll just figure out exactly what she needs." Merrilee brushed light fingers against the baby's hair as if she couldn't get enough of the silky texture. "I wonder what her name is?"

"Probably doesn't have one yet." He shifted her slight weight in his arms, steadying her head more.

"Well, we can't let her go without a name." Merrilee sat down across from him, her skirts brushing against the cuffs of his pants. "How does Aurora handle this kind of situation?"

The baby wrapped her hand tightly around his finger. "She usually asks the children what they think the baby should be called."

Merrilee frowned. "I'll bet that leads to some interesting names being suggested."

He leaned in toward her, and she followed suit, her face filling his vision. The freckles that had dusted her nose years before had faded, leaving him regretful that he hadn't been around to kiss them at least once a day. Hopefully soon he could make up for lost time. "Billy wanted to name Ellie 'Munchkin.'"

Her green eyes sparkled with laughter. "Oh, dear."

He glanced back down at the baby. "What would you name her?"

Merrilee tilted her head slightly, her straight white teeth worrying her bottom lip. "How about Sarah?"

Her Grandma Bailey's given name. Didn't she want to keep the name in case they had a daughter in the future? Or had Merrilee given up on the possibility of more children, of marriage, of a love that would last for the next forty or fifty years? She deserved better. She deserved every happiness life had to give her, and if he had to spend the rest of his life convincing her of that truth, then so be it.

"Sarah's a fine name, but I thought you always wanted to name your own girls after your grandmothers." Maybe one day, if he could convince Merrilee that they belonged together, they could have a baby sister for Claire. Or a little brother.

"If you haven't noticed, I'm going to have a teenager on my hands in the next couple years." She glanced down at the baby, who had awakened and was studying them both in wide-eyed wonder. "No, I think Sarah suits her, don't you?"

"Sure," John answered reluctantly. Had Merrilee given up all her girlish dreams of owning a farm and raising a small army of kids with a man who loved her to distraction? He'd known he was that man even before she told him her dreams, but when he'd gone away from her the first time, he'd let the manipulations of others keep him away from the only home he'd ever known. From the only woman he loved.

Not this time.

He frowned. How could he court Merrilee with his

hearing coming up? With the possibility of a jail sentence hanging over his head? But if he waited, he risked losing her. With the war over and the soldiers coming home, anxious to start their lives, many a man would take note of Merrilee's beauty and sweetness, of her steadfast faith, of that determination that ran like a rod of steel up her delicate spine. He'd be a fool not to declare himself.

And selfish if he did. No, he had to wait until he knew the outcome of the proceedings, until he knew with a certainty that he could come back to Marietta for good and claim Merrilee as his wife. *Lord, I only want Merrilee to be happy, and if that means letting her go, give me the strength to do it.*

But first, just one more memory. That was all he needed to carry him through the lonely years stretched out before him. John leaned forward, noting the hitch in Merrilee's breath, the pleasant flush that rose in her cheeks. Her irises turned into a smoky emerald, her eyelids falling slowly until the light reddish-gold lashes rested against the creamy crest of her cheeks. Her lips opened slightly, and John covered them with his own, ready to make a memory that might have to last his lifetime.

Chapter Seventeen

Any thoughts of names or anything else flew out of Merrilee's head the moment John lowered his lips to hers. He'd come to some decision, though what he'd decided she wasn't sure, only that there had been a shift in him, a heaviness that made the blue in his eyes darken, the flecks of newly polished silver that circled his irises dull into something akin to pain.

Without thinking, she lifted her hands to his face, tilted his head slightly to one side and pressed her lips fully against his. How dearly she loved this man, not with the mad giddiness of the girl she had once been but with a steadiness, a certainty that abided deep in the very heart of her being.

One hand crept around the back of his neck, her fingers brushed through his close-cut hair, holding him close.

A high-pitched mew tore through the space between them.

John broke off the kiss, resting his forehead against hers, his chest lifting in ragged sighs that matched her own. She didn't trust her voice so she waited, hoping he would break the silence.

"I forgot about the baby."

The slight catch, the rough vulnerability in his voice made her heart ache. She couldn't let him think he was alone in these feelings. "Me, too."

She lifted her gaze to his and found blue eyes blazing into hers and for the briefest of moments, she wondered if he would kiss her again. But then he straightened, his mouth flattened into a serious line, a tiny furrow buried between his blond brows as he handed the baby back to her and stood. "We'd better get that formula made before Sarah really pitches a fit."

Merrilee offered the baby her clean knuckle to suckle as she watched John return to the pantry. Why was he backing away from her? She wanted to ask him, but the infant in her arms refused to be ignored anymore. "I think that fit is going to be here sooner rather than later. What are we going to do if Aurora doesn't have the canned milk and sugar for the formula?"

"Don't worry. Pastor Williams knows what Aurora needs to keep on hand and encourages his members to donate a little each month." He grabbed several cans of evaporated milk and a bottle of Karo syrup and put them on the countertop before grabbing a pot and pumping water into it to boil on the stove. The efficiency with which he moved, the confidence as he measured out the ingredients caused a shiver of suspicion that had served her well in her "occupation," but did nothing to calm her growing concern. "Did Aurora teach you how to mix formula?"

John's movements stilled, and he turned toward her,

his eyes again dulled in the pain and conflict she'd witnessed in the fleeting seconds before he'd kissed her. A sense of foreboding slid through her, chilling her to the core. John didn't seem to think she was going to like his answer. It couldn't be as bad as all that, could it?

He leaned back against the counter, his fingers gripping the edges, his knuckles glowing white. "I had a friend I worked with in construction out in San Francisco by the name of Peter Oahu."

Japanese? Maybe, with a name like that, but the name wasn't the word she'd really noticed. "Had?"

"He joined the 442nd and was killed over in Italy last summer."

"I'm so sorry, John." Friends had never come easily to John, despite his kind and generous nature. Was it because he'd believed his father's lies that he, by association with Mattie's disabilities, was too damaged, too flawed to deserve friendship? Love?

"Anyway, Peter asked me to keep an eye on his children and wife. She was expecting, and they had relocated inland to an internment camp in Manzanar."

Merrilee had seen the newsreels at the movies, the black-and-white pictures of neat little plywood houses that had been hurriedly erected for Japanese Americans after Pearl Harbor. It had bothered her at the time, the thought of American citizens being held against their will. It smacked too close to the rumors coming out of Germany. "Death camps" the reporter on the radio had called them, with hundreds, possibly thousands killed.

How had John's friend fared there, locked away from home? "What happened?"

"I got a call a few days before I was supposed to ship out. The news of Peter's death had come, and it had caused Grace to go into labor early. No one could get a doctor to see her. By the time I hunted down and dragged her sorry doctor to the camp, she was almost dead, and the baby had been born. Peter's boy was small." The corners of John's mouth lifted in a tender smile. "But he was a stubborn little thing, bound and determined to live."

Tears clogged Merrilee's throat. John had done that for his friend? He'd looked past the color of Peter's skin, past the vile hate that spewed on both sides of the ocean and saw what really mattered: saving his friend's son, keeping his word. The words of the song Merrilee had sung with Claire took on new meaning. "Red and yellow, black and white, they are precious in His sight, Jesus loves the little children of the world!" Words to her, yet John had lived them in his kindness to his friend. "So that's how you learned how to mix baby formula?"

He blinked as if he'd expected a different reaction from her. "You're not mad?"

"Why? Because you did right by your friend and saved his son's life? To my way of thinking, you deserve a medal," she answered, gently bouncing the baby. She didn't have any gold or silver pins, only her heart as a token.

And the truth about her undercover work. She owed him that, only she wasn't free to tell him. There were personnel channels she'd have to go through, starting with filing her resignation with Major Evans. But that shouldn't be a problem, not with the war in Europe won.

Until then, she had to keep quiet, and pray that John could forgive her for keeping the truth from him.

Chapter Eighteen

Merrilee sank back into the leather chair, the hum of the bomber's assembly line on the other side of Major Evans's office lulling her—the staccato whirl of the riveters, the low murmur of the blowtorches working together to make this country safe for the next generation. For Claire, Billy and Ellie. For Gail and the twins. For Maggie's unborn child.

For her future with John.

She tilted her head to one side. When had that dream been resurrected? The moment in the kitchen when she'd learned the depths of John's goodness? Maybe that first day when he'd showed up on her doorstep, demanding to meet his daughter? Or had it only laid dormant all the years, waiting for him to make his way back to Marietta, back home to her?

What could be taking Major Evans so long? Merrilee glanced around the room, her gaze settling on the round, bold-faced clock hanging over the door. The man had kept her waiting for almost an hour. Well, she'd wait forever if it gave her the freedom to leave her spying behind and finally level with John. She patted her clutch bag, the resignation letter she'd written tucked neatly inside. If she had her way, she'd never have to grace these halls again after this afternoon.

The door behind her clicked open, and she stiffened to attention.

"Relax. It's just me." Edie Michaels Daniels's familiar voice washed over her as she closed the door. "Major Evans told me you were here so I thought I'd come and sit with you for a moment."

Merrilee turned to the young woman as she sat down in the chair next to hers. "Did he give you an idea of how much longer he'd be? I don't like being away from Aurora's too long."

"Is Aurora all right?" Edie's perfectly arched brows furrowed in confusion. "She seemed to be doing so much better the last time Beau and I came for a visit."

"She's fine, but you know how she can be sometimes, wanting to get back into the fray of things before she's ready."

"And the kids? How are they doing with all these changes?"

Merrilee didn't doubt her nephew and his new bride were concerned about the children. Both had taken a shine to Claire and had helped nurse the children in the black community during the polio outbreak last spring. Edie and Beau would never find a child less than lovable just because of their appearance or abilities. "Well, Ellie and the twins are still too young to understand much, and Gail seems to be handling it all right, but Billy worries enough for all of them. He's afraid Ms. Aurora is dying and will leave him. John spends some extra time with him in the evenings to help him talk through it. But that routine might have to change because Mack brought us another child yesterday, a newborn baby girl."

"Oh, how terrible. Is there anything we can do?"

Her nephew had chosen the perfect wife for himself, someone who shared his determination to provide medical care to the poor and underserved. Merrilee reached out and pressed her hand over Edie's. "I called and got her an appointment with Dr. Tripp. He's a doctor over at Henrietta Egleston Hospital that Ms. Aurora suggested."

"I've heard Beau talk about him. He's supposed to be very good."

Knowing her nephew thought highly of the man soothed any lingering nerves Merrilee had. "How is Beau?"

"Wonderful." The younger woman's smile bubbled over with sheer joy. "In fact, he was heading out to Ms. Aurora's to see John today."

"Really? John didn't mention it."

"That's because my husband has a habit of just dropping in on people." Edie shook her head disapprovingly but with a smile that revealed the deep abiding love she had for her new husband. "He was in town yesterday, talking over plans for the new hospital when Edith Watson ran over from the post office with a package for him to deliver to John. Beau said it was that box of letters we found out at his father's place last year."

A peace she couldn't have conceived of a month ago settled over Merrilee. She'd laid her heart bare in those missives, had spoken of all the hopes she had for her and John, for them and their unborn baby. Maybe one day soon they could read them together, reminisce without the pain of those long years apart, rejoice in the love they'd rediscovered.

That is if Major Evans would get in here so she could hand in her resignation!

"May I ask you a personal question?"

Merrilee looked over at Edie, surprised by the confusion clouding her expression. "You can ask me anything," Merrilee answered.

Edie's gaze shifted away. "Why are you here? I mean, I know you and Major Evans are good friends, and at one time, I thought it might turn into something more, but…" she hesitated "…it's unusual for nonauthorized personnel to be admitted into the plant."

Oh, dear. Merrilee hadn't thought how odd her appearance would be considered when she'd called and asked for this meeting earlier this morning. Obviously the major hadn't considered it, either, or he would have diverted her away from the plant. She couldn't tell Edie her true purpose—tendering her resignation as a home-front informant—at least, not until it had been accepted. But lying to her niece wasn't an option, either. She scrambled her brain for a viable excuse, then settled on the only reason she still dealt with the man. "The major and I have some business to discuss about getting Claire admitted into Warm Springs."

Edie relaxed, scooting back into the chair, her elbows resting on the leather armrest. "That's nice of him. How is our Claire Bear?"

Merrilee let go of the breath she'd been holding. How in the world had she ever thought she could be a spy? But not for much longer. "Better. You should see her with John. I think she's becoming a daddy's girl."

Edie bent her elbow and rested her chin in the palm of her hand, her smile suddenly silly. "You're in love with him again, aren't you?"

There didn't seem to be any reason not to be completely honest. "I don't think I ever stopped loving John."

"Oh, thank goodness. I thought for a moment when I heard you were here to see Evans—" Edie pressed her lips together and shook her head. "It doesn't matter. Maggie was right. She's been telling me ever since she moved into the house that you still had feelings for John, but I wasn't so sure."

Merrilee didn't know what to think. Her relatives and friends had been gossiping about her? "You two talked about me?"

"Only because we were concerned about you." Edie straightened, dark brows furrowed over worried eyes. "This past year with Claire has been hard on you, and the last thing any of us want is for you to get hurt again."

Merrilee opened her mouth to reassure her, then closed it. What promises did she have that John wouldn't break her heart again? He still planned to leave Marietta, still hadn't told her why he had to go and when.

She felt Edie's slender hand rest against her forearm. "I'm talking out of turn here," her niece said. "Anyone with eyes in their head can see the man adores you."

Merrilee nodded, the muscles in her chest suddenly tight. She'd known with every beat of her heart that John had loved her twelve years ago, and yet he'd taken the first job he could find, one that took him as far away as the east was from the west. How did she know with certainty that when he left this time, he'd keep his promise to return to her and Claire?

Merrilee thought back to that first day when John had shown up on her front porch, Claire's letter in his suit pocket. How hard it must have been for him, to have to face the wife he'd thought had abandoned him, a woman who'd run off to her daddy's house at the first sign of trouble. Yet John had never wavered in his determination to forge a relationship with Claire, never tucked tail and run. She shook her head slightly. John wouldn't abandon them again, not unless he had no other choice. And then he'd fight with every breath in him, in every way he could, to show his love and get back to them as soon as he could.

She sucked in a breath. The homestead! It had been John's love letter to her all those years ago, the only means available for him to show her that despite everything that had happened, he loved her. He'd loved her all these years, just as she'd loved him.

A knock behind them, followed by the door opening, spared Merrilee from any explanations as Major Evans entered the room. "Ladies, so sorry to keep you waiting, but I'm sure you've had a nice visit with Mrs. Daniels."

"Being called Mrs. Daniels still takes some getting used to." A slight blush stained Edie's cheeks as she stood. "I'd better get back to work." She glanced down at Merrilee. "Dinner at our place soon?"

"We look forward to it."

"Great." Her niece nodded toward Evans, then turned, the soft swish of her skirts keeping time with the high-pitched *clip-clop* of her steps.

When the door clicked shut, Evans pulled out his

leather chair and sat down. "Nice girl. Good to know that she's on our side."

Merrilee dug her fingers into the leather sides of her purse. Evans never gave anyone the benefit of the doubt. Must be the nature of his job, this distrust he seemed to have toward everyone. Another reason why she didn't make a very good spy. "Edie was always on our side. It was her father who was the problem, remember?"

He didn't linger on her question for very long, not that she'd expected him to. "So what information have you got for me today?"

So much for the niceties. "Nothing."

Evans blinked as if he wasn't quite sure he'd heard her correctly. "What do you mean, nothing?"

"Exactly what I said. Nothing. Aurora is no more supplying the black market around here than you or I am, Major."

"Do you have any proof to back up your statement?"

Opening her purse, Merrilee pulled out a small leather-bound notebook Aurora had given her and handed it to him. "Aurora has kept records of every donation she's ever received for close to twenty years. She's also made notes detailing when the war started, how many rations items she used each month along with a list of people who had donated their rationed items to her and the children."

"That seems odd."

"Not really," Merrilee answered, smiling at the memory of Aurora's explanation. Evans would probably be suspicious of the older woman's act of gratefulness, but Merrilee knew it was nothing more than the truth. "Aurora sends thank-you notes to everyone who helped, and that book was her way of keeping track."

He flipped the pages, probably noting the same tiny entries Merrilee had noticed when Aurora gave it to her. "And what about John? Are we sure he's the one who bought the old Todd place?"

She'd already explained all this to the major. "He wants to have a home closer to our daughter."

Evans flipped the notebook on his desk and leaned back in his chair, his fingers steepled over his chest. "Wondered when you'd get around to telling me he's the father of your child. But we still don't know how he got the money. That farm cost a big chunk of change."

The hairs at the nape of her neck stood at attention. "Why are you suspicious of John all of a sudden?"

Arched eyebrows rose over cunning eyes. "If I recall, you had your own suspicions about Davenport when he first rolled into town."

Merrilee felt her throat tighten. Yes, she realized she had, and in her blind determination to get to John's real reasons for coming back to Marietta, she'd pitched him up to Evans like a hanging curve ball. It was up to her to rectify this. "I admit, I had my doubts, but not anymore. As far as buying the Todd place goes, I'm sure John bought it by saving every nickel and dime he's made except for what he needed to live on."

Evans snorted. "I thought you were a smart woman, Merrilee, but you're not giving up on him, are you? Even after he left you and Claire to fend for yourselves?"

It was the closest thing she'd ever seen to an emotion in Evans, as if he found her actions disappointing. Well, she refused to rise to the bait. "What's your point, Major?"

Staring at her, Evans opened the top drawer to his desk, pulled out a folder and dropped it with a loud *thump* in front of him. "After you confirmed Davenport had set up an account for Aurora, I began digging a little deeper into your former husband."

Worry fluttered in her belly. John had been in and out of the Pacific for most of the past two years, and training Seabees before that. There was nothing dishonorable in any of that. So why did the major look so smug, like a alley cat who'd discovered another bowl of cream? "You're wasting your time, Major."

Evans flipped open the first page. "Interesting reading. Seems your fellow has been up to no good."

She refused to be taunted. Grasping the armrests, she pulled herself to her feet. "If you're just going to throw out accusations, I'm leaving."

"Did you know he's been relieved of his post while under investigation for aiding and abetting the enemy?" The sound of turning pages echoed through Merrilee. "According to this report, he gave a Japanese family rationed items without a reasonable explanation as to how he obtained them."

The patterned floor beneath her feet began to swim in her view. Why hadn't John told her about the investigation and the possible charges he faced?

But he had, hadn't he? At least to a point. John had always been up front with her about leaving, though he'd never shared his reasons, and he hadn't lied about what he'd done for Peter when she'd asked him about the baby formula. No, John had told her everything, except the possible punishment he faced. So why had he withheld that part of the story from her? Had he hoped to protect her and Claire? It was possible. More than anyone, John understood the censure that would follow them around like a dark cloud if the charges stood, the same storm that had followed him all those years because of Mattie. Tenderness for the man who'd captured her heart as a young girl stole through her.

The Lord moves in His own time.

Aurora's words came back to her with a clarity they'd never had before. Was that why she'd been placed in this position? So that God could use her to clear John? She bowed her head. *Lord, give me the right words to say. Soften the major's heart and let him recognize the truth. And, no matter what happens, let John know he's loved.*

A peace she hadn't felt in months slid through Merrilee as she settled into her chair again. "If you are willing to hear the truth about John, I need to tell you a story about a soldier with the 442nd. His name was Peter Oahu."

Merrilee should have been back by now.

John paced across the front porch, the sound of his boots pounding out a quicker beat with each passing moment. He stopped at the edge of the steps, cocked his head to listen, his ears honed for the high-pitched noise Merrilee's truck made when she coasted to a stop.

Nothing.

He frowned. Maybe he should have gone with her, but someone had to stay with Aurora and the kids. He just wished he knew why it was taking her so long to make a doctor's appointment for Sarah and check on things at the boardinghouse.

He walked toward the swing, the warmth of the evening settling over him like a humid blanket, drowning him in a sea of worry and regret, the letter about his trial that Beau had delivered burning a smoldering hole through his renewed hopes for a future with Merrilee and Claire. He knew only too well what people would say when the charges were made public. The snide remarks, the stigma. Guilt by association would stain his daughter and ex-wife.

John grimaced. Jacob Daniels must be turning in his grave.

The screen door creaked open behind him. "Worrying a path out on my porch floor, son?"

"Just thinking." He stared off toward the dirt driveway; a faint haze simmered along the edge of the rocky ground. The planted fields would need rain soon or the plants would die before rooting deep. Not that he'd be here to see them grow to harvest either way. By then, his fate for the foreseeable future would be sealed.

No sense feeling sorry for himself. It wouldn't do any good. John turned and leaned back against the railing. "What are you doing up? I thought you were going to rest while Sarah is down for her nap."

The older woman stretched to one side, her hand pressed against her rib cage as if to balance herself. "I'm more worn out from being in that bed than anything to do with my heart. Between that and you pounding up and down this porch like you were hitting the beaches of Normandy, I'm surprised the baby is still asleep."

John reached an arm around the woman and tugged

her into a maternal hug. "I'm sorry, Ms. Aurora. I didn't mean to keep you awake."

"I can sleep when I'm dead." She gave him a maternal shove to the chest. "So tell me. What's troubling you, son?"

Aurora had always been so good to him. He couldn't burden her with his problems. "Nothing for you to worry over."

"You always were a closemouthed little fella. Worried me to no end, especially after Mattie passed."

"You worried about me?"

She nestled her gray head against his shoulder. "Darling boy, there's not been a moment since that day I found you in that store that you haven't been in my thoughts. And every time I prayed, I asked the Lord to keep you safe and bring you back home if it was His will."

He swallowed against the hard knot forming in his throat. "But I stayed away for so long. Didn't you ever just give up on me?"

"Oh, John." Aurora tilted her head back until he stared into pale gray eyes sparkling with unshed tears. She gave his cheek a motherly pat. "Don't you see how much you're loved, how much you've always been loved?"

John leaned forward and pressed his cheek against her forehead, the strength of the emotions rolling around inside him threatening to choke the air right out of his lungs. "But, I've always felt…"

"As if you were all alone in this world. I know. I felt the same way growing up."

He frowned. Aurora couldn't know how he felt, could

she? But then again he'd never heard her speak much about herself. "What do you mean?"

John felt the sharp rise and fall of her rib cage against his side. "I had my first seizure when I was four years old—at least that's what I've been told. The next one happened when I was six. They started coming with some frequency after that."

John had a sinking feeling he knew where this story was leading, but he asked the question anyway. "What happened?"

"A few days shy of my eighth birthday, Mama and Daddy had me committed to the state institution down in Milledgeville." Her voice cracked and she hesitated for a few moments before continuing. "I don't remember much about that first year, except for wondering why Mama and Daddy had left me there. I figured I must have done something really bad because that place..." She swallowed hard. "Anyway, the seizures stopped as suddenly as they'd started. The state tried to send me back to my parents but they refused. I guess they were scared the seizures would start back up."

Dear Lord in heaven. She'd been so young, barely old enough to tie her shoes. And he'd heard whispers about the state institution, the stench and filth, patients dying in droves from dysentery and pneumonia. "How did you survive?"

He couldn't believe it when Aurora laughed. "The preacher from the local church started coming to the hospital once a week. I used to hide behind the long curtains near the patients' beds and listen to him talk about a Father who'd love even the least of these, someone who'd never leave. I clung to those moments when the preacher spoke about Jesus, about His unconditional love until one day, I asked Him into my heart."

"I've done that already, so why do I still feel lonely?" John asked.

Aurora wrapped one arm around his waist and hugged him close. "It's a struggle every day, son, to accept that the Lord is always there. At first, you may have to remind yourself of that truth every second of every day, but as time goes on, the reality of it sinks into your heart."

I will never leave you nor forsake you.

The verse he'd remembered from childhood seemed to shift the heaviness he'd always felt down in his bones. Maybe Aurora was right. Some time studying his Bible might help, too.

"So tell me, son. What's troubling you?"

John lowered his gaze to the ground, his thoughts suddenly turning to his daughter. How would he feel if Claire refused to share her worries with him? His gut twisted at the thought. Why would Aurora feel any differently? "I have to leave."

"Has something happened?"

Backing away from her, John shoved his hand into his back pocket, pulled out the folded envelope and handed it to her. The paper crinkled softly as she opened the folds and read. When she finally finished, she lifted her gaze to John's. "Does Merrilee know about this?"

"Everything except for the charges. I didn't want to tell her until I had a hearing date."

Aurora folded the letter and handed it back to John. "You have to tell her."

"I know." He rammed his fingers through his hair. "I just didn't think it was going to be this hard."

Aurora scoffed. "You remember those verses in Genesis, right after Adam saw Eve for the first time? 'And a man shall leave his mother, and a woman leave her home, and the two shall be as one.' The truth is that loving someone is hard at times, but it's going through that fire together, holding on to each other during those hard times, that forges two very different people into one mind and heart." She rested her hands on his forearm, her dear face lifted to his. "I've watched the way you and Merrilee have dealt with the past few weeks. Yes, you've disagreed at times, but you've listened to each other and worked through the problems. And, if I'm not mistaken, you've grown closer to each other."

Not just closer, but more in love with Merrilee than ever. "I don't want to leave her."

"Then tell her that. Give her your side of the story and let her decide if she wants to wait for you." Reaching up, Aurora cupped his face in her hands, pulled him toward her and gave him a kiss on his forehead as if he were still a young boy.

"Thank you, Mama."

A grinding noise from the front lawn turned his attention to the rickety old blue truck bouncing its way up the drive, a cloud of red dust trailing behind like wispy flames. Through the dirty window, Merrilee sat primly, her hold on the steering wheel unyielding, but even from his vantage point, John could sense a lightness in her eyes, a slight lift at the corners of her mouth that gave him hope.

"I'll watch the children while you two have your

talk," Aurora said, patting him on the arm before moving away. She was halfway to the door when she turned to him again. "I'm praying for you both, John."

He nodded. What had he done to deserve a mother like Aurora? *Thank You for my mother, Lord, and for never abandoning me. Be with me as I talk to Merrilee. Give me the right words to speak. Let Thy will, not mine, be done.*

With a deep breath, John waited at the top of the stairs as Merrilee pulled the truck up alongside the barn and cut the engine. A few long moments later, she walked across the yard, her navy blue skirts swaying with each step, her cream-colored purse tucked neatly under her arm. As she came closer, her lips lifted into a flirtatious smile that made his heart hammer against his rib cage. "Hey, you."

"Hey." His voice came out in a whispered growl, and he coughed before continuing. "I thought you'd be home before now."

Her smile dimmed just a bit. "I had to take care of some things. How are the kids?"

"Fine, Ms. Aurora's keeping them occupied in the parlor."

"And the baby?"

There was such tender concern in her voice. He wondered if his daughter knew how blessed she was to have this woman for her mother. "Down for a nap."

"Good." She stood at the bottom of the steps, a sudden awkwardness to her silence that John recognized as nerves. Had she picked up on his uneasiness? Was that why she seemed to be walking on eggshells now?

Or was she anxious about something else?

"Can we talk for a second?"

John blinked. That was supposed to have been his line. "Sure." He held out his hand to her, surprised by the slight tremble in her fingers before she grasped his.

"Did something happen while you were in town?"

She didn't answer, just clung to his hand tighter as she took the last two steps onto the porch. She tilted her head toward the porch swing. "You want to sit?"

John nodded, worry knotting in his stomach with each step he took. What could have Merrilee this wound up? Had something happened at the boardinghouse? Was something wrong with Maggie or Beau?

What's wrong? Why are you acting so funny?"

"I'm not sure where to start." Merrilee stared off down the length of the porch, white teeth worrying the pink flesh of her lower lip. "Maybe Daddy was right. Maybe it's better just to rip the bandage off rather than pull it off slowly."

"I don't understand."

"I know. I'm messing this up." She drew in a deep breath as if it might be the last one she'd take for a while. "The truth is I'm an informant for Major Evans over at the bomber plant."

This still wasn't making any sense to John. "But you don't work there."

"No, but I have a houseful of boarders involved in various stages of the B-29 development staying in my home." She hesitated slightly. "And last year, one of them was targeted by a German sympathizer to be kidnapped and sent to Berlin to work for the Nazis."

John stared off aimlessly. Beau had told him about his wife, how Edie's father had tried to press her into service for the Germans. He glanced back at Merrilee with new admiration. Why in the world had he under-estimated this courageous, determined woman who'd battled the worst life had to throw at her and still man-aged to love with her whole heart? John hoped one day he could be so brave.

Like today.

"I have to leave, Merrilee," John stated quietly, watching her expression for any response.

"I know. I went to M~~~ noon to resign my position, and he sho~~~ file."

The muscles in his chest contracted into crushing pain at a new thought. "Did you give him any infor-mation on me?"

She hesitated for half a second. "Yes."

John bounded up, the wooden swing pitching vio-lently, much like his warring emotions, his mind numb with the reality of what Merrilee had done. He paced the length of the porch, turned then marched back. "You resigned?"

She gave him a slight, sad smile. "Well, it wasn't as if I was good at it or something. And I hated the way I felt doing it, suspicious of every little thing, betraying the people I care about the most. That's just not who I am."

At least she recognized it for what it was. Maybe one day he'd understand why she'd felt the need to do it. Even now, in the midst of immeasurable pain, he knew he'd forgive her.

"Would you like to know what I told Major Evans?"

John blinked. There was compassion in her question, almost a sense that she wanted to make things right. But that wasn't possible now, was it?

All things are possible with God!

The swing shivered as Merrilee deposited her purse on the seat and stood, her hands folded in front of her, her lean fingers clasped as if in a desperate prayer. "Evans didn't have any of the information about Peter being with the 442nd. Once he put a call through to the War Department and received confirmation about Peter, he contacted one of his friends at army headquarters. They're sending your friend's paperwork to the Naval Command where your hearing will be held."

She hadn't thrown him to the wolves or abandoned him. Hadn't walked away from him when times got rough. No, she'd stood by him, done everything she could to help him. "Why did you do this?"

"Oh, John." Merrilee crossed the short distance that separated them and flung her arms around him, drawing him close. "I couldn't let you go to prison for doing the right thing."

He tightened his arms around her and pulled her in to his chest, close to his heart. "You believe in me?"

She gave him a watery smile. "Of course I do. You're the most honorable and decent man I know. What you did for Peter's son, that was just like Jesus commands us to do. To love one another." Merrilee lifted her hand to his face. "It's one of the reasons I love you so much."

Any remaining doubts he might have had crumbled beneath the glow of love lighting her eyes. She believed in him, probably always had. He turned his head slightly, brushing his lips against the tender flesh of her palm. "I should have never left you, Merri."

She stroked her thumb against his lips. "I made my fair share of mistakes then, mainly listening to everyone else but you. It's okay to seek counsel, but not at the cost of my husband's feelings."

He captured her face in his hands, loving the warmth that radiated beneath his fingertips as her cheeks bloomed into color. John brushed a kiss against her forehead. "I love you, Merrilee. You've held my heart ever since that first morning you came walking across your daddy's cotton field."

"I love you, too. Always have, always will."

He kissed her then, tilted her head ever so slightly so he could press his lips fully against hers, the intoxicating scent of vanilla and Merrilee floating around him, soaking down into his soul. This woman was his home, the other half to make him whole. He'd never walk away from her again.

When he lifted his head moments later, she tightened her arms around his neck. "Don't go. Not yet."

"I'm not going anywhere, sweetheart. Not unless you're there with me."

The contented smile that beamed back at him made his toes curl. "Then marry me."

John barked with laughter. "I thought I was the one who was supposed to do the asking?"

"You asked the first time around." She pressed up on her toes and brushed a brief kiss against his lips before settling back, one hand reaching for her necklace. "I've even got the ring."

He grasped the thin metal circle dangling from the

silver chain, his heart pounding in recognition. The old key ring they'd used for a wedding band the night they'd run off. "You saved it."

"It was the first gift you ever gave me."

She'd always surprised him, this woman who'd captured his heart so long ago. What would the next thirty or forty years have in store with her by his side? "What about the hearing?"

Her expression was somber, but held steadfast. "We'll face it together. United we stand, remember?"

John leaned his head against hers. No matter what life held for them, the good or the bad, they'd handle it together with the Lord's help. Always with the Lord's help. "Yes, Merrilee, united we'll stand."

Epilogue

A soft breeze fluttered through the lace curtains of Merrilee's bedroom window, the air cool and crisp like a Granny Smith apple from Aurora's yard. Merrilee pressed her satin collar into submission, then studied her reflection in the full-length mirror and smiled. She could have worn a feed sack today and it wouldn't have dimmed her happiness.

Within a few minutes, she would be Mrs. John Davenport.

Again.

It had been a long summer, waiting for the paperwork that would dismiss John of the charges filed against him. Every trip to the mailbox, every visit they made to the post office during June and July had ended in discouragement, at least for that moment. Then John would give her a flirtatious wink, reserved only for her, and Merrilee's heart would lighten.

The time spent waiting did have some advantages. John had opened up the package of Merrilee's letters Beau had found and they'd read them together, their love deepening with each envelope they opened. By the time

John's paperwork had come through, both had agreed they were ready to take their vows.

Merrilee lifted a small spray of white roses and baby's breath to her nose, then pinned it against the base of her upturned hairdo. Downstairs, the muted clatter of plates and glasses being carried into the dining room told her the ceremony was getting ready to start.

A slight knock on the door caused Merrilee to turn just as Claire hurried inside, the royal-blue skirts of her new dress bringing out the little flecks of gray in her eyes. Her daughter leaned back against the closed door. "Oh, Mama! You look so beautiful! Who would have thought an old parachute could turn out so pretty?"

A slight thrill of feminine satisfaction ran through her as she brushed a hand over the creamy-white satin of her wedding dress, a gift from Maggie and Wesley. "It did turn out quite nice, didn't it?"

"Daddy won't be able to take his eyes off you."

"Well, I don't know." Merrilee tried to give Claire her most serious look, but her lips wouldn't stop twitching upward into a smile. "I hear he's kind of partial to the maid of honor."

Claire laughed, her cheeks turning a rosy hue that matched the red sparks in her hair. "I still can't believe you asked me."

"Oh, Claire Bear, I can't think of anyone else I'd rather have walking me down the aisle." Tears crowded Merrilee's throat as she drew her daughter into her arms. The despair Claire had carried around for the last year had eased, replaced by a growing faith that amazed her and John with its depths, pushing Merrilee's own faith to expand. *Thank You, Lord. Thank*

You for leading us out of the darkness. Use Claire for Your glory no matter what her physical limitations are.

"Knock, knock." Maggie opened the door and lumbered into the bedroom, a bouquet of white roses clutched in one hand while the other rested on the thickening at her waist. "How are we doing in here? Almost ready?"

"I thought Edie was coming up with you," Claire said, her eyes on the door.

"She ran out to the kitchen to get some saltines." Maggie gave Merrilee a knowing gaze over Claire's head, her wide smile barely contained. "A little stomach trouble."

Another baby in the family! "Beau must be thrilled."

Claire shot her a confused look. "Thrilled with a stomachache?"

Maggie wrapped her arm around her younger cousin's shoulders and pulled her toward the doorway. "Come on, squirt. Let's get your mother married."

Merrilee had barely cleared the train of her skirt from the doorway when Aurora's voice drifted up to her from the main hallway. "It's traditional for the bride to be a little late for her wedding, son."

Another smile touched her lips, bubbles of joy filling her heart at knowing her groom was anxious for her arrival. The few steps it took to stand at the top of the stairwell seemed to take a lifetime. "I'm coming, John."

Merrilee felt everyone's gaze on her, but she had eyes only for John—the promises of tomorrow, of the home they would make together, the children they would raise, shining in his beautiful blue eyes. It felt as if she were floating, until suddenly she stood on the last step, John standing in front of her, waiting.

"Hi." He barely whispered the word, rough-hewed and low, as if she was the only person in the world.

"Hi." She rested a hand on his dark tie, her heart galloping to the same wild beat as his.

"Mama looks pretty, doesn't she, Daddy?" Claire asked.

The look of male appreciation on John's face made Merrilee's heart flutter as he leaned toward her, his gaze locked on hers as he reached up and touched her nose in a gentle caress. "The most beautiful woman I've ever known."

Maggie squeezed by them, holding tight to her growing waist. "Ms. Aurora, why don't we get everyone settled into their chairs and give the happy couple a few minutes alone with their daughter."

"Sounds like a fine idea." She held out a hand to the twins and Ellie. "It sure was sweet of the sheriff to help Billy and Gail hold our seats. But then again, it gives him a chance to hold Sarah, doesn't it?" Aurora led the three children down the hallway, Ellie skipping beside her, a basket full of rose petals tilting precariously on her chubby arm.

"Well—" Claire turned to her parents. "What are we waiting on?"

"Your daddy and I wanted to pray with you before the ceremony." After setting her bouquet down on the table, Merrilee held out her hand to Claire, then slid her hand into John's, nodding her head to him. "Sweetheart?"

The loving look he gave her before bowing his head

made her heart flutter, the words he spoke to the Lord giving her a peek into their future, inviting God to be part of this marriage.

Three strands were stronger than two.

The last words had barely passed John's lips before Claire slipped her hand from Merrilee's, reaching for her flowers.

John lifted Merrilee's bouquet from the table and handed it to her, his hand tenderly resting over hers. "Don't you think it's about time we got married?"

Merrilee threaded her free arm through his and smiled up at her soon-to-be husband as they walked down the hall to join their guests. "I think it's the perfect time."

* * * * *

Dear Reader,

I hope you enjoyed Merrilee and John's story of reconciliation and renewed love. These two have been on the fringes of my imagination for quite some time now, so it was a joy to finally give them the happily ever after they both deserved!

When I started writing *Hearts Rekindled,* I was sure this book was going to be about how marriage is hard work—no matter how much two people love each other! But as I dug deeper and kept writing, I began to notice how the issue of abandonment was something each of my characters battled with at some point in the story. It was something I could relate to, to a degree—for the past few years, I've fought severe back pain that left me unable to stand or sit for any length of time. It was a very lonely war, living in extreme pain, wondering if it would ever abate. Sometimes I'd cry out to God to take the pain away and, if that wasn't His will, to help me learn to deal with it. When the days turned into months without a response, I felt abandoned.

Just like Merrilee and John did.

In writing their story, God helped me see that He never abandoned me. He just used my physical pain to bring me closer to Him and to grow my faith. And, like Merrilee and John, my story also has a happy ending. After surgery and rehabilitation, I'm back to walking three miles a day, writing my stories and driving my family and friends crazy with all the activities I want to do!

My prayer for you is that no matter how alone you

feel, know that God is right there waiting for you, loving you more than the human heart or mind can imagine!

Blessings,

Patty Smith Hall

Questions for Discussion

1. In the first scene, Merrilee was forced into spying on a dear friend in order to secure her daughter Claire's polio treatment. How would you respond if faced with a similar situation?

2. How would you feel if your friend was investigating you? Would you be able to forgive them and remain friends?

3. John received Claire's letter introducing herself as his daughter a year after she mailed it to him. Look back over your life and recognize a situation where a delay would be considered God working in His own timing. Did those delays help build your faith or did you feel discouraged? How could you have reacted differently?

4. When John saw Merrilee with Major Evans, he felt jealous. Does jealousy have any part in a loving, Christ-centered relationship? Why or why not?

5. At the playground, John witnessed some children ignoring a young girl with Down syndrome and came to her rescue. How would you respond if faced with a similar situation? How would God want us to react?

6. Though they were married, Merrilee was surprised to learn John had a younger brother with severe

disabilities. Have you ever kept a secret from your spouse? How did it affect your relationship?

7. John had a lot of secrets: first his brother, then his friendship with a Japanese family that led to an investigation. Given society's discrimination against both of these groups, do you think John was right to keep those secrets close to the chest? What kinds of problems could he have possibly had if he had been honest? What does the Bible say about handling this kind of situation?

8. How do you feel Merrilee dealt with Ms. Davis after the older woman voiced her opinion that Billy and Ellie should not be allowed to come to church? Was Merrilee's response Christlike? Examine your feelings about people with mental disabilities having a place within the church. What does Ms. Davis's reaction say about her relationship with God?

9. Both John's decision to help his Japanese friend and Ms. Aurora's decision to shelter mentally and physically disabled children went against what society at that time period deemed morally right. Have you ever taken a stand for your beliefs in the face of stiff opposition? What does the Bible say about fighting laws that go against God's word?

10. When John and Merrilee caught the children smoking, John disciplined Billy and Claire by making them smoke the remaining cigarettes. Do you feel

that was a fair punishment? If not, what would you have done differently?

11. Merrilee forgave John for walking out on their marriage. Have you ever been in a situation where you've had to show grace to someone who has hurt you badly? Would you have been able to forgive John if you were Merrilee?

12. John felt that everyone he'd ever loved abandoned him, so he always left before he could get hurt. Do you understand why he would feel this way? What was wrong with John's thinking? What does the Bible say on this topic?

WINNING OVER THE WRANGLER
Cowboys of Eden Valley
by Linda Ford

Dodging his outlaw family hasn't left Brand Duggan time for romance. Breaking broncos at Eden Valley Ranch should've been another short stint before moving on, but a blue-eyed beauty may give him a reason to stay....

WOLF CREEK HOMECOMING
by Penny Richards

Dr. Rachel Stone has tried to forget the man who broke her heart. But now that he's returned home to make good, can she forgive him and reveal the truth about the child he never knew existed?

A BRIDE FOR THE BARON
Sanctuary Bay
by Jo Ann Brown

Edmund Herriott never prepared for life as a baron. As troubles on his estate mount, can the vicar's beautiful sister convince him he's worthy of a baronage—and a bride?

THE GUARDIAN'S PROMISE
by Christina Rich

Commander of the Temple Guard, Ari gave up his freedom to protect Judah's future king. Now he must choose between duty to his king and the woman who has stolen his heart.

REQUEST YOUR FREE BOOKS!

2 FREE INSPIRATIONAL NOVELS
PLUS 2
FREE
MYSTERY GIFTS

Love Inspired
H I S T O R I C A L
INSPIRATIONAL HISTORICAL ROMANCE

YES! Please send me 2 FREE Love Inspired® Historical novels and my 2 FREE mystery gifts (gifts are worth about $10). After receiving them, if I don't wish to receive any more books, I can return the shipping statement marked "cancel." If I don't cancel, I will receive 4 brand-new novels every month and be billed just $4.74 per book in the U.S. or $5.24 per book in Canada. That's a saving of at least 21% off the cover price. It's quite a bargain! Shipping and handling is just 50¢ per book in the U.S. and 75¢ per book in Canada.* I understand that accepting the 2 free books and gifts places me under no obligation to buy anything. I can always return a shipment and cancel at any time. Even if I never buy another book, the two free books and gifts are mine to keep forever.

102/302 IDN F5CN

Name	(PLEASE PRINT)	
Address		Apt. #
City	State/Prov.	Zip/Postal Code

Signature (if under 18, a parent or guardian must sign)

Mail to the Harlequin® Reader Service:
IN U.S.A.: P.O. Box 1867, Buffalo, NY 14240-1867
IN CANADA: P.O. Box 609, Fort Erie, Ontario L2A 5X3

Want to try two free books from another series?
Call 1-800-873-8635 or visit www.ReaderService.com.

* Terms and prices subject to change without notice. Prices do not include applicable taxes. Sales tax applicable in N.Y. Canadian residents will be charged applicable taxes. Offer not valid in Quebec. This offer is limited to one order per household. Not valid for current subscribers to Love Inspired Historical books. All orders subject to credit approval. Credit or debit balances in a customer's account(s) may be offset by any other outstanding balance owed by or to the customer. Please allow 4 to 6 weeks for delivery. Offer available while quantities last.

Your Privacy—The Harlequin® Reader Service is committed to protecting your privacy. Our Privacy Policy is available online at www.ReaderService.com or upon request from the Harlequin Reader Service.

We make a portion of our mailing list available to reputable third parties that offer products we believe may interest you. If you prefer that we not exchange your name with third parties, or if you wish to clarify or modify your communication preferences, please visit us at www.ReaderService.com/consumerchoice or write to us at Harlequin Reader Service Preference Service, P.O. Box 9062, Buffalo, NY 14269. Include your complete name and address.

LIH13R

A COWBOY WITHOUT A NAME

The only thing Brand Duggan's outlaw kin ever gave him was an undeserved reputation. Once he's through breaking horses, he'll leave Eden Valley. Staying means risk—and heartache. And he has no business falling for someone like Sybil Bannerman.

The rugged cowboy who rescues her from a stampede is just the kind of man Sybil Bannerman's editor wants her to write about. Yet she has no idea how big a secret Brand Duggan carries, until her life is threatened. Despite the evidence against him, Sybil can't walk away from the man who lassoed her heart....

COWBOYS OF *Eden Valley*

Winning Over the Wrangler

by

LINDA FORD

Available March 2014 wherever Love Inspired Historical books and ebooks are sold.